# A Time of Angels

# A Time of Angels

KAREN HESSE

HYPERION PAPERBACKS FOR CHILDREN/NEW YORK
An Imprint of Disney Book Group

The publishers have made every effort to locate the owners of all copyrighted material and to obtain permission to reprint the front cover iomage. Any errors made are unintentional, and corrections will be made in future editions if necessary.

First Hyperion Paperbacks edition 1997
Text copyright © 1995 by Karen Hesse

This book is set in Centaur

Library of Congress Cataloging-in-Publication Data on file.

ISBN 978-1-4231-1573-1

Visit www.hyperionbooksforchildren.com

*This book is dedicated to Frank Hodge—*
*How far and wide his wings spread, who can say*

# ACKNOWLEDGMENTS

*In this life many angels illuminate our paths.*
*Here are the names of a few:*

Gordon H. Anderson, Helvi Anttila, Bessie Barber, Harold Barry, Pauline Barry, Laura Batcha, Julian "Ben" Bednarcyk, Bernice L. Boyce, Mary Burke, Eileen Christelow, Katherine Condron, Seretta Corl, Lila Cranmer, Isalene Crow, Mary Dewey, Alvin Donald, Geraldine Donald, Betty Doncaster, Elaine Driver, Celia Ettl, Mary Ficken, Victoria Fogg, Evelyn M. Gass, Jaya Green, Dorothy W. Guy, Helen Haddad, Sheila Hargrave, Tom Hendrickson, Christian Hess, Kate Hesse, Rachel Hesse, Randy Hesse, Veronica Keely, Gladys Kennery, Liza Ketchum, Georgia Kimball, June Knight, Olinda Kuhlman, Frank Lavine, Randy Letzler, Fran Levin, Sarah Liston, Robert MacLean, Tink MacLean, Albert L. Maguire, Kathi Maio, J. E. McAdam, Doris McManaway, Jean E. Mitchell, Catherine Morrison, Cynthia Nau of the Moore Free Library, Marilyn Nee, Frank Ober, Georgie M. Paschal, Harriett Petrie, Leverettte V. Pierce, Cecelia Pollack, Richard Ross, Rosa Sand, Irene Schantz, Deidre Scherer, Vernita Schmalz, Arthur L. Smith. Johnny Smolka, Blanche Stepanian, Howard Stevenson, Lillian Swan, Dorothy Symes, April Wachtel, Heather Wachtel, Helen Wachtel, Dennis Wade, Mary Ward, Inez M. Warren, Walter Weber, the *West Ender*'s editors: James Campano and Joseph LoPiccolo, Gracie Westmoreland, and, of course, Andrea Cascardi and Barbara Kouts.

Over the night streets of Boston, angels fly. Angels soar in their shimmering robes. Their eyes shine. Their wings stretch tip to tip across the broad avenues: Beacon and Boylston and Commonwealth. Angels glide slowly on the warm currents of wind, while beneath them the city murmurs in its sleep: the rich in their high beds on Louisburgh Square, the poor in their crowded West End tenements. Bare floors are brushed by golden light as angels drift past North Station. Along the Charles River, the water gazes skyward in hushed wonder, reflecting angel light. A thousand children sleep sweetly, the breeze from angel wings tickling over their lids. A grocer dreams of golden cod; a scholar dreams, debating God; and a young girl dreams of a mother's kiss, weightless as silk——while angels sweep over alleys, over rooftops, over spires. In the moist September night, angels sing like rain weeping down the lavender panes of Beacon Hill.

# part one

chapter one

*Tuesday, September 10, 1918*

Y APRON HEAVY WITH COINS, I pushed
open the front door of our tenement and raced down the steps.
Hesitating a moment in the dark stairwell, I breathed in the
odors from the other apartments. Ham. Bacon. Smells that made
my mouth swim with hope. But in our apartment only the foul
stink of weeds waited for me.

Vashti sorted her roots and leaves in the sitting room. Her
two-colored eyes, the blue and the brown, swept over me, glaring,
as I entered.

"There's an article in today's paper," I said, brushing a stray
curl back from my face with newsprint-stained hands. "A hundred sailors, sick with influenza."

Vashti, the companion of my Tanta Rose, was like a great
buzzard. She enjoyed news of other people's illnesses. It gave her
the chance to descend on them with her weedy cures. A plant
hung limp in Vashti's fist. "I have heard."

Rubbing the side of my nose, I waited for her to say more.
Of course, she did not.

"Hannah?" The high voice of Tanta Rose floated under the

3

door between the sitting room and the kitchen. "Hannah? Home so soon?"

It surprised me to hear Tanta Rose still in the apartment.

Usually she left for the factory before I returned from North Station.

Pushing open the door, I entered the kitchen.

My sisters, Libbie and Eve, dawdled over their oatmeal— Eve dropping the cooling lumps back into her bowl, Libbie grumbling about sugar. I came up behind my sisters and stroked their talcum-powdered heads, Libbie's red head and Eve's brown one.

Tanta Rose rested her hand on my dog-eared sketchbook. Most of the time I kept the book in my apron pocket, but in my haste to meet Pilasky that morning to pick up our bundles of newspapers, I'd left it behind.

My sketchbook didn't come from a stationery shop; it wasn't store bought like the ones we used at the Settlement House for art lessons. I'd made my sketchbook myself, cutting and sewing together the unused wrapping paper from Mrs. Schwartz's fish shop.

With one hand, Tanta Rose held my sketchbook open on the kitchen table. The other hand wrapped around her blue flowered teacup. She was half in, half out of her overcoat. She did not need an overcoat, not on such a mild morning. But Tanta Rose wore her coat starting the first of September, no matter the temperature.

The door swung open, and Vashti strode into the kitchen. I gripped my sisters' shoulders; Eve and Libbie stopped their bickering instantly. Eve's hand closed over the tattered piece of silk she always kept in sight. In the suddenly silent room, Vashti passed Tanta Rose on her way to the shelf beside the stove. She counted the number of empty glass jars stored there, jars she used for her infusions and decoctions, then silently she returned to the sitting room.

As soon as the door swung shut behind her, I relaxed my grip on my sisters, and they immediately resumed their argument over who had eaten the most oatmeal.

The stack of folded khaki trousers on the kitchen chair was twice as tall as it had been when I went to bed the night before. "How late were you up sewing, Tanta Rose?" I had to shout over the squawks of my sisters.

Tanta Rose shrugged and raised her eyebrows. "Not so late."

I opened the icebox door, slipped my newspaper earnings into the jar on the bottom shelf, and nosed around, looking for something to eat.

"Hannelah, please, you're letting out the cold. Girls, you will each finish two more bites of oatmeal." Tanta Rose showed no sign of hurry. She kept staring at my little book of drawings.

Libbie teased Eve, inching her bowl away each time Eve tried spooning up some oatmeal.

Tanta Rose inspected me through her thick glasses. "Hannah. What are these pictures?"

I knew which pictures she meant. She'd found my drawings of angels. "They are—they are just pictures, Tanta Rose," I said.

Tanta Rose raised one eyebrow. She stared again at my drawings.

At night, when Eve and Libbie, Tanta Rose and Vashti slept in the big bed, out the window I saw angels. The angels I saw weren't the fierce angels of the Torah. But they were angels just the same.

Tanta Rose cocked her head sideways. She looked like a small bird, her russet eyes magnified by the thick lenses of her glasses. "You don't really *see* angels, Hannelah."

I didn't know what to tell her.

"Hannah?"

My sisters stared at me, too.

I shrugged.

Tanta Rose's hand trembled as she shut my sketchbook. "Don't think about it. Maybe they'll go away."

How could I not think about it? I rubbed my nose with my stained hand.

"Girls, you will listen to Hannah today? Eve?"

Eve looked up at Tanta Rose, affection shining in her wide green eyes.

"Don't leave your *schmatte* at school again, darling. The janitor didn't like when Hannah made him open up yesterday afternoon."

Eve lowered her eyes and held her silky in her lap.

"And Libbie?"

Libbie's dark eyes blinked behind her wire-rimmed glasses. She looked like a miniature Tanta Rose, except Tanta Rose's hair had turned from wooly red to wooly white.

Tanta Rose placed her empty teacup on the table and hobbled over to Libbie. She stroked Libbie's cheek, looked fondly into the round pouting face, then turned back to me, fishing for her other coat sleeve. "Hannah, make certain Libbie gets *inside* her classroom this morning, yes?"

"Yes, Tanta Rose."

I turned to Libbie; freckles covered every inch of her face.

6

Tanta Rose had freckles, too, though hers had faded and blurred. Papa used to call Libbie's freckles angel kisses. Angel kisses and angel whispers. That was my sister Libbie and my Tanta Rose.

*"Oy, Gottenyu,* look at the time!" Tanta Rose cried. She surrounded us each with quick hugs, filling our noses with the smell of balm of Gilead. Then, scooping her night's work of hemmed trousers into her arms, she headed through the swinging door into the sitting room.

"Be good," she called over her shoulder. She exchanged a quick good-bye with Vashti, and then she was out the sitting room door and up the steps leading from our basement flat to the street above.

"Okay, you two," I said.

But instead of getting ready to leave for school, Eve and Libbie raced from kitchen to sitting room to bedroom in our long narrow apartment. I followed them, tucking my sketchbook into my apron pocket.

In the bedroom, one small window looked up to street level. Tanta Rose emerged in her dark coat and sensible shoes. She hobbled down the front tenement steps, and started up Chambers Street.

"Tanta Rosie," Eve called, making her small voice heard through the glass.

Tanta Rose turned, glanced down at the three of us, blew us a kiss.

Libbie, grabbing Eve's hand, ran giggling back toward the kitchen.

But I stayed at the window and slid out my sketchbook. I drew quickly as Tanta Rose walked away. I was still drawing when Vashti came up behind me.

"Hannah!"

7

I jumped.

With Vashti it was always the same. The stern glare. The silent reproach. She held her hand out.

I pulled myself up as tall and stubborn as I could manage.

Vashti never approved of anything I did—particularly my drawing.

Taking the sketchbook from me, she glanced over it, then carelessly threw it onto the bed. "A waste of time," she said. "A waste of paper." Turning sharply, she left the bedroom. Moments later her footsteps snapped out of the apartment. I watched her out the window until she passed from sight.

"Hannah?" Eve appeared at the bedroom door.

My sketch of Tanta Rose had creased along one side. I made it worse with my fist of anger.

"Hannah, be careful," Eve cried. Wisps of brown curls escaped her braids. Eve always looked a little tattered, like a soft old collar, but a sweetness about her made people smile. "May I see the picture?"

I tore the page out of my sketchbook and handed it to my little sister.

Smoothing the paper on the bed, Eve touched my drawing of Tanta Rose, the lines that formed her head, her swayed back, her long coat.

"Oh, Hannah," she said. "May I keep it?"

"Just don't let Vashti see it."

Eve nodded.

I took her hand and led her through the apartment. In the kitchen, Libbie sat at the crusty table, surrounded by dirty dishes, her nose in a copy of *Tarzan of the Apes*. In her school notebook, she had just written a new word. *Countenance.*

8

"Libbie, put the book away," I said. "You'll make us late."

Libbie glared at me. "So what."

"Oh, Libbie. Please."

Libbie closed her book on her thumb. "I can get myself to school, Hannah," she said. "You don't need to take me."

My nose itched, a nose just a little too big for the rest of my face. I rubbed the side of it. In my parents' absence, my sisters' care fell to me. "If I don't take you to school, you'll find a nice little corner and read all day—"

Libbie crossed her stubby arms over her chest.

"Why don't you want to go to school?" I asked. "You know how important it is to Mama and Papa we get an education."

"I don't like school, Hannah. It's a waste of time and paper."

The hairs rose on my neck to hear her sound so much like Vashti.

Eve said, "At school they call us orphans and Libbie fights."

"Libbie, you shouldn't fight," I told her.

Libbie looked defiant. "We're not orphans."

"Of course we're not," I said. "Papa and Mama will be home as soon as the war ends."

Libbie's chin stuck out stubbornly. "Hannah, I could stay home. Tanta Rose would never know."

Eve's eyes widened in horror. "God would know."

Eve worried about God, especially right before Yom Kippur, when God prepared to write our fate in the book of life and seal it for the coming year.

"Oh, pooh," Libbie said. "You and your God."

Vashti spoke this way of God, too.

"All right," Libbie grumbled, slamming her book shut.

9

"Fine." Snatching her schoolbag off its peg, she ran out the back door, into the alley. "But you don't want to go to school any more than I do, Hannah," she called back to me. "You just go so you can see Haaaarrryyy."

Eve and I grabbed our own bags and ran after her. I tucked my sketchbook inside my pocket as we raced out of the apartment. We caught up to Libbie at the corner of Brighton and Chambers.

The fruit peddler with his loaded pushcart brushed flies away. "Apples," he called, his pushcart wheels rattling over the cobblestones. He held a large red apple for Libbie to see. It shone in the mild September morning

Libbie took a step toward him, her hand outstretched.

"No, Libbie."

"I want an apple."

"I have no knife to cut it. How could we share?"

Libbie puckered her face into a frown. "Who said I wanted to share?"

Holding her by the back of the neck, I steered her past the pushcart. "Chip Pilasky says there's a greasy pole at Vaccaro's this afternoon."

Libbie forgot about the apple. "A greasy pole today?"

From time to time the Italian grocers would set up a greasy pole in honor of some festival, usually on *Shabbes* when we couldn't go to watch.

"I want to see," Libbie said.

I frowned. "We can't. We have classes at the Settlement House this afternoon."

Libbie pulled away from us, racing around the corner. I caught sight of her stocky body just as it wriggled its way into a crowd gathered around the newly erected pole at Mr. Vaccaro's store.

His trousers rolled above his knobby ankles, Mr. Vaccaro sang in Italian as he climbed a ladder leaning against the wooden pole. A rope hung loosely around his middle.

Mrs. Vaccaro shouted from the bottom of the ladder. "Juley, get down before you hurt yourself!" She was a big woman with a voice that rumbled like loose gravel.

"Today is my birthday. Today I fix the pole myself," Mr. Vaccaro called down to his wife.

Kids clapped each time he climbed another rung on the ladder.

"Let the boys take care of it, Juley!" Mrs. Vaccaro cried.

"Today I take care of it," Mr. Vaccaro called to her. He looked out over the small crowd gathered on the street. "You kids coming back later to see who makes it to the top?"

Rocky Keegan shouted, "I'd rather watch you fall now."

"You should be nice," Mr. Vaccaro called down to Rocky.

I caught sight of Harry halfway down the block.

From the time we'd moved in with Tanta Rose and Vashti on Chambers Street, I had been aware of Harry Weitz. He would watch when Rocky Keegan made fun of my wild curls or my pencil-smudged nose. Then one day I'd had enough. I told Rocky to quit or I'd smudge *his* nose. Harry backed me up. He started walking with me. He said he liked my hair. We kissed on the roof once, but it was only for a second, just to get it over with.

I waved to get Harry's attention; he came down the block to stand beside me. His arm slipped around my waist.

Mrs. Vaccaro bellowed, "Julius, you'll make me a widow!"

"I'll bet you your Jewish star Mr. Vaccaro gets all the way to

I I

the top," Harry whispered in my ear. "Even with Mrs. Vaccaro yelling at him."

Harry had often admired the six-pointed Star of David resting in the hollow of my throat. Papa had given it to me in March, right before he left for the Great War.

"The star will remind you to always take care of Eve and Libbie while Mama and I are gone," Papa had said. He gave stars to my sisters, too. Once I nearly lost mine. The clasp would get tangled in my curls. During art class at the Settlement House, as I leaned over my drawing, the star had dropped right onto my paper. It frightened me to think how easily I might have lost it. Libbie did lose hers, two months ago, the same time Papa's letters stopped coming. Eve asked if it was Libbie's fault Papa had stopped writing. Tanta Rose said Libbie losing her star at the same time Papa stopped writing—that was a coincidence. Papa would write as soon as he could. Libbie added the word *coincidence* to her list of words.

I looked into Harry's eyes. They were the same dark blue as the Charles River.

"He shouldn't be up there," I said. "He's an old man to climb a ladder. Look how his knees are shaking."

"Old man maybe, but I bet he makes it," Harry said. "And if he does I get to keep your star for a week." Harry's dark hair, parted on the side, lay softly on his broad forehead. When I looked at Harry I forgot about seeing angels.

Just then Mr. Vaccaro's foot slipped. He scrambled to regain his balance.

Mrs. Vaccaro shrieked, "Juley!" and thumped her fists against her breasts.

I held my breath. But the next moment he was climbing again, grinning.

12

"That's just to make it exciting," Mr. Vaccaro called down to us.

Harry nudged me with his elbow. "Straight to the top."

"But he slipped."

"Slipping doesn't count."

At that very moment, Mr. Vaccaro reached the top of the pole. With his wife's help, he pulled up the basket holding a salami, a cheese, and a ten dollar bill and set them in the hoop.

As he climbed down the ladder, he spread black, miserable axle grease all around the pole. When his feet touched ground again we all cheered. Mr. Vaccaro turned to Mrs. Vaccaro. "You see?"

"You big fool, you could have killed yourself up there."

Mr. Vaccaro stretched his greasy hands toward us. "You come back this afternoon."

He cleaned one finger at a time on a towel Mrs. Vaccaro held for him, then rolled down his pants cuffs and squinted up at his handiwork. Carefully he removed the ladder and carried it away. Mrs. Vaccaro flapped her apron at us.

"Shoo," she called. "Show is over till this afternoon."

In one motion, we broke away, like a flock of birds, flying around the corner toward school.

I grabbed my sisters' hands so as not to lose them in the rush.

Harry kept pace with us. "You owe me that star," he called. "You owe me your star, Hannah Gold."

"I owe you nothing, Harry Weitz," I answered, running. "Not a single thing."

After school I picked up Eve and Libbie and walked them to the

Settlement House. They took dance lessons while I attended art class.

On our way back home, we bought an orange from the street peddler, and Eve carried it to our front stoop. We sat outside the tenement in the sunshine. The smell of Mrs. McCarthy's ham wafting out the open window twisted my stomach inside out. Pork, ham, bacon—all forbidden to Jews. At that moment my stomach did not want to know from oranges. It only wanted to eat something that smelled so good.

Eve stared up at me. "What are you thinking, Hannah?"

"I'm thinking I wish Mrs. McCarthy would invite me to dinner. The smell of her ham is driving me crazy."

Eve looked horrified.

"Don't worry, Evie. I wouldn't really eat it. Can you imagine how fast that news would get around the West End? Extra! Extra! Read all about it! Hannah Gold Eats *Trayf*! Mama would probably hear about it all the way in Russia."

Eve pushed up close to me. "What do you think Mama is doing right now?"

I imagined Mama on the other side of the world in a little house with a dirt floor. "I don't know."

"I hope God is writing a good fate for her this year," Eve said.

Mama had been trapped in Russia for four years.

"Well, he won't," Libbie said. "God is writing a bad fate for Mama because she went away and left us." Libbie's mouth, crammed with orange, shot out bits of juice as she talked, spotting the pages of her book.

I glared at Libbie. "God is doing no such thing. Mama went to Russia to take care of Bubbe. How was she to know the war would come?"

Eve was only three when Mama left. Three is very young to go without a mother. I'd taken good care of my sisters all these years. It wasn't so difficult while we lived in the old apartment on Wall Street with Papa. But Papa had gone to fight Bolsheviks. Now Libbie sounded more like Vashti every day. And Eve, she stayed a baby, never going anywhere with out her silky. I wished Mama and Papa would come home, and we could be a family again. Not that Tanta Rose wasn't good to us, but Vashti— Vashti was like something burning in your chest when you eat too fast.

Libbie, Eve, and I sat on the tenement steps, sharing the juicy sections of orange. Eve chewed slowly.

Across the street, in Mr. Murry's window, Hebrew books, brass candlesticks, and copper dishes collected dust. They had been pawned by neighbors selling their valuables for quick cash. Since we'd come to live with Tanta Rose, some of her own things had passed through that shop. Nothing of Vashti's, though. Vashti gave up nothing for us.

Mr. Bones steered his soap wagon past. Outside Mr. Izzy's butcher shop, boxes of green vegetables crowded the sidewalk. People yelled, horns blared.

Blocking it all out, Libbie licked her fingertip and turned the page of her Tarzan book. At eight years old, Libbie was some kind of brain. She could read anything. Bent over the pages of her book, her wire-rimmed spectacles slipping down her nose, she would make lists of words as she read, carefully spelling them out and memorizing them.

Looking through the drawings in my sketchbook, Eve rubbed her silky, a scrap from the baby blanket Mama had made for her. She made up a song as we sat on the stoop.

I 5

"Pickles and fish,
Pickles and fish,
Apples in barrels
and pickles in fish."

I leaned back with the sun on my face and shut my eyes.

"Are you tired, Hannah?" Eve asked.

I nodded.

Eve lifted her silky and rubbed it against my cheek. "If I stay up late, will I see angels, too?"

I opened my eyes for a moment, and looked down at my sister. She had stopped in my sketchbook at the drawings of angels. "You can't stay up late, Eve."

Eve rubbed her silky over her own cheek. "Do you see angels while you're helping Tanta Rosie?"

"No. I see them later. Much later. When everyone's sleeping."

"I see them, too," Eve said. "When it's very, very late."

I studied her a moment. Shut my eyes again. "Maybe you do," I said.

With my eyes closed, I tried imagining Mama in the apartment making kugel and Papa, in a suit, on his way home from work. The clop of horse hoofs, the leather creak of a harness, a deep familiar voice drove the fancy from my mind. Instead, behind my closed lids I saw Mr. Shaw in his ice wagon. The sharp tang of horse sweat mingled with the smell of baking ham and orange rinds.

Keeping my eyes shut, I concentrated on the ice wagon, trying to pull all the details into my mind. My fingers twitched for pencil and paper.

16

Opening my eyes, I adjusted what I'd seen behind closed lids to fit the real lines of the wagon.

Mr. Shaw waved to us and made a quick bow. "Good afternoon, ladies."

"Hi, Mr. Shaw," Eve said.

Mr. Shaw glanced up at the card in the third-story window above the Weitzes' apartment.

"Ten center for Mrs. Rubin," he said, making a note on a scrap of paper.

With a grunt, he lifted a block of ice with his tongs, threw it onto his shoulder, and held it there as he headed for the Weitzes' building, resting the ice on his rubber cape. He entered the dark vestibule beside Mrs. Weitz's dressmaking shop.

As soon as he disappeared from sight, Rocky Keegan hopped into the back of the wagon, reappearing a moment later with a stolen sliver of ice.

Libbie, looking up from her book, fixed Rocky with a scowl. I glared at him, too.

He glared back. "You got a problem, Banana Nose?"

I held my temper. "He'd give you a piece if you asked."

"So there ain't nothing wrong with my taking it, is there?" Rocky snarled, running off before Mr. Shaw could come back.

More West End boys wandered over and started a ball game. They'd gone straight from school to watch the greasy pole at Vaccaro's. Someone from the North End beat out a kid from Vaccaro's own neighborhood.

Naomi and Nathan Strauss came out of their building. They crossed Chambers Street and minced down the block toward us. Nathan, at twelve, was plenty big enough to play ball

17

with the older boys, but he didn't. His brother, Ovadiah, for-
bade it.

Before they reached us, I stood and walked to the curb and
back, glancing at Rocky Keegan to see if he'd noticed Naomi and
Nathan's approach.

Ovadiah always sent Naomi to sit beside us in the balcony
of our synagogue, too. On Rosh Hashanah, we would all stare
down at her brother through the wooden screen. The men wor-
shiped downstairs in the main sanctuary, women in the balcony.
We all stared at Ovadiah because his voice was so big he over-
powered every other voice in the congregation. It could give you
a headache, Ovadiah's singing. I felt sorry for Nathan, standing
right next to him. But Tanta Rose said Ovadiah had the voice of
an angel.

Harry came out of his apartment last. Mr. and Mrs. Weitz
insisted Harry's studies came before play. Mrs. Weitz said if
everyone else in Harry's class did two hours of homework, Harry
should do four. She watched him, checking every paper. "Think,"
she always said. "Think, Harry. Not only about how to do it, but
why to do it."

When Harry caught sight of us he waved. He took off his
jacket and then his overshirt in the warm September afternoon,
and I studied the muscles in his arms and his back, how they
moved as he swung the stick, wondering if I could draw muscles
like that, moving under skin.

I sat on the stoop, took up my sketchbook, turned to a
blank sheet, and started drawing.

Mrs. Gantz and Mrs. Rizzoli, leaning out their windows,
gossiped over our heads. Their voices made music in the back-
ground.

But suddenly their voices stopped. I looked up from my sketching.

Ovadiah was coming out of his tenement, down the steps. He moved slowly, shambling in his dark coat like a bear.

Nearly every man from the West End who was not too young, like Harry, or too old, like Mr. Yankel, had enlisted to fight in the war. But not Ovadiah. He was the right age to go, but he stayed home anyway.

"Why doesn't your brother go off to fight like everyone else?" Libbie asked.

Nathan watched his brother coming down the street. "He's a scholar, not a soldier," Nathan said. "Besides, he promised our parents he wouldn't. Anyway, who would take care of us if Ovadiah went to war?"

"I don't know," I told him. "Tanta Rose looks after us."

Nathan shrugged. "But what if something happened to your aunt? She's an old woman. Who would look after you then?"

I was at a loss to answer. Who would look after us then? Certainly not Vashti.

"Rocky Keegan says your brother doesn't go to war because he's a coward," Libbie said.

"My brother isn't afraid of anything."

Ovadiah shambled down the block, coming closer to the stickball game. Rocky, seeing Ovadiah's approach, stopped the game and raced toward us, most of the other boys following on his heels. They pushed Libbie, Eve, and me up the steps and inside the tenement.

Rocky had spread a rumor about Ovadiah. He said Ovadiah could turn boys into cowards just by looking at them. Rocky didn't want anything like that happening to him. He planned on enlisting in the army on his sixteenth birthday. His parents were signing.

Rocky led the way down the inside steps of our tenement.

I looked back at Naomi and Nathan, alone outside on the stoop. Their expressions made me pause.

"Hey, why don't you hide in your own place," I called down to Rocky.

"Your place is closer," Rocky said. "Besides, my pop's sick. Ma said I should keep away."

I looked again outside at Nathan and Naomi, and they looked back at me. I should have stood up to Rocky.

I didn't.

Rocky and the other boys crowded through our sitting-room door, spilling into our apartment, and I followed them. Harry stood in the street, watching me disappear into the tenement.

With Tanta Rose still at work at the factory and Vashti out gathering weeds, the apartment was my responsibility.

Rocky raced from the sitting room into our bedroom, where he watched at the window until Ovadiah, Nathan, and Naomi had gone. Then he pushed his way into the kitchen.

"Hey, I'm hungry, Banana Nose. What you Jews got to eat?"

I pulled up straight. Libbie's face turned red enough to blend her freckles together.

Rocky poked around the kitchen, peering inside our cabinets, letting the icebox door hang open. The rest of the boys took his actions as an invitation to turn everything in our kitchen upside down.

Fury boiled up inside of me. "Get out of here!" I grabbed for Rocky's shirt, but he shrugged me off.

He headed back to the cabinet between the stove and the sink, as Harry came through the kitchen door.

I grabbed at Rocky again.

This time he pushed me away, hard.

Tripping over the cracked linoleum, I hit the kitchen table with my hip, and Tanta Rose's teacup, her precious blue-flowered teacup, skipped toward the table's edge. Throwing myself across the top, I lunged to catch it. I missed.

But Harry was there. He caught the cup as it fell. The whole thing happened in a matter of seconds. If Harry had been just an instant late, the cup would have smashed to bits on the floor.

I took the cup from Harry and placed it high on the shelf without even thanking him. My hands trembled. The thought of having almost broken Tanta Rose's cup, the thought of Rocky's comment about Jews, made me furious.

"All of you out," I cried.

"Get out!"


I stood at the sitting-room door, waiting for Tanta Rose, whose slow footsteps announced her arrival. She dragged herself inside the apartment with a fresh bundle of trousers to be hemmed, hobbled into the kitchen, and sat in the chair closest to the stove. I took the unhemmed trousers from her and piled them on an empty seat. Tanta Rose rubbed at her neck. She eased off her shoes one at a time and sighed.

"Here. Let me make you a cup of tea." My sisters and I exchanged glances. I retrieved the cup from the high shelf.

Tanta Rose sagged in her seat, her spotted hands resting in her lap. Pouring off hot water from the reservoir in the stove, I fixed the tea strong, the way she liked it.

While the leaves steeped, I rubbed Tanta Rose's back, working at the tension in her shoulders the way I'd seen Vashti do.

Tanta Rose sighed. "Ahh, Hannelah. That's very good."

In the still of the early evening, we had Tanta Rose all to ourselves. Libbie and Eve played quietly beside the stove. Vashti had not yet come back with her weeds.

Tanta Rose listened as we told her about our day.

"Miss Levy is planning an art show at the Settlement House," I said.

Tanta Rose nodded, sipping her tea from the blue-flowered cup. She tipped her head back and drained the last swallow down her throat, delicately picking the bits of tea leaves from the tip of her tongue. Carrying her empty cup across the kitchen, Tanta Rose sighed again. I studied the hump of her back as she stood unmoving in front of the porcelain sink. My fingers itched to draw her.

Slowly Tanta Rose turned.

"Can you wait for supper, girls?" she asked.

My stomach burned hungrily, but I nodded. Libbie made a face, but she nodded, too.

"Why?" I asked.

"Even the insides of my bones ache tonight," Tanta Rose said. "I'm thinking a bath would be an extra we could afford. President Wilson hasn't rationed baths yet, has he?"

I smiled. The president of the United States rationed our sugar and our coal because of the war. But he had said nothing about baths.

"Will you help me get the tub ready, Hannah?"

"I want a bath, too," Libbie said.

"You do?" Tanta Rose asked.

"Me, too," said Eve.

We heated extra water on the coal stove in the kitchen.

Tanta Rose rubbed her hands together and laughed mischievously as Libbie undressed. "Won't we be something? Spanking clean on a Tuesday."

Eve and I stole oats from Vashti's stash, and I tied a handful into a cloth bag. We put the oat bag in the bottom of the tub, then poured hot water over it, the milky white cream from the oats easing into the water. The oats soothed our itchy skin, making it soft and smooth. I hoped Vashti didn't come home too soon and catch us.

Libbie climbed in first. She let me wash her hair, fussing the whole time. And then out she came and in went Eve.

Tanta Rose, who had the idea for a bath in the first place, waited patiently. While I washed my little sisters, she took a pair of trousers onto her lap in the steamy kitchen and started hemming.

When Eve and Libbie scurried back to the bedroom for their nightgowns, I prepared the tub for Tanta Rose.

"Don't you want a bath, too, Hannah?" Tanta Rose asked.

"I can wait until Thursday," I said.

If I did not wait, Tanta Rose would get no bath at all.

She nodded. "Thank you, darling."

Slowly, Tanta Rose unfastened her clothes, folding layer after layer neatly over the kitchen chair. At last, naked, she stepped into the tub. I loved Tanta Rose's body, freckles on white skin, her breasts saggy, her belly and thighs round and dimpled. I wanted to draw her like that, naked, inside the washtub, but what would Vashti have said about a picture like that?

Mrs. McCarthy's piano played above us.

"Why don't you brush out my hair, Hannelah." Tanta Rose sat with her head back against the hard lip of the tub, her glasses off.

Usually, brushing Tanta Rose's hair was a family activity. Every night before bed we took turns with it. Vashti always got to brush first. I loved having it to do all myself. I loved having Tanta Rose and my sisters all to myself. Running the gilded brush through Tanta Rose's white hair, I pretended Mama and Papa would be coming through the door any minute, that when they arrived we would have a great celebration and eat three kinds of sweets for dinner. And from Russia, Mama would bring ham that was kosher. And none of us would ever be separated from each other, no matter what happened, ever again.

## chapter two

## Saturday, September 14, 1918

STANDING IN THE CHILLY PREDAWN SHADOW of North Station. I shivered until the sun rose high enough to reach me. Hawking my bundle of newspapers, my voice rasped. Business was slow. Some Saturdays were like that. Actually, all business had slowed since the influenza hit town.

Pilasky yelled at me between customers, "Hey, Gold. Stay out front where I can see you."

Chip Pilasky looked out for me. A girl selling newspapers in Boston could find herself in trouble; newsgirls got beat up, robbed.

"I like it better around the side," I yelled to Chip. "I'm selling papers like crazy over here."

I shouldn't have lied on the Sabbath; I shouldn't have lied so near Yom Kippur. But Chip Pilasky drove me crazy. He kept such a close eye on me it made me itch. It didn't seem right a ten-year-old kid like Pilasky should be protecting me. If women ever got the right to vote, it'd be different.

Between customers, I found plenty to read: about the war—the movement of battle lines in France, the casualty lists, ads for Liberty Bonds—and about the influenza.

Not only sailors had the grippe, but also civilians, some as far away as Brockton and Rutland. With so many doctors overseas, not enough remained stateside to tend to us.

Vashti stayed out most of the time now, treating those who couldn't afford a doctor. Some people, even if they could afford one, felt uneasy with doctors and hospitals. Like Harry's mother, Mrs. Weitz, they preferred Vashti.

After selling his last paper, Pilasky plunged his hands into his pockets and fell into step beside me. "You all done?"

I jangled the coins in my apron pocket with my empty newsprint-stained hands.

"I'll walk you as far as the library," he said. Chip went to a special library, one just for newsboys. It stayed open all the time.

"How's the new baby doing?" I asked as we walked.

Chip Pilasky's mother had given birth to her eleventh child a week ago.

"It ain't too good," Chip said. "It never gives up crying. I don't think it's eating right. I'm gonna look in the library about babies."

If Mama had been here, I could have asked her about Mrs. Pilasky's baby. "Hope you figure something out," I called as Chip pulled open the library door.

I dreaded coming home to an empty house. Tanta Rose and my sisters spent every Saturday morning at the synagogue. And then Saturday afternoon they visited neighbors. Sabbath visiting. That always meant good food to eat. Having to sell newspapers every Saturday, I didn't miss going to services, but I sure did miss the food.

I came in through the front door and found Vashti settled in the sitting room, sorting weeds. She didn't even look up. I pushed through to the kitchen, and after putting more coal on the stove, emptying the drip pan from under the icebox, and slurping down a bowl of broth, I opened my sketchbook to a clean page. Drawing kept me from feeling lonely. When I worked on my pictures, any worries I had disappeared. I planned on doing some drawings from the roof, but the view out the kitchen window caught my eye: the clotheslines strung across the alley, the piles of ash cans, the dark and sooty backsides of the tenements. I started sketching right there in the kitchen, losing track of time, when I heard banging at the sitting-room door. The noise startled me. My hand jerked, spoiling the picture. Why didn't Vashti answer the door? Annoyed, I burst into the sitting room.

Yanking the front door open, ready to take out my anger on the person doing the pounding, I found Harry standing before me.

"Harry!" I rubbed the side of my nose with my finger. Too late I remembered the pencil stains. Now my nose was smudged black.

"Harry?"

He looked uneasy, his dark hair messy.

"Harry, what is it?"

"My mother sent me to fetch Vashti, Hannah."

At that moment, Vashti came down the steps behind him. She must have been upstairs using the toilet.

"Vashti. My father is sick."

As she listened to Harry, Vashti gathered bottles of tinctures and decoctions from her shelves and placed them in her bag.

Harry and I followed along, a little distance behind her, to Mrs. Weitz's shop.

Mrs. Weitz looked up from her sewing machine as Vashti approached. "Oy, that Max, what a kvetch. That man could make a *tsimmes* over a hiccup. I can't keep running up and down the stairs, Vashti. But I'm worried—he shouldn't have flu."

Vashti rested a reassuring hand on Mrs. Weitz's shoulder, calming her. Then she turned, and still not noticing us, she climbed the inside stairs to the Weitzes' apartment.

Bent over her sewing machine again, Mrs. Weitz also missed seeing the two of us creep up the inside stairs. We watched from the shadows as Vashti examined Mr. Weitz.

"Oy, Vashti," Mr. Weitz whimpered, catching hold of her arm.

Vashti moved her fingers so she could take his pulse. "Yes, Max."

Mr. Weitz began coughing. He couldn't speak for nearly a minute because of the coughing. "I was coming home from the factory yesterday. Before I reached Hanover Street my head, my eyes—such an ache."

Vashti continued her examination with a gentleness that surprised me.

The Weitzes' apartment, usually bright and cheerful, seemed dark and gloomy behind closed curtains. It smelled stale, like a sweatshop. Vashti parted the curtains. She pushed open the windows, letting the crisp autumn air rush in. The breeze sweetened the sour smell of the room.

Vashti spread another blanket on the shivering Mr. Weitz.

"I couldn't go to Sabbath services, Vashti."

"God will understand," Vashti said, listening to Mr. Weitz's chest. "Rest awhile, Max. I'm going to the kitchen and fix something for you to eat."

"Don't bother," Mr. Weitz said. "I couldn't eat a thing."

"Of course you can."

Mr. Weitz always protested he couldn't eat, only to sit down and polish off a heaping platter of whatever sat before him.

In a few minutes Vashti brought back a bowl of fresh greens. She sprinkled a tonic from her bag over the contents of the bowl. I smelled vinegar, horseradish, onion. The stink made my eyes water.

Shoulder to shoulder, Harry and I watched Vashti feed Mr. Weitz one small forkful at a time. We did not talk, pressed against each other in the narrow stairwell. Harry held my hand, surprising me with the coldness of his fingers. I looked into his face and saw lines of worry. Squeezing his hand, I tried to reassure him everything would be all right.

Mr. Weitz had eaten only half of the greens Vashti prepared when he put up his hand for her to stop. Groaning, his forehead breaking into large beads of sweat, he grabbed for the bucket beside the bed and emptied from his stomach the food Vashti had just put into it.

We didn't wait to see more. Harry and I crept down the stairs and through the shop out onto the street. I expected him to take my hand again, but when I looked over, he'd jammed his fists deep into his pockets. He kept his head down.

"Would you rather be alone, Harry?"

"No. No, Hannah," Harry said. "Please, stay with me."

Relieved, I moved a little closer to him. If Harry had sent me away—I don't know. I think I needed him as much as he needed me.

We kept silent for a long time as we walked through the busy West End. I couldn't get the sound and sight of Mr. Weitz retching out of my mind.

29

"Do you think it's really influenza?" Harry asked as we walked along the bank of the Charles.

"It might be," I said. "Your mother is crazy to send for Vashti. Why didn't she call a real doctor?"

"My mother thinks Vashti is better than a real doctor."

I shook my head.

"It's true, Hannah."

Sixteen years ago, Harry's mother didn't think she could have children, and then she met Vashti. A year later she gave birth to Harry. Mrs. Weitz believed Vashti worked miracles.

Harry reached for my hand.

I pulled away. "You'll get smudged."

"I don't mind, Hannah. Pencil washes off."

His hand stretched toward me again and this time I took it. "The other day Nathan Strauss asked what would happen to us, to Eve and Libbie and me, if Tanta Rose died. Tanta Rose could never die, but—I don't know, Harry. I wish Mama and Papa would come home."

Harry was silent for a moment. Then he let out a ragged sigh. "What will I do if my father dies?"

"Your father won't die, Harry," I assured him. How could Mr. Weitz die? How could Tanta Rose die? Such things could never happen.

"Mr. Weitz has influenza, Tanta Rose," I announced, coming through the kitchen door. The light outside had faded to gray.

Tanta Rose looked up from her sewing. On the stove simmered kasha in water and chicken fat. "Is it bad?" she asked.

"It's bad."

Libbie and Eve sat on the linoleum playing the card game "war."

"Since we got home from Sabbath visiting," Eve said, "we had to send three people away. They were all looking for Vashti."

"Are we going to get influenza, too?" Libbie asked. *Influenza* had made it onto Libbie's list of words days ago.

"This question you should ask Vashti," Tanta Rose said.

"But Vashti isn't here," I said, coming close to my aunt. "So we are asking you. Are we going to get it?"

Tanta Rose's fingers moved skillfully around the hem of a trouser leg. The sounds of Mrs. McCarthy at her piano reached through to our apartment.

"We might," she said, clipping a piece of thread with her teeth. "Influenza you get easy. Maybe you're on the streetcar and someone coughs; maybe you're selling newspapers and someone spits near you. Or you touch somebody's hand and then you rub your nose. You know how you rub your nose, Hannah?"

I nodded.

"Then you, my darling, might very well get influenza. So be careful. If anyone is coughing or sneezing or spitting, move out of the way. If they want to shake your hand or give you a kiss"—my sisters exchanged knowing glances and mouthed the word *Harry*—"say, 'I'm not feeling very sociable today.' You understand?"

"How do you know if you've got it?" I'd been feeling queasy ever since Mr. Weitz.

"Oh, you'll know. You'll get a chill, such a chill your bones shiver, and then the fever comes. It spreads through your body so fast. Your head aches, your back aches, your eyes ache—everything."

Tanta Rose turned to Libbie and Eve. "If you feel that way you come straight home, you understand? You'll be fine. You'll rest a few days, drink Vashti's concoctions. You'll see. Vashti will make you all better."

I nodded. "What about you?"

"Don't worry about me."

"Every day you work at the factory next to sick people. And Vashti could—"

Tanta Rose lifted her eyebrow. "Vashti could what? Are you concerned for Vashti?"

"No," I said, bluntly. "I'm concerned she could bring the illness into our house."

Tanta Rose nodded, looking tired. "Don't forget, Hannelah. This is Vashti's home, too. But yes, you're right. Vashti could bring it in, I could bring it in, any of us could bring the illness here."

Shortly after dinner, Vashti's footsteps creaked down the front stairs. Tanta Rose put down her sewing in the middle of a hem.

Libbie and Eve played on the kitchen floor in front of the stove.

I followed Tanta Rose into the sitting room and watched as Vashti came to the door, her back straight, her bag of tinctures and syrups gripped in her fist.

"Have you been all these hours with Max Weitz?" Tanta Rose asked.

Vashti stood in the doorway. "I have seen others."

"Take Vashti's bag from her, Hannah," Tanta Rose said, striking a match to light the lamp in the sitting room. "I'll warm up the kasha for you, Vashti."

Vashti shrugged me away.

"I'm not hungry, Rose. Just some tea if you would."

Vashti, exhausted, had left the front door open. Kneeling, her long legs folded beneath her, she unpacked the remains of her tinctures and syrups. Immediately she refilled and repacked the bag again, preparing for her next round of patients.

Tanta Rose returned from the kitchen, shut the front door, and placed a cup of tea beside Vashti. She settled herself in the big chair, surrounded by shelves of Vashti's jars and bottles and bags. Tanta Rose studied Vashti with a concerned look.

Vashti returned her gaze. "I haven't seen anything like it, Rose. Entire buildings filled with influenza. I am seeing not only my regular families but dozens of others." Vashti unscrewed the lid of a bottle and sniffed. "I've never seen an illness fill a city so quickly. Whole families taken sick at once. And the illness comes on so suddenly, so violently. The people, most of them, too poor to call a doctor. Too weak to prepare the simplest meal."

"I'll make soup," Tanta Rose said. "You can bring it with you. Good chicken soup."

Tanta Rose. She was ready to feed half of Boston without a thought to how she would feed the five of us.

But to imagine the delicious aroma of chicken soup filling our apartment made me light-headed.

I closed my eyes, picturing myself eating soup with big white portions of chicken and potato-filled kreplach and golden circles of fat gliding across the surface of the bowl.

"Hannah!" Tanta Rose's voice rang with alarm. "What's the matter, Hannah?"

My eyes snapped open. I swallowed. "Nothing, Tanta Rose."

"You're not sick? You're not coming down with the grippe?" Tanta Rose exchanged glances with Vashti.

"No, Tanta Rose. I'm fine."

"Examine her, Vashti," Tanta Rose ordered.

Vashti put aside her bottles and stood, then came over to me, her blue eye and her brown eye studying me as she approached.

Vashti touched the back of her hand to my forehead and my cheeks, ran her fingers behind my ears, under my jaw, down the sides of my neck. She told me to stick out my tongue. She listened to me breathe, counted my heartbeats.

"She's fine." Vashti turned her back on me, returning to her inventory.

Tanta Rose sighed. "You work too hard, Hannah. Between your newspapers and your schoolwork and your sisters and helping me with the sewing. A child of fourteen should not work so hard. What would your mother say? Go. Go into the kitchen. I almost forgot I have a surprise for you in there. And you, Vashti, drink your tea," Tanta Rose ordered.

Vashti took the cup in her hands, but before she could sip from it someone knocked on the sitting-room door, and a few moments later she was gone again.

Tanta Rose lit the lamp in the shadowy kitchen and sent Libbie and Eve to bed. The kitchen door swung shut behind them.

In Tanta Rose's coat pocket, wrapped in paper, was a little package. She thrust the package into my hand, and I unwrapped it carefully. Inside the paper sat a doughnut.

"Where did you find a doughnut?" I asked. My mouth watered.

"Eat," Tanta Rose said. "It's from Mrs. Rubin, for you."

"But it's a doughnut, Tanta Rose."

"So?" Tanta Rose asked.

"Is it kosher?"

"Hannelah, it's from Mrs. Rubin. Of course it's kosher. You think I would bring something trayf for you?"

"What about Libbie and Eve?"

"Libbie and Eve went Sabbath visiting with me. They had their doughnuts already."

I broke off a piece, offered some to my aunt.

"No, you eat."

Nibbling the edges of the fried treat, I let the taste spread across my tongue. The sweetness made a singing below my ears. My mouth danced with pleasure.

Tanta Rose moved her half-finished hem from the table and dug out the big soup pot.

"You brought home a lot of sewing," I said.

Tanta Rose nodded. "It's the weekend."

"But what of preparation for Yom Kippur?"

"If I don't work, Hannah, we don't eat."

While Tanta Rose bustled around the kitchen, filling the big pot with water, preparing to make chicken soup for the sick, I took up the hemming. Tanta Rose settled herself across the table from me to peel and slice carrots.

"Have you finished your lessons for Monday?" she asked.

"I still have mathematics to do."

"Which you haven't started yet?"

"Not yet, Tanta Rose."

Tanta Rose lifted her eyebrow. "Well, what are you waiting for? The war to end?"

My hands stretched across the table to Tanta Rose. "It's not that much homework."

"Do it."

I tied a knot and broke the thread with my teeth. Taking my schoolbag from its peg, I bent over the math paper at the kitchen table. It took only minutes to complete the problems. Passing behind Tanta Rose, I hung my schoolbag back up.

Tanta Rose flicked thin carrot peels onto a piece of newspaper. "All done?"

I nodded.

She eased the scraped carrots into the boiling broth. "All that trouble I gave you for a few minutes of homework?"

I shrugged.

"Good," Tanta Rose said. "Remember, in case I forget to give you trouble some other time." She left the stove long enough to come over and give me a kiss. "So, take out your drawings and show me what made your fingers and your nose so dirty today, my little da Vinci."

I pulled my sketchbook from my pocket and slid it under the pool of light from the lamp. I didn't show her the ruined picture I'd been working on when Harry came. I turned instead to another page.

Tanta Rose's thick-lensed eyes studied the drawing resting on the oilcloth. "That's Eve," she said, tapping the lacy dark curls framing Eve's small face. Tanta Rose returned to the stove and stirred the pot. "Eve dancing. It's a beautiful picture, Hannelah."

Smiling, I put my sketchbook away and picked up the hemming again.

"Tanta Rose, what's an epidemic?"

"Epidemic is when a lot of people get sick at once. When I

was a girl in Russia there was cholera. Very bad. We would have died, but my mother sent me and my sisters away. We stayed with relatives on a farm in the country."

She continued stirring, her glasses fogged with steam.

"Is cholera like influenza?" I asked.

A shiver rattled Tanta Rose as she stood at the hot stove. The spoon clanged against the side of the pot. Tanta Rose lost her grip, and the spoon dropped into the simmering broth.

"Oy, Hannah, now look what you made me do."

She made a big fuss about the spoon. She never answered my question.

chapter three

*Friday, September 20, 1918*

L IBBIE AND EVE SLEPT UNCOVERED in the balmy morning, their bottoms pushed up against each other in the big bed.

Coming into the kitchen, I pressed a kiss against Tanta Rose's cheek. The kerosene lamp burned at the table, casting long shadows. Tanta Rose simmered more soup, always more soup for the sick. She stirred carrots, celery, and onion into the chicken broth. Inside a bowl, yeast bubbled slowly, the beginnings of our Sabbath challah. I filled my apron pocket with money to buy a bundle of morning papers.

"Is it all right for Hannah to go out, Vashti?" Tanta Rose asked. "With so much illness?"

Vashti sat at the table, crushing dried leaves. She nodded.

A shadow approached our back door from the alley. I thought for a moment of angels.

The shadow took shape as it came down the back steps to our kitchen. There was a soft knock.

Vashti rose from her work to answer.

Standing in our doorway was no angel. It was Ovadiah.

Bug-eyed, bear-shaped Ovadiah.

Vashti stepped aside to let him in.

"You're out early," Tanta Rose said, as Ovadiah entered the flickering light of the kitchen. "Who would guess scholars did their visiting this time of day."

"I am helping Hershel Yankel," Ovadiah said, in his thick accent. "The regular delivery boy is sick with influenza."

"Who is looking after Nathan and Naomi?" Tanta Rose asked.

Ovadiah shifted the crate with Tanta Rose's Sabbath order. "They are outside in the alley."

I looked. Sure enough, Nathan and Naomi leaned sleepily against one another in the grainy dark.

"I will take them to school later. If you think it is safe for them to go, Vashti."

Vashti opened the door and summoned Naomi and Nathan into our kitchen.

Naomi looked like Ovadiah: protruding eyes, a body too large, taking up too much space. Nathan was different. He was tall for twelve, and wiry. His hair curled wildly around the edges of his cap, and his eyes were wide apart and green like mine. People mistook us for brother and sister.

Ovadiah and Nathan and Naomi dressed as if they still lived in the old country, Naomi always in a kerchief, Ovadiah and Nathan always in their hats. They were out of place in America. Out of place in our kitchen.

"Put the crate down on the table," Tanta Rose instructed.

Ovadiah, relieved of his load, straightened his broad back.

"Sit," Vashti ordered, pointing at chairs for Ovadiah and

Naomi and Nathan. Then, sorting through the groceries Ovadiah had brought, she reached for the apple strudel and opened the wrappings.

I stared at her. What was she doing? That was our dessert. Our Sabbath dessert.

"Vashti!" The harsh cry escaped my mouth before I could call it back. "That's for us for Shabbes!"

Tanta Rose frowned at me.

Vashti lifted her head and glared. "Who do you think you are, Hannah Gold?" Vashti used each word like a knife to stab me.

I knew exactly what she was doing. I had seen her generosity before, generosity heaped into the outstretched arms of strangers. Yet not a shred of that kindness did she save for us, for my sisters and for me.

"We are not hungry," Ovadiah said. "Strudel is too sweet to start the day."

Nathan's pinched face, however, said something different.

Vashti picked up the knife and cut the apple strudel.

"Just a small piece," Ovadiah said, embarrassed.

Vashti cut Ovadiah a large slice of apple strudel. Bigger pieces went to Nathan and Naomi.

I couldn't believe she was feeding him, the coward, the man who would not fight in the Great War. Ovadiah, that big bear of a man, sat at our kitchen table, preparing to eat our apple strudel. A man who would rather sit and read Torah all day than defend his country. While my father risked his life, while my mother remained trapped by Bolsheviks, while hundreds of West End boys rushed to serve their country, Ovadiah sat comfortably in America reading Torah and eating our strudel. Vashti did not just feed him the soup we saved for ourselves after the best soup was distributed among the sick. No! She was feeding him our precious apple strudel, the strudel we should have had for our Sabbath.

Ovadiah wiped his hands clean before eating. "Thank you, Vashti," he said, offering a prayer to God as well. His dark bulging eyes disgusted me.

"Thank you," Nathan and Naomi mumbled.

"It is very bad?" Ovadiah asked, looking with concern at his sister and brother. "This influenza?"

Vashti nodded. She cut him another piece of strudel to take with him. And two more pieces for Naomi and Nathan. She pushed it into their hands. "You'll eat it later," she said. "You'll eat in your sukkah up on the roof, yes?"

Unable to watch the strudel disappear completely, I flew out of the kitchen in a rage, out to Chambers Street. Racing across the West End, I tried running off my bad mood. A scowl was no good for business. All through the neighborhoods, soft rectangles of light brightened the early morning in tenement window after tenement window. After buying my bundle of papers, I hustled to catch up with Pilasky at North Station.

"Hey, Gold," he called, as I came into sight. "You kept me waiting this morning. Couldn't you get your stockings on straight?"

"My stockings are fine, thank you, Pilasky. How's the baby today?"

"It don't cry so much anymore, but my ma thinks maybe it's sick."

"Don't *you* get sick," I called.

"Don't worry about me. Just be here when you say you will. We don't want no one else beating us to the station."

A crowd of customers headed toward me. North Station topped every other place in the West End for selling the news.

"Paper! Paper!"

Some customers preferred taking their paper from me. Others went out of their way to avoid me. They muttered about girls doing a boy's work.

"Paper! Paper!"

Any customer who came within ten feet of me I looked directly in the eye. Sometimes I followed them straight into the station. That's the way to sell papers. By looking a person in the eye.

The sun was up already, and my papers nearly all sold, when Rocky Keegan came running along Causeway Street. "Hey, Banana Nose," he called across traffic. "A kid in your building just rode off in an ambulance."

"What?" I yelled back.

"Someone from your apartment house just took a one-way trip to the hospital. Too bad it wasn't you."

"Who?" I called. "Who was it?"

There were dozens of children in our building. Every bed on Chambers Street overflowed with children. But what if the sick child was Eve, what if it was Libbie? They were sleeping so soundly when I left. What if when Tanta Rose went to wake them she found one of them ill?

I ran into the street without looking. "Rocky," I yelled. "Which kid?"

I didn't see the trolley coming toward me. I was thinking only of my sisters. Someone yelled. I think it was Pilasky. Only then did I realize I stood in the path of an oncoming streetcar.

My legs froze. In front of me, behind me, crowds of

people, automobiles, horses, carts. I stood paralyzed, watching the trolley bear down on me.

And then, from nowhere, a girl appeared.

She ran across Causeway, weaving in and out of traffic. What she was doing was impossible, and yet, she was moving toward me even faster than the trolley. With a slam, her two palms hit my chest and forced me backward. She pushed me out of the trolley's way. Violet eyes. In my brain I saw violet eyes.

Sprawling backward, I landed on the sidewalk. My papers flew from my hands. The trolley clanged past.

For a few minutes I heard only a buzzing in my ears.

When the buzzing cleared, Pilasky was there, kneeling beside me.

I sat up, brushing myself off. The palms of my hands bled a little where they had scraped against the concrete. I looked around for the girl with violet eyes, the girl who had pushed me to safety, but she was gone.

All that remained was a handful of ruined papers and my fear for my sisters. What would I do if anything happened to my sisters?

"I'll sell the rest of these," Pilasky said. "You'd better get cleaned up. Just watch what you're doing, Gold, would ya?"

My legs jittered as I raced for home along Lowell, over to Brighton. My feet and heart pumped harder the closer I got to Chambers.

Instead of going the front way, where Harry usually watched for me at his window, I headed for the back. It was shorter.

Running through the alley, I jumped over garbage from the

building next to ours. A cat, frightened by my approach, slipped behind a stack of ash cans.

"Eve, Libbie," I cried, tearing down the steps and through the kitchen door.

I burst into the shadowy room. It took my eyes a moment to adjust from the brightness outside.

Slowly, like ghosts, Libbie and Eve emerged from the shadows. They sat at the kitchen table, dressed, hair combed, bows tied, ready for school.

I sagged backward against the kitchen door, sighed, and gave the side of my nose a good rub.

Libbie rose from her chair and grabbed her schoolbag. "You missed the excitement."

Eve looked sorrowful, wriggling under my arm and staring up at me with her large green eyes, so much like my own. "Mrs. McCarthy's baby went in an ambulance."

So it was Mrs. McCarthy's baby.

With relief I put one arm around each sister, and without another word, I led them to school.

All through classes I couldn't get the girl with violet eyes out of my mind. On our way home, I looked for her in every face we passed. Preparations for the Sabbath were nearly finished. The smells of chicken and kasha and challah wafted out onto the streets.

The neighborhood spun with colors, sounds, smells. Crowds everywhere. On foot, on bicycles, in automobiles, the creak of wood and leather, the clopping hooves of horses.

I walked with my sisters home along Chambers Street. Naomi and Nathan Strauss carried dried cornstalks for their sukkah, hurrying to finish it before the Sabbath started.

Mrs. Weitz came scuttling up.

"Hannah," she said warmly. Her brown hair strayed wildly around her flushed cheeks. "Eve. Libbie."

"Hello, Mrs. Weitz."

"What were you thinking about, Hannah? You had the strangest expression on your face. You have a pain, darling?"

I shook my head. "No. No pain."

She patted Libbie's red head.

"How's Mr. Weitz feeling?" I asked.

Mrs. Weitz smiled, and sighed with relief. "Better. He's better. I don't have to tell you how I worried."

I nodded. The crowds of people flowed around us. Children shouted; horns blared.

Mrs. Weitz beamed at me. "Harry says soon you are having a little show of your drawings at the Settlement House, Hannah."

"Yes. But everyone in my class will display their work, Mrs. Weitz. Not just me."

"Ah, but yours will be the best, Hannelah, yes? You'll tell me when your pictures are hanging? Max and I will come see."

I rubbed my nose, looked down at the sidewalk.

"Oy, I've embarrassed you. But look at you, Hannah. You are growing into a beauty. Just like your mother, may God keep her safe in Russia until she returns. My Harry has very good taste in women. All three of you, three Gold beauties." Mrs. Weitz whispered in my ear. "If you have any questions, Hannah, you know, about woman things, you can come to me. Of course, I don't know why you'd need to talk to me when you have Vashti, but just in case."

"Thank you, Mrs. Weitz," I mumbled.

"Well, I have shopping. And I don't want to leave Max too long. Good Shabbes, Hannah." She brushed a kiss across my forehead. "Good Shabbes, girls." Bending down, Mrs. Weitz hugged first Libbie, then Eve.

"Good Shabbes, Mrs. Weitz," we called, watching her disappear into Leo's Grocery.

I continued walking my sisters home. We passed Hershel Yankel's, with the barrels of pickles lined up in front of the store.

"I want a pickle," Libbie said.

Breathing in the vinegar and garlic made my mouth wet. I wanted one, too. But I shook my head. It was always the same walking home with the two of them. They wanted everything. I could give them nothing.

Mr. Izzy, the butcher, with his shop full of dead chickens hanging upside down from clothesline, waved from inside the door. "Good Shabbes, Hannah," he called through the window. "Good Shabbes, children."

"Good Shabbes, Mr. Izzy," I called, waving back.

At the fish market, Mrs. Schwartz reeled us in. Libbie stood at the door, her fingers pinching her nose shut against the fishy smell. "You need more paper, Hannelah?"

I nodded. "I can always use more paper, Mrs. Schwartz."

Mrs. Schwartz kept one of my drawings pinned up behind the fish counter.

"When are you going to make me another picture?" she asked.

"I don't think anyone notices the first picture I drew for you, Mrs. Schwartz. It's just a bunch of fish."

She stared at me in disbelief. "Just a bunch of fish?" She

looked at Eve, and Eve shook her head slowly. "It's a master-piece. We know about these things, don't we, Evelah? You think I know nothing but fish in this world? Mark my words. Someday everyone on Chambers Street will be bragging how they knew Hannah Gold when she was a little *pisherke*, and I will have the one and only first genuine picture Hannah Gold ever sold in trade for the ends of fish paper. I'll be the envy of the block."

Mrs. Schwartz made me smile.

Glancing over at the real fish kept on ice in the window, their glazed eyes fixed and staring at nothing, I wished Tanta Rose would serve a fresh piece of cod for Sabbath dinner. Of course, if she did, with our luck Vashti would invite Ovadiah and his brother and sister, and they would eat it all.

My arms loaded with nearly empty rolls of fish paper, I called a good Shabbes to Mrs. Schwartz.

Back at our tenement, Libbie, Eve, and I thumped up the stairs to the bathroom to wash. My brown curls, still damp around the edges, tickled my cheeks as we returned to the apartment.

In the kitchen, Vashti and Tanta Rose stood ready to welcome in the Sabbath. Tanta Rose placed a shawl over her head. Two white Sabbath candles waited, straight and tall, in their brass candlesticks.

Outside, the traffic slowed, and the street grew quieter as in tenements up and down the block the Sabbath began. Even the Irish and Italian families quieted down in the solemn moments before the sun set on Friday night.

Tanta Rose struck a match and touched it to the candlewicks. Her hands, making ghostly circles over the candle flames, looked like angel wings. Closing her large eyes behind their thick lenses, she cupped her hands in front of her face, whispering in a private conversation with God, *"Baruch Atah Adonai—*Blessed are You, O Lord our God."

"My beautiful Hannah, come," Tanta Rose beckoned.

I stood before her.

"May God make you as Sarah, Rebecca, Rachel, and Leah," Tanta Rose said, her hands resting lightly on my bowed head.

She repeated the blessing over Libbie and then Eve.

Eve loved being blessed. She looked up at Tanta Rose, her eyes shining as the words faded in the double candlelight.

Tanta Rose removed the embroidered cover from the challah and sang, *"Hamotzi lechem min ha'oretz."* Softly, Eve sang with her.

Two tiny flames danced in the shiny crust of the braided loaf.

Vashti broke the challah in half and from each half tore us a piece.

At last, with all the prayers and blessings out of the way, we sat down to eat. Greens, chicken soup. Boiled chicken. No strudel.

"It is a blessing you are with us tonight, Vashti," Tanta Rose said. "You have been away too much."

Vashti rested her two different-colored eyes on Tanta Rose, and her face softened. "It is good to sit and relax and eat your delicious matzoh balls," Vashti said.

Tanta Rose nodded. "You want more?" She started after the pot. Vashti touched her hand, shook her head no.

Tanta Rose settled back in her chair. "Vashti . . ."

Vashti looked down gently on Tanta Rose.

"I need to speak with you," Tanta Rose said. "It's about the children."

The muscles in Vashti's jaw jerked, tightening and loosening.

"I should let you have your Sabbath in peace, but you could be called away at any moment, and I cannot wait another night to discuss this with you. I am thinking, Vashti, that the girls should leave town." Tanta Rose stirred her spoon around in her soup, causing a piece of parsley to dance on the edge of a bubble of fat.

I watched first Vashti, then Tanta Rose. Eve sat back in her chair, wrapping a stray curl around her finger. Libbie, elbows on the table, shoveled food into her mouth, ignoring the conversation. She squinted at the Hebrew letters embroidered on the challah cover.

"It's the influenza," Tanta Rose said. "It's everywhere. We must send the children away to the country. To my cousin Frank outside Albany. My mother sent me and my sisters to country relations when cholera struck. We must do the same."

I put my spoon down. My appetite had suddenly left me.

Tanta Rose reached a hand out to Vashti. "We should get them out of the city now. Frank would take them."

Vashti looked furious. "We send them nowhere."

In the months we had lived with them, I had never heard them argue.

Tanta Rose's eyes grew moist behind the thick lenses of her glasses. "They are my responsibility. People are dying from this influenza, Vashti. The manager of my factory died this afternoon. Mr. Bushey. A big healthy man. Healthy as a horse. He stayed home with influenza two days ago, and today he is dead."

Vashti crossed her arms in front of her, stubborn. "What would people think if we sent them away? If they get sick I will care for them the way I care for everyone else. I will not hear another word about their leaving."

"Then promise me," Tanta Rose said, "promise me nothing will happen to them."

Vashti looked at her. "I promise."

Pounding, pounding. I woke suddenly to the sound of some one beating on our front door. My heart leaped in my throat as I followed Tanta Rose and Vashti to the sitting room. It was Mrs. Weitz.

"Vashti, come quick," she cried.

"What is it, Zilla?" Tanta Rose asked, her long white braid hanging down her back against her nightgown.

"It's Max," Mrs. Weitz cried.

Tanta Rose sat with Mrs. Weitz in the kitchen while Vashti quickly dressed. Libbie, Eve, and I watched from the sitting room, wide-eyed.

"He was so much better, Rose," Mrs. Weitz said, pulling a handkerchief through her fist as she spoke. Her brown hair stuck out wild all over her head. She paused only long enough in her fretting to wipe her eyes.

When Vashti reappeared, dressed, her short salt-and-pepper hair smoothed down, Mrs. Weitz began to cry in earnest.

Vashti wrapped one arm behind Mrs. Weitz in support. She carried her bag of remedies over the other arm. As they left our apartment, Mrs. Weitz repeated what she had told Tanta Rose. "He was sitting up and eating supper. He took a walk around the room after he ate." Her voice faded. Their footsteps faded.

"Enough, girls. Go back to sleep. Hannah, stay with your sisters in the big bed."

The catch in Tanta Rose's voice frightened me. I tucked my sisters in, stayed with them until they slept again, then came back to stand in the kitchen doorway. I could not believe what I saw. Her hands trembling, Tanta Rose was ripping out a hem. In all the time we'd lived with Tanta Rose, she had never ripped out a hem.

"Tanta Rose?"

She looked up, rested her work in her lap.

I came into the kitchen to sit with her. Wait with her.

Very softly, from above, came the slow, grieving notes of Mrs. McCarthy's piano.

I knelt before Tanta Rose. "Please don't send us away."

"I made a promise to your parents, Hannelah," Tanta Rose said. She took my face in her stubby fingers. "Oh, God, my precious child, I don't want you to leave. Do not think for a moment I want to send you away. You and your sisters, you are three shining lights in this dark cellar. But I must keep you safe. And if sending you to the country is the only way, then you will go." Tanta Rose shut her eyes for a moment. "Do you understand?"

"Understand?" I cried. "How can I understand? You love us, yet you want us to go away, and Vashti, who wishes we never came, insists we stay."

"For Vashti it is a matter of pride, Hannah," Tanta Rose said. "You must learn tolerance, my darling girl. And patience. Vashti is not what you think she is."

"You can't imagine what I think she is. She glares at me and doesn't speak. She scowls at me no matter what I do. I am never good enough. And Eve and Libbie. It's as if they don't exist. They need to be loved."

"They are loved, Hannah." Tanta Rose stared into the single lamp flickering in the kitchen. The Sabbath candles had long since burned down, but the kitchen was still warm, still filled with the smells of soup and bread. "Vashti's mother died after

51

giving birth to her. Her father, he was a rabbi, a very scholarly man, very severe. He treated Vashti the way Vashti treats you, Hannah. He believed to raise self-reliant children, you must raise them in silence, in the absence of affection. He said it is not what you do for the child but what you teach the child to do for itself that makes it succeed. Vashti was only ten when her father died. Maybe he knew death was coming. Maybe he knew he had little time to make her strong. Maybe this is why he was so stern with her. Who knows. But what ever you might say about his method it worked. At ten, Vashti was strong and self-reliant. She arranged a position for herself in a wealthy home where she worked from sunrise to sunset."

I sat on the floor beside Tanta Rose, resting my head in her lap.

"She had no one. At ten, Vashti was completely alone, cut off from everyone, from everything.

"There was a woman who taught her the ways of healing, passing on the names and uses of all the plants in the woods outside their village. But even on her Vashti would not depend. She accepted the first proposal of marriage that came to her and sailed with her husband to America. Five years later, that husband left her."

Tanta Rose's fingers moved comfortingly through my hair. My eyes grew heavy, and I think I slept.

I tried hard to rouse myself, to listen.

"We became friends, Vashti and I. Vashti moved in to help me care for my parents. After they died, she stayed."

Tanta Rose's words made a strange picture in my head, a picture that ended with Vashti's footsteps creaking down the front stairs.

I shook myself awake and stood stiffly.

"Vashti?" Tanta Rose called, heading toward the sitting room.

Vashti moved like a sleepwalker, past Tanta Rose, into the kitchen. She pulled out a chair and sat at the table. She smelled of camphor and sweat.

I could see. I could see right away that it was not good with Harry's father.

Vashti's hands trembled.

"Go to bed now, Hannah," Tanta Rose ordered.

"But—"

"Now!"

I went as far as the sitting room, then peered through the gap made by the hinges of the swinging door

Vashti rested her elbows on the table, dug her long fingers into her short hair, and moved her scalp back and forth over her skull.

Tanta Rose stood behind her, wrapping her short arms around the unyielding shoulders. Her enormous eyes squeezed shut as she rested her chin atop Vashti's head.

Vashti sagged in her seat. She raised her hands and gripped Tanta Rose's fingers.

And I knew. I knew without anyone saying the words.

Mr. Weitz, Harry's father, was dead.

## chapter four

### *Monday, September 23, 1918*

Schools were officially closed until further notice, to slow the spread of influenza. Tanta Rose had given strict orders that we must stay inside. "You are not to play on the street, not even out back," Tanta Rose warned. "Hannah, forget your newspapers until I say you can go back again."

"But—Chip waits for me. What will happen when I don't come?"

"The least of our worries is Chip Pilasky. Keep Libbie and Eve out of the bedroom. Vashti needs her rest."

Tanta Rose had not been gone an hour when someone knocked at the door. It was a girl, my age, but shorter. Her dark hair slapped at her shoulders. She reeked of fish and filth. Her torn dress showed patches of skin, raw and red and wheeled up in hives. She did not look directly at me when I let her in.

"I need Vashti," she said to her wretched boots.

Libbie and Eve hung on to my skirt.

Vashti, hearing her knock, stumbled wearily out of the bedroom, her short hair flattened on one side, her skirt and blouse rumpled.

The girl gazed up at Vashti, hope and despair mixed in her eyes.

We stared at Vashti, too. Never before had she slept in her clothes.

Vashti picked up her bag of salves and tinctures. She glanced over at me once, a look of dead exhaustion in her eyes. And then she put an arm around the girl's shoulders and led her out of the apartment.

For a while I entertained my sisters by rereading Papa's letters. Then carefully, I gathered in my lap the packet from Mama. When I held her letters, I thought how Mama touched the paper and the envelopes with her own hands. How she put her lips to them. Mama's letters came at first in the mail, and then carried by strangers who managed to escape from the village in Russia that trapped her. And then, when the war made escape to America impossible, the letters from Mama stopped coming.

"Remember how Mama made faces for us out of grapes and pears and cherries and she would cry, 'Oh, oh, oh,' every time we ate a nose or an eye?" Libbie asked.

Eve tried, but how could she remember?

"When Mama laughed, she had a dimple here," I said, touching Eve's cheek. "Her skin was softer than your silky, Eve."

"What color were her eyes?" Eve asked.

I couldn't remember.

My sisters looked up at me, waiting for an answer.

"Brown," I said. "Greenish brown."

I lied to my sisters. I couldn't remember. Mama slipped farther away from us with each passing day. But I refused to let her go, even if I had to make her up. I would not let her go.

I listened in crowds for voices deep and textured, like Mama's voice. She used to take us around the neighborhood, so proud, showing us off. I tried drawing her, but the drawings looked nothing like Mama.

"Read the part about me again," Eve said.

I went through the letters.

*My little Eve, you must be so grown-up now. Going to school! Be a good girl and listen to Hannah. Do you still sing your little songs, Evie?*

I reread every passage that mentioned any of our names.

*Libbie, your hair grows so fast. It must be all the way down to your little freckled tushie.*

Eve giggled.

Libbie tried not to, but she giggled, too.

*Hannah, my dear Hannah. Whenever I peel eggs here, I think how you made little carvings with a butter knife in the soft solid white of a hard-boiled egg. We tried to keep your egg carvings, but they always started to stink. Pew, how they'd stink. Hannah, take good care of your sisters for me. You must be their mama until I return. I know you will do a good job.*

Oh, Mama.

After several hours with the letters, Libbie and Eve grew restless. They bickered and snapped at each other. I tried teasing them into good moods; I tried tickling them, hugging them. Nothing worked.

"Let's climb up on Ovadiah's roof to see the sukkah," Libbie suggested.

I frowned. "Tanta Rose said we go nowhere."

"Then draw pictures for us," Eve said.

I wanted to slip out and check on Harry. My heart broke for him. Harry had buried his own father. But I could not disobey Tanta Rose.

"Only one or two," I said. "Until Vashti gets back."

Eve pushed me down on the bed and slipped my drawing book from my pocket.

As I picked up the pencil and began sketching, I forgot Harry, and Mama and Papa, and the war, and the influenza. My pencil got comfortable on the paper, and my hand knew what to do.

I drew silly pictures of neighbors, exaggerating Ovadiah's eyes, Mr. Izzy's nose, Rocky's teeth.

Libbie made up a story about each drawing, and Eve made up a song, and an hour more slipped by.

We were climbing off the bed, heading toward the kitchen for lunch, when the fire engine turned onto Chambers Street. A great clanging sounded outside the window, and we rushed to look out. Two white horses appeared, blowing, striking sparks on the cobblestones as they flew past. The shining fire truck belched smoke; the steel-rimmed wheels clacked and spit out stones. A dozen kids tore after the engine, followed by barking dogs.

Before I could grab her, Libbie was after them, running through the sitting room, up the front steps, out of the tenement.

"Libbie!" I yelled. "Come back"

Eve looked out the bedroom window as Libbie raced past.

"Oh, Hannah," she cried. "Tanta Rose said."

"I know what Tanta Rose said."

Tears swam in Eve's eyes. "Will Libbie catch influenza?"

"We'll go after her and bring her right back." I looked at

Eve's face, puckered up with fear, and pulled a fresh hand ker-chief out of the dresser. "Keep this over your mouth until I say to take it down."

I pulled Eve out of the bedroom, across the sitting room, and out the door in pursuit of Libbie. We ran up Chambers Street, following the path of the fire engine. My heart banged against my ribs as we reached the corner of Chambers and Cambridge Street. I'd lost her.

But then Eve tugged on my hand. She pointed halfway up the block. There on the marble steps of the church on Cambridge Street I saw a flash of red hair. Libbie.

I didn't know whether to yell at her or hug her.

She didn't apologize. As we rushed up, she didn't look the least bit concerned at the worry she'd caused. She simply peered at me through her wire-rimmed glasses, tossed back her red braids, and frowned. "I want a hot dog," she said.

I stared at her in disbelief.

"We're almost to Joe and Nemo's, Hannah. Please, can we split a hot dog three ways?"

"No," I told Libbie, still trying to catch my breath. "We are not going to Joe and Nemo's. We are going straight home. We shouldn't be out here in the first place. What if you get sick?"

"I won't," Libbie said. "How about we go over to Parson's and get cat pie? Cat pie only costs two cents."

My mouth watered at the thought. Mr. Parson spread raisins and nuts and apples on a sheet of pastry and topped it with sugar and cinnamon, baking it in his oven till the smell filled your mouth with spit. That was cat pie.

Eve tugged at my sleeve. "Can I take the handkerchief off my face yet?" Her voice came out soft, muffled.

"We're going straight home, Libbie," I said. "Straight home."

"But cat pie—"

"Parson's is probably closed."

"Why would it be closed?" Libbie asked. "It's early."

I tried to be patient, the way Mama would be. "Because of the influenza."

"They wouldn't close Parson's for influenza, Hannah," Libbie said. "Parson's is a bakery. The health officer didn't say anything about closing bakeries. If they closed bakeries we'd all starve to death, wouldn't we? I bet Parson's is open. We have to go that way anyway."

"All right, we can walk past there." I would have said any thing just to get her going.

"And get cat pie?"

"We'll see."

Parson's was open. Libbie ran inside before I could stop her, lifted the glass lid on a jar of powdered crescent cookies, and stuck her nose deep into the opening. Her face shut into a squint as her hot breath came back at her from inside the jar, bringing with it the sticky smell of powdered sugar.

"Can I smell, too?" Eve asked, coming up behind Libbie. Their giggles echoed through Mr. Parson's empty store.

"Close that jar now!" I ordered.

Mr. Parson appeared from the back of the store. He ducked under the door frame as he came into the front shop, holding his yarmulke on his head with one hand. He had a gold tooth in front that flashed when he smiled.

Libbie stomped over to me, the evidence of confectioner's sugar around her lips. She was still chewing.

I wanted to cry. She had taken a cookie without permission, without paying. What would become of such a girl?

"Libbie, how could you?"

Libbie shrugged.

"May I have a cookie, too?" Eve asked.

I opened the jar and picked out a powdery crescent for Eve. Then I pulled the pennies from my pocket and paid Mr. Parson. My empty mouth watered. There would be no treat for me.

"What are you children doing out?" Mr. Parson asked, putting my pennies in his cash register. "You shouldn't be roaming the streets. Hannah because you get a day off school, you think you should run around wild?"

"Libbie heard the fire engine."

"*Nu?*" Mr. Parson said. "The dead could have heard it. But the fire engine didn't stop in my shop." He looked at Libbie. "You did."

"We're leaving now," I said.

"What about my cat pie?" Libbie whined.

I glared at her.

She crossed her arms in front of her, and pouting, she marched out of Mr. Parson's bakery.

"Go home and lock the door," Mr. Parson called after us. "I don't want to hear you children got sick."

Heading home, Libbie sulked past Solomon Derby's, where only last year she had learned to tell time. Closed.

Angelo's Barbershop. Closed.

Yaffee's Dry Goods. Closed.

Russo's Funeral Parlor. Not closed. Open, And very busy.

"Hurry," I said, rushing my sisters back to the tenement.

The smell of ham hit us as we came through the front door.

"Let's go upstairs and visit Mrs. McCarthy," Libbie said.

"No school, no movie houses, no McCarthys," I repeated.

We were only in our apartment a few minutes when Yossel Yankel, the insurance man, brother of Hershel Yankel, the grocer, knocked at our door.

"So there you are," Mr. Yankel said. He wore his dark overcoat and held his hat in front of him. "I was knocking before and no one answered. I knew you should be in here with school closed. You scared me when you didn't come. I thought, What if the girls are lying on the floor, all sick with the grippe? I'm glad to see the three of you so well."

I smiled at Mr. Yankel and wished I had some cake to offer him, but we had nothing sweet in the house. "How much do we owe this week?"

"A dime, my *shayna* Hannelah," Mr. Yankel said. The silvery stubble of a beard showed on his chin and cheeks. Mr. Yankel's hair grew everywhere but on the top of his head, which mostly he kept covered with a hat. "You missed last week. You got a dime?"

I reached into the jar where Tanta Rose kept our household money.

"Only a nickel." I rubbed the side of my nose, then started toward the icebox and my newspaper jar.

Mr. Yankel frowned, scratching his stubbly chin. "Your aunt refuses to touch that money, Hannah. She says it is yours. For your education. She wouldn't like if I took it for insurance."

"It's my money, Mr. Yankel," I said. "I have the right to decide what to use it for."

Mr. Yankel pushed his two lips together so they stuck out. Then he bent over Eve and pulled a nickel out from behind her ear. "Look what I found."

Eve took the nickel from Mr. Yankel's hand and gazed at it in wonder. She checked carefully behind her ears with her own fingers, hoping to find another coin. Of course, she found nothing but a little ear crust.

"Look, Hannah," she said. "God must have put the nickel behind my ear so you wouldn't have to use your money."

I couldn't make Mr. Yankel take my money now. Eve would think I was ungrateful to God.

Mr. Yankel marked in his big collection book, *Rose Aronson. Paid. Ten cents.* "Put that nickel back in your newspaper jar," he told me. "And give your Tanta Rose my warmest regards."

"I'll do that, Mr. Yankel. Thank you."

"Think nothing of it, my *shayna* Hannelah."

Mr. Yankel climbed up out of the basement and out the front of our building.

"I'm hungry," Libbie whined.

"You just had a cookie."

"I'm still hungry."

"I can make oatmeal. You'll be happy with oatmeal?"

Libbie nodded.

I made a pot of oatmeal on the coal stove and filled each of their bowls.

"I want sugar in my oatmeal," Libbie said.

"You finished our sugar ration weeks ago. No more till October, Libbie."

"I don't like it plain," Libbie whined.

I dripped into their bowls a little bit of the honey Vashti kept on her salve shelf.

"You gave Eve more than you gave me," Libbie complained.

I drizzled a little more honey into Libbie's bowl.

"Now Libbie has more," Eve said.

They kicked each other under the table. The bowls and spoons jumped each time my sisters swung their legs.

It was nearly time for dinner, and I hadn't even cleaned up the breakfast dishes.

"Stop it before you break something," I snapped. I, who never lost my temper with them, who loved them enough for Papa and Mama both. "And finish your oatmeal so I can clean up."

I drained some hot water from the stove reservoir into the washtub and started scouring the crusty dishes in the sink.

Turning for a moment to check on them, I saw Eve screw up her face and give Libbie a hard kick to the shins.

Libbie rose out of her chair, howling. She chased Eve around the table. A chair tipped over as Eve struggled to stay out of Libbie's reach.

Round the table they flew, screaming like factory whistles, their braids streaming behind them.

When I stepped between them, Libbie slammed into me with such force that I stumbled sideways and hit the kitchen table with my hip. Tanta Rose's teacup, her precious teacup, jumped to the table's edge, and this time, Harry was not there to catch it. The sound of the cup smashing against the linoleum filled the kitchen.

Libbie and Eve froze.

A blizzard of black flakes floated in front of my eyes, and for a moment I saw nothing. Then, slowly, the blackness cleared.

Tanta Rose's cup was in pieces on the kitchen floor.

I bent down and touched them. One, two, three, four, five. Five impossibly separate pieces.

Eve's eyes filled with tears. "What are we going to do?"

"Hannah can fix it," Libbie said.

I sat down on the floor, tried fitting the pieces together. Each time I reconstructed Tanta Rose's cup, I'd let go and it would fall apart again.

How could I fix it? How? This cup had traveled all the way from Russia. Now, in this place where everything should be safe, Tanta Rose's cup had shattered.

A chill crept up my spine as the slow shuffle of footsteps sounded in the front hall. Footsteps coming down the stairs.

"Tanta Rose," Eve whispered in panic.

"Hide the pieces," Libbie said without breathing.

We placed the five blue-flowered pieces inside a tea towel and shoved the bundle up on the shelf behind Vashti's empty bottles.

Guiltily, we rushed into the sitting room, opened the front door. Tanta Rose stood in the doorway but she didn't come inside.

"Tanta Rose?"

No response.

"Tanta Rose?"

Still no response.

Then suddenly, coughing, uncontrollable coughing. From Tanta Rose. Mr. Weitz's cough.

I came to her, took her arm, and gently led her to the bedroom.

Libbie and Eve watched from a distance.

"I don't feel good, Hannelah," Tanta Rose whispered.

"Let me take these off for you," I said, removing Tanta Rose's heavy shoes.

She shivered. "I'm so cold."

I covered Tanta Rose with every blanket we had in our flat and pushed Libbie and Eve into the kitchen.

Coming back, I placed a cool rag on Tanta Rose's burning forehead.

"Everywhere I hurt, Hannah," Tanta Rose said. Her eyes, as dull as the eyes of the fish in Mrs. Schwartz's shop, frightened me. She started coughing again.

I tried making her more comfortable.

Libbie and Eve crept to the bedroom door. "I'll get a doctor, Tanta Rose."

She grabbed my hand. "No. Find Vashti, Hannah."

"But—"

"Vashti," Tanta Rose insisted.

"I want you to stay away from Tanta Rose," I told Libbie and Eve, leading them back to the kitchen. I hugged my arms tightly around myself to quiet my trembling. "I'm going out to get Vashti and bring her back. You stay right here in the kitchen and wait. You understand? I need you to take good care of each other."

"What should we do?" Eve asked.

"Play cards, tell stories. Libbie, read your book out loud to Eve. Just stay quiet and keep away from Tanta Rose. We don't want you getting sick, too."

My voice frightened them. Tanta Rose so sick frightened them. Wide-eyed, they agreed to do as I asked.

I began knocking on doors, asking for Vashti.

"I think she's at the Rubins'," Mrs. Fleishman informed me. Mrs. Rubin said, "She went to the O'Brians'." Mr. O'Brian wouldn't even open the door to me. He spoke through the keyhole. "She was here until Flora Goldstein came. Go away quickly, child. There is terrible sickness in this place." At the Goldsteins' apartment I discovered Vashti had just headed over to the North End, led by a dark-haired girl in dirty clothes.

My fears grew as I searched the North End. I should have fetched a doctor. Right from the start, as soon as Tanta Rose came through the door, I should have fetched a real doctor.

I had finally given up and turned back toward home, when suddenly I spotted her, coming out of a building on Clark Street. The rumpled clothes hung on her tall, straight back.

"Vashti," I called, running toward her. "Vashti." I wanted to cry with relief at finding her, but I knew I mustn't. I made my voice calm; I forced it to be calm. Inside, my heart hammered with rage at her. For wasting hours making me find her.

"What is it?" Vashti asked. A muscle twitched below her blue eye. The skin on her face sagged even though her back remained straight.

"Tanta Rose," I said. "She's sick."

Vashti and I flew back to the West End.

Rushing down the front steps of our tenement, we found the door wide open.

I raced to the kitchen to check on my sisters while Vashti headed toward the bedroom. Something was wrong. My sisters were not in front of the stove where I'd left them. Tanta Rose was in the kitchen. She slumped over the table, her head cradled in her crossed arms.

"Tanta Rose?" I asked gently. "Where are Eve and Libbie?"

I had a horrible feeling. Why wasn't Tanta Rose in bed where I'd left her, and my sisters, where were my sisters?

Tanta Rose didn't answer. She didn't move. I placed my hand on her forehead. "You're burning up, Tanta Rose. You should be in bed."

"No," Tanta Rose protested, weakly resisting. "No, it doesn't matter for me. See to the babies." Tanta Rose focused her eyes on me for a moment as we moved toward the bedroom. "Hannah, Hannelah. Do you see the angels now? I see one. It's taller than the ceiling."

A shiver ran through me. "Tanta Rose," I asked again, guiding her through the sitting room, "where are Eve and Libbie?"

Tanta Rose looked at me. Her eyes suddenly filled with alarm. She stopped outside the bedroom door but would not go in.

It was then I saw them.

Libbie and Eve asleep in their clothes on the big bed.

"Vashti." Tanta Rose stumbled toward the tall, straight woman. "You promised." She lifted her fists to beat on Vashti's chest, but she never delivered the first blow. Tanta Rose collapsed on the bedroom floor.

Gently Vashti lifted her, gently she placed her on my cot. After giving her a quick examination, Vashti joined me beside the big bed, placing her hand on Eve's forehead. She examined both my sisters in their fitful sleep, listening long and carefully at their chests.

Vashti closed her eyes. The late-afternoon light sifted through the high window.

"Is it influenza?" I asked.

Vashti nodded.

My sisters, they looked so tiny and helpless in the bed. Their cheeks aflame, their lips scarlet.

"I just left them. Two hours ago, maybe three. They were fine. How could this happen?"

Vashti did not answer. She disappeared into the sitting room, returned with a small brown bottle.

"What is that?" I asked. Vashti ignored me. She took the bottle of syrup to Eve, then Libbie, then Tanta Rose, waking them, lifting them, urging them to swallow.

As the hours passed, awake or asleep, they coughed, horrible coughs, and they shivered.

"I'm so cold, Hannah," Eve wept, reaching her burning arms out to me. "I'm so cold."

"I'll get more blankets, Evie."

Racing upstairs, I pounded at Mrs. McCarthy's door.

Mrs. McCarthy came to my knock. "Hannah, what is it?"

"Is there any more illness here?" I cried. "Do you have any more influenza?"

"No," Mrs. McCarthy said. "Just the baby." Her chin trembled.

"Mrs. McCarthy, may I have your extra blankets. I need blankets. Please. Anything you can spare."

When I returned, my arms laden with tattered covers, I found Vashti at the stove, fixing an onion poultice. She divided the hot onions into three piles; wrapping them quickly, she hurried back to the bedroom and placed them over each laboring chest.

As soon as Vashti left the bedroom again, I spread Mrs. McCarthy's blankets over my sisters and my aunt.

Vashti returned with rubbing alcohol.

"Let me help," I pleaded.

Vashti looked at me for a moment, then nodded.

Every hour, we sponged alcohol over their necks, under their arms, trying to cool them. I could see Eve's heart tapping wildly beneath her ribs; her tiny chest instantly pimpled with gooseflesh the moment we uncovered her.

6 8

Thrashing, she cried out, "Papa. Papa."

Libbie lapsed into a deep sleep, so deep she did not move. Her breath rasped in her throat. We lit the lamps against the night.

"Vashti? There has to be more we can do."

Vashti's shadow stretched and shrank in the lamplight as she moved back and forth between my cot and the big bed.

We spooned chamomile tea between their parched lips, placed more poultices on their chests. We kept the doors open through to the kitchen, where pans on the stove steamed the air to help their breathing.

Nothing worked through the long night. All three of them, desperately ill.

And Vashti exhausted. Both of us exhausted.

Six, seven times, people knocked at the door, asking for Vashti. I sent them away.

Eve had grown quiet, too. Almost as quiet as Libbie.

I rested my head on her chest to count her heartbeats, little taps, so weak, so irregular. One, two, three, four, five, six . . .

Gently, someone shook my shoulder. For a moment I felt full of brightness, as if I'd swallowed a bowl of sunlight. But when I opened my eyes, night still curtained the bedroom window. I lifted my head, confused.

What was I doing on my knees in the bedroom in the middle of the night?

And then I remembered.

Libbie. Eve. Tanta Rose.

The lamp dimly lit the room.

I looked over at Vashti. She knelt by the cot, tending to Tanta Rose.

Vashti couldn't have shaken my shoulder. Who shook me awake?

"Eve? Libbie?"

My sisters were silent, side by side, on the big bed.

A corner of the silky poked out from between the small fingers of Eve's fist. Libbie's glasses lay on the nightstand. I lifted her chunky little body in my arms. Such heat. Libbie's red braids fell back away from her face.

"Libbie! Eve!" I cried. "Vashti, do something!"

Vashti ignored me. She knelt beside the cot where Tanta Rose lay. Her back remained straight.

"Vashti! My sisters!"

Finally she turned to stare at me. Her eyes reflected a haunting despair in the lamplight.

I became aware of a new sound. It came from Tanta Rose. A horrible sound, like a baby's rattle lodged in her throat. It went on and on and on. Grew softer, weaker. And then the rattle stopped. All sound stopped. And Tanta Rose was dead.

In that moment Vashti's stiff back folded. Her hands curled into tight fists. She lifted one of those fists, and I thought she would shake it in rage at the heavens.

But I was wrong.

Vashti took that fist and jammed it instead into her own mouth. I could watch no more. Tanta Rose was dead. I had to do something to help my sisters. If I didn't do something my sisters would die, too.

Turning my back on Vashti, turning my back on my dear Tanta Rose, I concentrated on Libbie and Eve. I wet a cloth and pressed the cold rag against their burning faces.

"Fight, Libbie," I pleaded. "You can read books all day and never go to school. You can have a whole sheet of cat pie. I'll pay. Just fight, Libbie."

I spooned a tincture that smelled of licorice between Eve's lips. "Please, Evie—"

Suddenly Vashti was standing over me. She took the bottle of tincture from me. "Get out of here," she said. "Go!"

My heart pounded. "What have I done wrong? Vashti, what am I doing wrong?"

"Rose wanted you to go. She wanted all three of you to go. Go now. Take your money, get out of here."

"I can't. I wont leave my sisters—"

"I said go. Here." She scribbled words on a slip of paper, handed me money from her apron. "Go to Albany!" Vashti cried. "Go to Rose's cousin."

"You can't make me leave them."

"Hannah!" Vashti's voice flashed. It was like the voice of God. Her hand closed over my arm. She pushed me across the room, toward the door. "You will go now!"

I pulled myself up straight. "No, Vashti. I wont leave my sisters."

"If you want them to live you will," Vashti said. "You are an intrusion, a distraction. I must not be distracted now. I promised Rose no harm would come to you. I will keep my word to her." Vashti's voice wavered when she spoke Tanta Rose's name. "But you must leave. Leave now. Leave this apartment. Leave Boston."

Could I trust her to save my sisters? If Tanta Rose could die, my sisters could die, too.

I would get a doctor. I would bring a doctor to help. Vashti's pride had already cost me Tanta Rose. I would not lose my sisters.

7 I

Flying up the steps of the tenement onto Chambers Street, my feet pounded the sidewalk along Auburn, around the corner to Poplar, past the Peabody House to Brighton, then through the maze of buildings of Massachusetts General. A man pointed out the building I needed, and I burst through the doors and into the waiting room. Breathless, I pushed into line. There were so many in front of me. At last my turn came. "My sisters are dying," I told the woman seated at the desk. "My aunt is dead."

The receptionist hardly reacted. "Influenza?" She had dark circles under her eyes. She smelled of sweat.

"We have money to pay for a real doctor. It's in the jar inside the icebox."

The receptionist took a fresh sheet of paper and made a note. "Is anyone with your sisters? Have they received any care?"

A woman in a stained apron and cap passed behind the receptionist on her way to a boy, lying on the floor.

"Nurse," an old man moaned from a pallet only a few feet away. "Nurse."

"Did you leave them alone?" The receptionist looked wearily at me.

"No," I said.

"Good, then they're being taken care of."

"Yes, but—"

"We can't do anything more. You can see what it's like here."

The hospital groaned with patients; they spilled out into the hallways; they sprawled on the floors.

Tears swelled the pouches beneath my eyes. "My sisters need a doctor."

"Write down your address," the woman said. "Someone will get there."

"How long?" I scribbled our address on a piece of paper from my apron. On the back was the address of Tanta Rose's cousin outside Albany. "How long until someone gets there?"

But there was a line behind me. I was dismissed.

Running back to Chambers Street, I stooped and touched my fingers to the window, looking down into our bedroom. Tenderly, just as she had done with Mr. Weitz, Vashti nursed my sisters. She sponged Eve with alcohol. Libbie tossed restlessly at her side.

Tanta Rose lay alone in death. Nothing more could be done for her.

Would my leaving really save my sisters?

I backed away from the window.

Away from Libbie and Eve.

Looking up at the darkened front windows of Harry's apartment, I wanted nothing but to go to him. To be comforted by Harry. Protected by Harry. But Harry and Mrs. Weitz had sorrow of their own. They were sitting shivah for Harry's father. How could I put any more on them?

My hands shook as I tucked wild curls behind my ears.

Papa put me in charge when he left. He trusted me to take care of my sisters. They were my responsibility.

I walked without thinking, ending up on the bank of the Charles. "Mama, Papa, you took too long. You took too long to come home. Now there is nothing to come home to." My words slipped away on the wind. Just two weeks ago I had come to this river on Rosh Hashanah to cast my sins into the water.

I pressed my knuckles against my eyes, hard, until I saw patterns in the pounding darkness.

But when I took my hands down, the three rooms on Chambers Street filled my vision, the big coal stove in the kitchen, the sitting room lined with Vashti's tinctures and extracts. And the front room, with the big bed and the little cot. Tanta Rose and Vashti, Eve and Libbie, the four of them slept together in the big bed. In the big bed Tanta Rose kept my sisters warm.

The pain washed over me. "It is my fault, my fault they got sick."

If only we'd left Boston when Tanta Rose wanted us to go, everyone would be all right. If only I'd kept my sisters inside the way Tanta Rose said. If only Mama and Papa would come home now. Then everything would be all right.

A branch floated down the Charles River. It drifted slowly, then caught in an eddy. It spiraled in tighter and tighter circles. Finally, breaking lose, it drifted downriver again.

All I ever wanted was for my family to be together.

I had to trust Vashti. If I wanted Libbie and Eve to live, I had to do what Vashti said. Vashti said Libbie and Eve could only be saved if I didn't intrude, if I didn't distract her.

Shivering, I turned from the river. A barefoot girl moved toward me in the autumn light. Putting my hand to my throat, I touched my Jewish star. My fist knotted around it, holding it so tightly it pierced my skin.

The girl came closer. Closer and closer. She had black hair. She had violet eyes. She beckoned to me, and my hands dropped to my sides.

We walked together to North Station. I couldn't get to Albany from North Station. But what did it matter where I went as long as I was not around to distract Vashti. I was without suitcase, dressed in my everyday clothes, without my sketchbook even. The girl with violet eyes hovered at my side as the clerk handed me a ticket. I didn't remember asking for a ticket; I didn't remember paying for one.

The girl stood by me on the crowded platform as the train screeched into the station.

Stacks of coffins waited to be loaded. Coffins filled with soldiers who came to Boston prepared to fight in the Great War. Soldiers who died instead before they ever saw battle, died of influenza.

The conductor's hand reached out, helped me up the steps into the train. I turned, looking for the girl with violet eyes. She had vanished.

What was I doing? I was leaving my sisters. How could I leave my sisters?

I snapped out of my fog and saw a large sign hanging on a board outside the train window. It was a list of safety precautions.

To Prevent the Spread of Influenza
- Wash hands before each meal.
- Don't go to crowded places.
- Avoid the person who sneezes.
- Smother your cough in your handkerchief.
- Keep out of dirty restaurants.
- Warmth is necessary; be well clothed.
- Soda is unnecessary; why run the risk of infection from a dirty glass?
- Safety lies in boiled dishes.
- A common towel is only for filthy people.
- Sleep well, eat well, play well, don't worry.

I closed my eyes again, dropped into a seat. My head spun. No. The train was moving. Rubbing my fist against my nose, I saw Libbie and Eve, still and silent in the big bed. How could I have left them? How could I have left them to Vashti?

So she could make them well again. She promised Tanta Rose they would be all right. She promised her all three of us would be all right.

I thought of Eve, her wispy brown curls plastered to her face with sweat. Libbie's bright red braids, unraveling like broken rope. In my mouth spread the metallic taste of fear, fear that I would never see them again. I tried to stand. I tried to leave the train. But the train was moving.

The last sound I heard in the apartment, after Vashti's roar stopped echoing in my ears, was the sound of my sisters' breathing, like the suck and scrub of a wave over stones. The sound of their breathing filled the bedroom, it filled the entire flat. Libbie, Eve. I should have stayed in spite of Vashti.

The train moved out of the city. Faster, faster. Where was I going? I didnt know where I was going.

Rocking side to side, the steady clack of the train filled my head. I felt so tired. The train stopped, started. At one station we waited a long time. I dragged myself out of my seat and down the aisle. Go back to Libbie and Eve, I thought. I left the train, boarded another. We started moving again and I shut my eyes. I awoke to find someone in the seat beside me.

The girl next to me, she sat with her knees bent, her ankles crossed, her bare feet pressed against the seat in front of her. It seemed perfectly normal for her to be on the train barefoot.

The girl's black hair fell to her shoulders and flipped under softly on the ends. In her hand she held a harmonica.

I looked at her, but she did not look back. Instead, putting the harmonica to her mouth, she played softly. I recognized the song. I had heard Mrs. McCarthy play it on her piano. "Amazing Grace." The sound of the harmonica soothed me. I fell back to sleep.

When I woke again, my whole body hurt, my legs, my back, my eyes burned, my head throbbed. I tried changing position and heard someone groan. I think it was me.

The girl turned toward me.

She had violet eyes.

Images swarmed into my head. Images of being pushed out of a trolley's path, of being led from the river to the train station. It was the same girl. I didn't know how, but it was the same girl.

"I'm sick."

She nodded.

A heavy coat covered me. It had a peculiar odor to it. Like the first breath of fresh air that blows through the tenement in the spring. But it was not spring. It was fall. The wind bristled the trees outside the window of the train.

The girl with violet eyes wore only a thin blue dress, belted with a piece of dark ribbon. No coat. Nothing on her feet. How could she be warm enough? I couldn't stop shivering. My teeth chattered. "It's so cold."

A conductor passed.

"Are we almost to Boston?" I whispered.

"Boston? Child, your ticket says you're going to Saint Albans, Vermont."

Vermont?

I shook my head. It banged with pain.

Vermont.

"I have to get back to Boston."

The conductor looked down at me. "Next stop I'll see what I can do for you." He bent down closer, whispered. "You feel all right?"

I groaned in answer.

As we pulled into a train station the girl got up from her seat and moved down the aisle. I squeezed my eyes shut and opened them again. She floated.

A dark fog closed over me. I sank down into it.

"Here we go." Someone lifted me, a tall woman in a Red Cross uniform. The whiteness of her apron stung my eyes.

"Here we go." She repositioned herself, helping me stand.

"Who are you? Where are you taking me?"

She led me down the narrow aisle of the train. People leaned away from us. I had trouble hearing over the buzzing in my ears. Someone yelled, "You shouldn't let them on the train sick. She'll infect us all."

The Red Cross woman helped me down the steps of the train and into a waiting ambulance. She wrapped me in a wool blanket.

I moaned.

"It's all right," she said. "You'll feel better once you're settled in bed. You're our first case of influenza."

I wanted Tanta Rose. I wanted Papa. I wanted Mama. I wanted Eve and Libbie. But I couldn't have them. None of them. Would I ever have them again?

My head hurt. And my back. Every part of me hurt. I couldn't hold my legs still.

Influenza.

I didn't care if I had it. I didn't care that I might die. I didn't care about anything.

In my delirium, the girl with violet eyes pushed me out of the way of a train. As her hands hit my chest, the girl disappeared inside of me. My chest hurt from the weight of her.

"Get off my chest," I cried.

Someone whispered, "Shhhh."

Wantastiquet Mountain rises in the dark. Trees along the summit extend their long fingers, stroking the black underbelly of the night.

The moon rests her chin on the rugged shoulder of the mountain, gazing lazily across the river toward Brattleboro. She hums a haunting song. Her music ripples across the sweeping surface of the sky.

Dim stars pick up threads of moon song and add their harmonics, creating a concert of night music, a celestial symphony, until without warning, everything stops.

The moon disappears.

The stars wink out.

And then the sky opens.

Heaven is revealed through the breached seam, a billowing of colors, a pulsing dazzle of light.

And through this shining breach, figures stream, descending on silken ladders, the colors of heaven reflected in their robes.

*In that mote of light from heaven, angels descend to earth.*

*Tens of angels, hundreds of angels, thousands of angels.*

*They descend until the heavens close again.*

*The curtain of night drops into place.*

*And the moon reappears, balanced on the tip of a pine.*

*The moon picks up the thread of her song where she left it. Humming softly, she soothes the troubled brow of the night.*

part two

chapter five

*Tuesday, October 8, 1918*

O PENING MY EYES, I found myself on a cot, surrounded by white screens. An enormous ceiling of intricately
patterned tin stretched above me.

Where was I?

Sounds of coughing reached my ears. A woman's voice
spoke. "Fifty-eight Jewish workers to fight on the western front."

"I didn't think Jews knew how to fight." A man's voice, dry
and vicious.

I inched my hand to my throat. It took forever to complete
the long journey. I felt for my star. It was gone. My clothes were
gone, too. In their place I wore a thin hospital gown.

More coughing, the clink of metal and glass, the sound of
long skirts brushing through close spaces.

I tried sitting up. Too weak.

"Hello there, are you awake, love?" A woman wearing a
gauze mask on the lower half of a round red face appeared at the
side of my cot. A white apron covered the front of her generous
body; printed on the brim of her headdress—a red cross.

I trembled.

"It's all right, love," she said. "You've been very sick but you're going to be just fine now."

In a rush I remembered the train, Tanta Rose, my sisters.

My sisters.

I looked up at the nurse in desperation.

"There, there, love," she said, stroking my curls back from my forehead. "There, there." She leaned around the screen. "Miss Carpenter," she called softly to someone unseen. "Come. Your Miss Doe is awake."

The soft shush of skirts reached my ears. Around the corner of the screen a young woman appeared, Miss Carpenter, also in a mask, also in a Red Cross headdress. She was very tall.

"There you are, awake at last. You're in an emergency hospital. Do you understand?"

Weakly, I nodded.

"How about something to drink?" Miss Carpenter lifted a glass of water to my lips

I was thirsty, but I stopped after a few sips, too tired to take more.

"Good," Miss Carpenter said, putting the glass down. "You can go now, Miss Sullivan. I'll stay with her."

Miss Carpenter turned to me. "We're a little shorthanded, or I'd have been here the moment you opened your eyes."

She perched lightly on the edge of my bed. Miss Carpenter could not have been more than nineteen. Under the white headdress, thick auburn hair framed her face. "You've been one sick poppet since I brought you in two weeks ago."

Two weeks? Had I been in this place two weeks? What had happened to Libbie and Eve in two weeks' time?

Miss Carpenter said, "No one on the train knew you. Were you traveling alone?"

For a moment I saw the girl with violet eyes so clearly. "We'll want to let your family know right away that you're all right. They must be out of their minds worrying. Who should the telegram go to?"

Was Vashti still working to save my sisters?

I tried to speak. No sound came out. I tried again. Grasping my throat, I panicked. My heart pounded with alarm.

Miss Carpenter's brow creased. "Just stay calm. I'll get the doctor."

She disappeared behind a screen and came back a few moments later followed by another woman, equally tall, with soft brown hair and a kind smile. The woman wore a white coat over her long black skirt. "This is Dr. Grace Burnett," Miss Carpenter said.

After examining my throat, my chest, my ears, my eyes, the doctor took my hand. "The secondary infection has caused some damage," she said, speaking directly to me. She smoothed the skin on the back of my hand. Her palms were hard, callused—a lady doctor with laborer's hands. "If you take good care and follow directions, you should be chattering like a magpie by spring."

Leaving my screened space, Dr. Grace called Miss Carpenter to follow her. I heard their voices on the other side of the divider. "She's doing better than I'd hoped."

"But she can't talk, Dr. Grace."

"Maybe she never could."

"No, she spoke when I took her off the train. I heard her. I'm certain I heard her."

Their voices sounded like bees.

I shut my eyes, lulled by the drone.

8 7

*Wedneдday, October 9, 1918*

THE NEXT TIME I WOKE, my nostrils twitched with the odor of wood smoke and horse sweat. Automatically, my hand reached to rub the side of my nose. For a moment the image of Mr. Shaw and his ice wagon formed in my head. I turned toward the smell, opened my eyes.

An old man with a long white beard sat beside my cot in the hospital. He looked like Santa Claus, a very thin Santa Claus.

"So they spoke true," he said. "They told me you were some better." He had a tangy way of talking. Like the people from New Hampshire and Vermont who got off the train at North Station. Vermont. Somewhere in the haze of my memory, a train conductor had told me I was going to Vermont.

The old man leaned toward me. He wore a mask across his mouth and nose. A gentleness lit his gray eyes, but I pulled back anyway. He was a stranger, as odd to look at in his own way as Ovadiah.

"Whoa now," he said. "Steady, gal. I won't hurt you."

My breath sounded fast and shallow in my ears; it burned in my chest.

"I'm Klaus," he said slowly, calmly. "Klaus Gerhard."

A German name. Our country was at war with Germany.

I swallowed. My throat hurt.

He thumped a delicate hand across his chest, causing his long beard to bounce. "You can call me Uncle Klaus."

Why would I do that? Even if I could talk, why would I call him "Uncle" anything? You call someone "Uncle" when they're family. This Klaus Gerhard was no kin of mine.

"Let me look on you, gal." He moved closer to the bed.

That was when I saw his hair. White hair cascading down his back. It was nearly as long as Tanta Rose's hair, when she loosened it from the braid, and just as thick.

Crumbs clung in the soft curls of his beard. His breath smelled sharp but clean. "Drink this."

He held a flask up to my lips.

I drew back. The smell of vinegar stung my nostrils.

"Don't turn your nose up, gal. This is what's been keeping you alive."

Miss Carpenter peeked around the edge of the screen. "That's long enough for now, Uncle Klaus." She hunched down and spoke in his ear. "What are you doing? Forcing more vinegar down her throat?"

"It's vinegar saved her."

"It must have been. I don't know what else could have."

"I'll leave the flask here," Klaus Gerhard said. "You sip it until I get back tonight."

He turned to leave. He wore a mud-stained vest over baggy trousers. His boots were caked with dirt. The cap, held in his weathered hands, looked like the kind fishermen wore down at the wharf. "You drink that."

"I'm certain she will, Uncle Klaus," Miss Carpenter said, watching him limp away.

She stood over me. "He took a shine to you the night I brought you from the train. He's been helping ever since. Most people are afraid to work on the ward. But not Uncle Klaus. I don't think that man's afraid of anything." She made some notes on my chart. Gently turning my wrist, she nodded her head with each heartbeat as she took my pulse. "He's lonely, though, with his mother gone this past year." She entered more notes after listening to my chest. "Your heart sounds a little better today. How's your voice?"

I tried talking. I wanted to answer her questions. I wanted to ask questions of my own. But the pain of drawing breath brought tears to my eyes. And no sound came.

Miss Carpenter disappeared for a moment and returned with a fresh pencil and a small book, a store-bought book filled with clean unmarked pages.

I had always admired little books like that. My fingers tingled as she handed the notebook to me.

"Since you can't talk, I thought maybe you could write. Tell us what you need. Who you are. You must have a name."

I took the book and weakly wrote, "Hannah." My shaky hand spoiled the clean white page.

"Hannah. It's pretty. It suits you."

On Chambers Street, no one ever said anything nice about my name. Rocky made fun of it.

I wrote, "My mother named me."

"Your mother. She'll be worried sick about you I'll wager. Where can we find her?"

I wrote, "My mother's in Russia. Trapped by the war."

Miss Carpenter's face dropped. "And your father?"

I didn't know what to write. I sketched a man in uniform with Papa's mustache and the smile wrinkles around his eyes.

"You're an artist, Hannah," Miss Carpenter said with surprise. "Your father. He's a soldier?"

I nodded. "No word in a long time," I wrote.

"Then you're alone?"

I looked down at the book.

"Oh, Hannah," Miss Carpenter said. "Will no one be looking for you?"

Vashti. A burning liquid rose in my throat. She sent me away, drove me away. For the good of my sisters, she said. For my own good, she said. For Tanta Rose.

"No," I wrote. "No one looking for me."

But then I thought of my sisters As soon as they recovered, they would be looking for me. And Harry. He would be looking for me, too.

I turned to Miss Carpenter.

She had already moved toward the edge of the screened divider. I couldn't speak, couldn't call her back. Couldn't tell her about Libbie and Eve and Harry.

"I'll let the authorities know right away."

She caught something in my expression.

"Don't worry, Hannah. I won't let anything bad happen to you."

Something bad already had happened to me.

Miss Carpenter said, "Rest awhile. I'll find you something to eat. Are you hungry?"

Hungry?

My stomach felt empty enough, I would have swallowed the crumbs from Klaus Gerhard's beard. How could I be hungry when I was hundreds of miles from home, surrounded by strangers. How could I be hungry, not knowing if my sisters were alive or dead? But I was hungry.

## chapter seven

# *Thursday, October 10, 1918*

KLAUS GERHARD SHOOK the vinegar flask, found it full. "That ain't no way to get better, gal." His mouth frowned behind the mask, moving the beard on his chest.

I had tried the concoction in the flask the night before. The sharp bite of vinegar had turned my stomach. I couldn't swallow more than the first sip. As I lay on my cot, alone, staring up at the ceiling, I wondered if he might be trying to poison me. After all, he was a German.

He slipped the full flask into an enormous pocket in his grease-stained pants. As he did, a cracked button on his sweater let go and slid out of its hole. Tanta Rose would have fixed that button in a second. Tanta Rose.

Red suspenders kept Klaus Gerhard's trousers from falling down. Out of another pocket he pulled a peach and held it out to me. "Picked it off the tree in August," he said.

August to October. Two months. I stared at the peach, expecting a shriveled, rotten piece of fruit. But it was perfect.

"Prettiest peach in the root cellar, gal."

My mouth watered. I thought of the meal Miss Carpenter

had brought me yesterday. I didn't know what I could eat here. She had brought applesauce. I knew apples were kosher. But what about the crackers? What if they were made with lard?

Klaus Gerhard handed the peach to me and crossed his arms over his beard

It worried me, taking anything from him, but the peach looked so good. Before I knew what my hand was up to, it had lifted the peach to my mouth. I bit into it. Closing my eyes, I let the taste of sweet peach juice roll over my tongue.

Down to the stone, I used my fingers to pick out the strings clinging inside the deep trenches and ate them, too, one at a time. My hands weren't stained with newsprint anymore. Miss Carpenter and Miss Sullivan must have washed me often to get my fingers so clean.

As I swallowed the last of the peach, I remembered the peddler who held the apple out to Libbie. Why hadn't I bought that apple for her? I should have bought it for her.

Wiping my hand on the top of my blanket, I took the pencil and book and wrote a sticky, "Thank you."

Klaus Gerhard nodded. "I'll take that stone. The army uses all these fruit pits for making their gas masks." He placed a handkerchief over my peach pit, wrapping it carefully and tucking it down into yet another pocket. "I don't approve of this war, gal, but I approve even less of them boys over there dying from mustard gas."

He didn't approve of the war?

"Florence Carpenter tells me you draw pretty good. I used to draw some myself." He had his eye on my notebook. "Can I see?"

I shrugged.

"Shy, are you?"

9 4

What business was it of his?

He picked up the book. I'd done only a few sketches: one of Papa, one of the girl with violet eyes, a small picture of Miss Carpenter. "Ever take drawing lessons, gal?"

I nodded.

"Me, too. When I was a boy, about the same age you are now. I thought drawing beat everything. I skunked out of work every chance I got just so I could get away and draw. I'd have rather sketched than eat."

Thin as he was, it looked like he still spent most of his time doing something other than eating.

"You ain't half bad," he said, studying my drawings. "This bit of Miss Flo's chin under the mask is good." Miss Carpenter had a broad jaw even the mask couldn't hide. "But them eyes."

I frowned. I always had trouble with eyes.

Klaus Gerhard took the pencil, put the point to the paper, then stopped. "I ain't got no right drawing in your book," he said softly. "I ain't got no right drawing at all." He handed the book and pencil back to me, removed another flask from his shirt pocket. "Drink this," he said, placing it on the stand beside my bed. And then he left.

All alone, I listened to the emergency hospital sounds. The bustling never stopped. All through the night, more cots and mattresses moved in. More patients. More influenza.

The ward filled with coughing, moaning, weeping.

I heard whispers. On the other side of my screen a man had died.

Leaning on one elbow, I reached for Klaus Gerhard's flask. Opening it, slowly I drank down the entire contents, one vinegary sip after another.

# chapter eight

*Friday, October 11, 1918*

DR. PUTNAM, a pink-faced man with pale blue eyes, examined me briefly, then moved on. Dr. Grace, who had left during the night to call on patients in their homes, had not returned. Miss Carpenter was so busy, I held my own bucket as I brought up the bloody phlegm from my lungs.

There were children on the ward now. Little children. Their weeping tortured me with fears for Libbie and Eve. I thought I would lose my mind with worry.

I had to get back to Boston, to my sisters. But how?

And what about Vashti?

Remembering the look on her face when she sent me away, I was convinced Vashti never wanted to see me again. I had distracted her, she said. I had been an intrusion. When I would sit at the kitchen table, sewing with Tanta Rose, Vashti would leave, resettling in the sitting room. Tanta Rose made excuses for Vashti's rudeness then. There was no one to make excuses for Vashti now.

Miss Carpenter and Miss Sullivan talked softly on the other side of my screen.

"I'm thinking of volunteering in France," Miss Sullivan said. "I could work in a hospital hut. The Red Cross needs girls."

"Oh, Hattie," Miss Carpenter whispered.

The sound of glass clinking against metal blotted out the next words. The two nurses worked as they talked, washing up instruments.

"They want strong women," Miss Sullivan said.

I struggled to sit up, then reached for my pencil and note book. Listening to them speak, I clearly saw Miss Sullivan, her rosy cheeks above the mask, her round, soft body in the white apron.

"My brother is over there already," Miss Carpenter said. "My parents couldn't bear to have me go, too."

We couldn't bear to have Papa go, either, not with Mama gone. But Papa went anyway.

"What of the danger, Hattie?"

"We may be in more danger working here," Miss Sullivan said, "what with the influenza. Look at Annie Clapp and Lizzie. And Mrs. Elmore. And then last night Dr. Brooks taking ill. We've had three patients die in the last twenty-four hours, Flo."

"But we're taking precautions. We're burning what we can't boil. We go through iodine and carbolic like they were water."

Their voices grew muffled. Then Miss Sullivan whispered, "Did you see the notice on the board? We're over capacity and more coming this weekend. We have to send recovering patients home starting tomorrow."

"What about Hannah?" Miss Carpenter asked. "We can't let her leave yet. She barely eats. She's too weak."

Their voices dropped even softer. Only the clink and slosh of their work reached through the screen to me.

Where would I go? This emergency hospital, these people, had taken me in. And now I'd overstayed my welcome and they planned to put me out. Was I strong enough to make it back to Boston?

Miss Carpenter stopped to visit on her rounds. She acted cheerfull, full of good tidings. "We have wonderful news for you, Hannah," she said. "This is the last day you need look at these screens. You're leaving us tomorrow. What do you think about that?"

I shut my eyes. If I was well enough to leave the hospital, I was well enough to return to Boston. How far could I walk, I wondered. "Where are my clothes?" I wrote.

"I'm sorry, Hannah," Miss Carpenter said. "We had to destroy them."

How could they? Tanta Rose made that dress for me. And my star. Did they destroy my Jewish star, too?

Miss Carpenter took my hand. "Don't worry, Hannah. We won't put you out on the street."

I looked up at her.

"One of the seminary teachers, Miss Grant, has offered to care for you in her home. She'll be by after dinner to meet you. It'll be fine, you'll see. I'll find you a dress to wear before you leave."

My gaze locked onto Miss Carpenter's face. For an instant I saw in her eyes something unsure. My chin trembled and tears tried slipping past my lashes. They ended up swimming back and forth over my eyes.

"There, there, Hannah," Miss Carpenter said. She took my face between her two hands and looked at me. "It will be all right. Honest. Listen, Dr. Putnam wants you out of bed and moving around before you leave tomorrow. How about we take a little stroll to the window right now, okay?"

As she helped me stand, she continued to whisper to me. "Miss Grant's not so bad, just a little on the stiff side. And I'll check on you every few days. It'll be fine. Honest, Hannah. It's better to get you out of here. With so much illness and you in such a weakened state, what if you came down with tuberculosis? And it's so noisy. You can't possibly get any rest. No, it's really better to get you out."

I nodded.

"Do you know anyone else you could go to? Anyone?" Miss Carpenter asked.

I thought about Tanta Rose's cousin Frank outside Albany. How far away was Albany? How would I even know where to go once I got there?

I shook my head.

The cold floor curled my toes. A draft blew under the hem of my hospital gown. We left the row of screened-in cots and headed for the window. My legs wobbled like jam. My head pounded. How could I walk to Boston? I couldn't walk across the room.

"Here, you lean against the window and rest while I bring over a chair. Can you stand on your own for a moment or two?"

I nodded, sagging as Miss Carpenter let go.

But she was back quickly. "You sit and look out on Main Street awhile, Hannah. It's Friday afternoon, you should see plenty comings and goings. That brick house right there belongs to the Clapps. And that tower is the Brooks Hotel. Have a look. I'll be back soon."

From where I sat I could see a tall white steeple, trees blazing with autumn color. A memory flashed into my mind. Mama. Pushing a black pram with Libbie inside. Or maybe it was Eve. Me helping her, holding the handle of the pram, my small hands next to Mama's. "What a good sister you are, Hannah," Mama had said. We strolled through the West End, across the Common and Charles Street, through the Public Garden, over the little bridge with the swan boats gliding beneath us.

I shut my eyes. For the first time in years I could see Mama clearly. Her eyes were green. Green like mine and like Eve's. I could answer my sister's question. I wished I'd had pencil and paper to draw Mama right then and there. But the notebook was too far away, all the way back at my bed.

A brick building, directly across the street from the emergency hospital, had flaming ivy scaling its walls.

"That's the First Baptist Church." Miss Carpenter, at my side again, handed me a cup of hot lemonade. "We're in the Congregational Church's parish house. The town converted the parish house to a hospital just to handle influenza cases.

That made two churches in this small town. Where was the synagogue?

Automobiles and horse-drawn wagons moved slowly up and down the road. A street cleaner pushed his barrel along, leaning over his shovel, scooping up after the horses.

If a street cleaner tried walking down Beacon or Boylston or Commonwealth like that, he'd have been run over. I shuddered, remembering the trolley nearly hitting me.

Brattleboro was a pretty town, a tiny town. Smaller than the West End. Smaller even than Chambers Street. There were no rows of tenements stitched to each other, no crowded sidewalks spilling with shoppers and crates of vegetables and barrels of pickles, no mobs of kids shoving and shouting, no Mrs. Rizzoli hanging out the window, calling down to the street. Brattleboro was just a quiet little town, with lots of grass and trees.

I leaned my head against the side of the window frame, trying to see the hotel a little better. Exhausted, I slept like that until Miss Carpenter woke me and guided me back to bed.

Miss Lydia Grant came while I slept. I'm certain if I'd been awake I wouldn't have reacted so rudely. But she startled me.

I had been dreaming about brushing Tanta Rose's hair. We were taking turns, Libbie, Eve, and I. In my dream Vashti glared at me. She insisted I count each stroke out loud, but I couldn't get sound to come from my mouth. Eve sang a nonsense song about vinegar. Libbie recited her list of words.

"Hannah?"

A voice jerked me out of the dream. I saw a woman bending over me. She smelled of peppermint and wool. My eyes traveled up toward her face, above her mask, to her eyes. She had two different-colored eyes. One brown, one blue. I panicked, pulling the blanket over my head.

"Now, now," the woman said. "Lower the blanket, child, and let us get acquainted. I'm Miss Grant."

Those eyes remained imprinted on my closed lids. Lydia Grant had Vashti's eyes.

"Hannah, I cannot speak to you through a blanket."

My fingers hurt from gripping the edge of the blanket so tightly.

"Don't be foolish," Miss Grant said. A sharpness crept into her voice. "You're acting like an infant."

I couldn't, I wouldn't budge.

Finally, she grew frustrated, so frustrated she left. Her footsteps retreated from the big room. "Please inform Dr. Putnam," she told someone at the door to the ward, "that this arrangement will not work after all." And she was gone.

"Hannah?" Miss Carpenter's voice spoke softly above me.

I felt her tug gently at the blanket covering my head.

"Hannah?"

She had to pry the blanket from my stiff hands and help me to lower my arms. I blinked at Miss Carpenter's familiar face behind the mask.

"She's gone, Hannah," Miss Carpenter said, smoothing back my curls. "Why did you act that way?" She handed me my book and pencil.

I wrote, "She frightened me."

Miss Carpenter looked confused.

"Her eyes," I wrote.

"What about her eyes?"

A voice called from the other side of the screen. "Miss Carpenter? Mr. Williams needs you."

"I have to go, Hannah," Miss Carpenter said, tucking the blanket tenderly around me. "There are so many new patients. I'll come back and check on you before I leave for the day."

I nodded.

"It will be all right."

Suddenly she was gone, and I was alone, surrounded by nothing but white screens and my fear.

Dr. Putnam poked his head in after supper. "Let's see how you're doing, young miss," he said, listening to my lungs.

I took as deep a breath as I dared, deeper than yesterday. A pain cut through my chest like a quick knife.

Dr. Putnam frowned, then bent closer. "Now, what's this I hear about you and Miss Grant?"

I watched him carefully, his pink skin, his white eyebrows, his yellowed teeth. I wished Dr. Grace would come back.

"I've spoken with Lydia Grant, and she's willing to give it another try. So mind yourself tomorrow. You're not likely to get a better offer."

I shuddered at the thought of going anywhere with Lydia Grant. It wasn't her different-colored eyes that worried me the most. It was the coldness behind them, the distant coldness of Vashti.

I fretted in bed, thinking what I might do, where I might go, when Klaus Gerhard came. As soon as I caught sight of him, I held out the empty flask. It still smelled of vinegar. Turning the flask upside down, I showed him I'd finished every drop.

"Good gal," he said, genuinely pleased with me.

A rush of embarrassment warmed my face.

Standing in silence for a while, he flipped the brim of his cap back and forth with his fingers. "Miss Carpenter tells me you're leaving with Lydia Grant tomorrow."

Panic seized me. I reached for my book. "I can't go with her," I scribbled.

He studied my words, then me.

"What should I do?" I wrote.

"You ain't strong enough to do much of anything, gal. You need more bed rest. Three, four weeks to build your strength up. And you need a little meat on them bones." He thought awhile.

"Well, I guess if you ain't going home with Miss Lydia, you'll have to come on home with me."

I dropped my pencil.

On Chambers Street, I would have had nothing to do with him. No more than I would have had to do with Ovadiah Strauss. Not only was Klaus Gerhard a stranger and odd to look at but he was a German and against the war. Back in Boston, about the most I'd have done for Klaus Gerhard was sell him a newspaper. But this wasn't Boston, and if my only other choice was Lydia Grant, Klaus Gerhard might not be too bad.

"You're mighty weak to be moved, yet. But they need your bed."

"Would Miss Carpenter let me go with you?" I wrote.

He crossed his arms over his beard. "She don't know what else to do with you. It's one thing if you had family nearby. They'd have to take you in. You ain't got anyone local, have you?"

"No," I wrote.

"Well, bless you. It looks like you'll be rooming with me a while then, gal, don't it?"

Bless me. Miss Carpenter had said it was Friday night. Shabbes. In Boston, clean white tablecloths would be spread in coal-warmed kitchens; brass candlesticks would reflect the flicker of golden flames. Children would be blessed by their mothers as families all over the West End observed the Sabbath.

Life had gone on without me. Without me, without Tanta Rose. Without Mr. Weitz. What about Libbie and Eve? Was life going on without Libbie and Eve? And what about Harry? I had to know.

I had to get back to them.

After Klaus Gerhard made arrangements to fetch me the

next day, he went home. In the late hours, the busy hospital quieted down some. Behind the privacy of my screen, I took my pencil and paper and I wrote:

*Dear Harry,*

*I write to you and not Vashti because she is angry with me. She told me to leave. She doesn't want me back.*

*I think about Eve and Libbie all the time. And about you. I hope you are well.*

*I have been ill with influenza.*

*Tell Eve and Libbie as soon as I can I'll come back.*

*Yours truly,*

*Hannah*

I wanted to sign it love. Love, Hannah. But maybe Harry didn't feel that way about me anymore. I left him while he was in mourning. I left him without saying good-bye.

## chapter nine

*Saturday, October 12, 1918*

PLUMP MISS SULLIVAN slipped me licorice bits wrapped in a paper cone. "Now, don't you go hungry, love," she said.

Sitting on the side of my bed, I took the paper cone of candy from her, though I was not at all certain I could eat it. Mr. Parson's licorice bits were okay for me to eat, but were all licorice bits okay?

Helping me stand, Miss Carpenter wrapped her long arms around me and pressed me against her. "I'll be checking on you."

Dr. Putnam and Dr. Grace joined the nurses to see me off.

Klaus Gerhard threw a blanket across my shoulders and helped me out of the emergency hospital, down the walk to the street. The brisk outside air smelled of wood smoke.

A single horse and wagon sat at the curb. The back of the wagon, a large flat box with a narrow lip all the way around, held scattered piles of hay.

Gently, Klaus Gerhard lifted me onto the hard plank seat. He limped around the wagon and climbed up the other side.

"Gup, Big Train," he said softly, and the huge chestnut horse in front of us twitched its ears, stretched its neck forward, and began to move. Klaus Gerhard's wagon creaked as we rolled along Main Street, past a new brick building on the left and several large houses. Within minutes the town lay behind us. The road grew rougher.

We hadn't gone far when we came to a covered bridge. A sign above the bridge entrance read WALK YOUR HORSES. Klaus Gerhard slowed the enormous Big Train with a touch of the reins. To the right and the left, railroad bridges over powered the smaller covered bridge. Beneath us a brook flowed to join a large river at our right. A mountain rose above the river's far bank.

"That river there is the Connecticut," Klaus Gerhard said, pointing. "Across t'other side is New Hampshire."

Occasionally I spotted a house situated back from the road, a curl of smoke drifting out of a chimney, but mostly the view was of fields and pastures, river and mountain. Trees blazed in colors from orange to red, from yellow to green.

"That pretty piece of mountain you're staring at there is called Wantastiquet," Klaus Gerhard said. "That's an Indian word. Means West River Mountain."

Wantastiquet. Libbie would insist he spell it. Eve would make a song of it.

I repeated it in my mind. Wantastiquet. I wanted to remember it so I could bring the word back with me to Boston.

The morning held so many smells and sounds, so many sights: horses and cows, the rush of water, the rustle of leaves. It was all so different from the comforting din of Chambers Street.

Up a hill and down we bumped in the early morning chill. We turned left and climbed a road that followed pastureland. As the hill leveled off, we turned left again across from a cemetery,

107

and Big Train trotted along a rutted drive where a white house and several barns sat.

"Here we are, gal," Klaus Gerhard said, pulling up in front of the house.

His place looked across open land, out toward the mountain—Wantastiquet. In the field to the front of the house, cornstalks huddled in groups like soldiers in rustling khaki. To one side of the house stood a grove of crimson trees, to the other side an autumn garden. Behind Klaus Gerhard's little house spread an orchard—I remembered the peach he brought me. And beside the orchard, beehives, lined up in neat rows.

"Hey," a voice called, "Klaus!"

We both turned. A horse and buggy came around the corner from the road, into the drive, heading toward us.

"Hey, Ott." Klaus Gerhard lifted his arm and waved.

The buggy drove up and stopped beside us.

"This the little girl you've been courtin' at the hospital?"

"Sure is," Klaus Gerhard said, a note of affection in his voice. "Hannah, this here's Ottiwell Wood. One of the cuspiest scoundrels north of the Mason-Dixon line. I wouldn't look at him twice except the government went and hired him to bring the mail while the regular carrier is down with the grippe."

Ottiwell Wood took off his hat and mopped his sparse hair with his hand. He reached out the other hand to shake with me.

I pulled back. The hand he offered was missing two fingers. "Ottiwell Wood," he said, ignoring my reaction. "*O*, double *t*, *i*, double *u*, *e*, double *l*, double *u*, double *o*, *d*."

I stared at him, baffled.

He grinned. "Think about it. You'll get it in time. I'm

pleased to meet you. See what you can do with this old man. I've barely heard him rub two sentences together since the Boss left us."

The Boss—that must be Klaus Gerhard's mother. Miss Carpenter had told me that she'd died this past year.

Ottiwell Wood unfolded a leather roll and brought out a newspaper.

My fingers inched under the blanket and latched on to the letter I'd written to Harry. I had folded it into a small square and tucked it inside the sleeve of the charity dress Miss Carpenter had found for me. Ottiwell Wood was the mail carrier. He could send Harry's letter.

Watching, listening, I waited for the right moment to pass my letter to him. No one else knew I had anyone left in Boston. It'd gone on for so long, I didn't know how to tell them now.

"Got a Christmas label from my grandson," Ottiwell Wood said.

"Walt sent that label to you, did he? " Klaus Gerhard asked.

I'd heard something about Christmas labels in Boston, at the Settlement House. Each soldier was only allowed one Christmas package. I wondered what Papa would do with his Christmas label. Would he send it to Chambers Street? Would he even get a Christmas label on account of our being Jewish? And if he did send it to Chambers Street, who was left to make a Christmas box—a Hanukkah box—for him?

"He didn't send that label to his ma or his pa, did he? No siree. He sent it to me. Wants Grampa Ott to put together his Christmas package for him and send it over there to France. I guess Walt knows who has good taste in our family." The booming man puffed up as he talked about his grandson.

109

"When you get ready to send off that package let me know," Klaus Gerhard said. "I'm making fruit leather up in the attic. Peach and apple. That boy always loved my fruit leather. I'll pack some up in a tin for him soon as it's ready."

"That's kind of you, Klaus," Ottiwell Wood said. "I'm sure Walt'll be pleased." He patted the leather pouch filled with the mail on the buggy seat beside him. "I'd best let you get that little girl to bed. Looks half dead if you ask me. You sure you didn't bring her home too soon? I know you were eager for company but—"

"They've got them at that hospital looking a lot sicker than this one," Klaus Gerhard said. "Matter of fact, this little gal has looked a lot sicker than what she looks right now."

"Well, you keep pouring that vinegar down her throat. She'll either get better or get pickled."

"Ha!" Klaus Gerhard shouted. "Pickled! I'll get you pickled."

Ottiwell Wood winked at me. "Keep your old vinegar, Klaus. The only thing I'm interested in today is a few of your sumac smokes."

Klaus Gerhard grinned. "I just rolled some day before yesterday. You okay a little longer out here, gal?"

I nodded.

My heart raced as he limped toward his house, disappearing from sight. I pinched my fingers over the letter to Harry, held it out to Ottiwell Wood. He stretched his long arm toward me and took the paper.

"What do we have here?" Ottiwell Wood unfolded the tightly creased sheet and looked it over. "Ahh. U.S. mail." He tipped his hat toward me and placed my letter to Harry in an inside pocket of his great coat.

Klaus Gerhard, still chuckling to himself as he came out of the house followed by two big dogs, carried a handful of neatly rolled cigarettes. "Pickled," he muttered, handing the smokes to Ottiwell Wood. "You're the only one pickled around here."

The mail carrier tipped his hat to me, turned his buggy around, and headed back out to the road.

"Don't pay no mind to old Ott," Klaus Gerhard said, lifting me down off the hard seat. "I don't intend to pickle you. But I do intend to get you to bed before you come chilled. Here we go."

Though I came up to his chin, he carried me anyway, effortlessly, slung over his shoulder like a sack of flour. The two dogs circled around us. Tails wagging, they stood on their back legs, trying to get a good look at me.

"Down Orville, down Wilbur," Klaus Gerhard said.

A warm blast of air hit my bottom as we stepped through the door. The house smelled terrible, like dirty socks and dead mice and filthy roots. Plants filled every room, some potted, some hanging upside down from the ceiling, some spread out across the floor. I caught sight of the messiest kitchen I'd ever seen, with big pans sitting out, and more plants spilling off barrel tops, over the edges of the kitchen table onto the chairs. It didn't look as if Klaus Gerhard had cleaned in a year.

Vashti insisted on cleanliness. After she harvested her weeds she'd come back to Chambers Street and tincture the leaves or make a syrup from the roots, and once she'd sealed the newly filled bottles and lined them up along shelves in the sitting room, she made me carry the waste, what there was of it, into the alleyway behind the tenement.

Limping, Klaus Gerhard hauled me away from the kitchen, through the sitting room, picking his way over piles of oat straw.

The sitting room equaled the kitchen in size and in mess. A big stone fireplace and some old sofas and chairs pushed up through the plants at odd angles around the room. The furniture was covered with hairy blankets and throw rugs. Klaus Gerhard tromped on a seed pod with his boot, causing a puff of pollen to fly.

I gave a soundless sneeze.

"Bless you, gal. The weeds do get thick in here from time to time," Klaus Gerhard said. "The Boss was always after me about picking up. Never did get the hang of it."

The dogs jumped onto the dirty blankets on the sofas and settled themselves, sighing.

Klaus Gerhard carried me down a flight of three stairs, turned to the right, and there he stopped. I moved my head, wondering what waited next. I glimpsed a room filled with light, a clean room looking out over fields and pasture.

There was a dresser. A stack of old magazines on a trunk. And along the wall under a big window, a high bed covered with a frayed quilt.

He pulled back the bedclothes and eased me down into the cool sheets. The mattress felt wonderfully soft. It smelled like the banks of the Charles River.

Leaving me alone, he limped up the three stairs, his foot steps heading across the sitting room. Coming back a minute later, he held a towel, wrapped around a small bundle. I thought for a moment of the broken pieces of Tanta Rose's teacup.

"Here, little gal." He lifted the blankets at the end of the bed and tucked the towel under my feet. Warmth. Klaus Gerhard had heated a brick for me.

My eyes closed, heavy with comfort. I fought to open them

again, but couldn't. As I floated down on a cushion of sleep, a girl floated beside me. I reached out and touched her hand. She was the girl with violet eyes. I tried to speak to her. But I couldn't make a sound.

chapter ten

*Monday, October 14, 1918*

S WIMMING UP from the depths of sleep, I heard the sound of a train whistle in the distance, the crowing of a rooster, the scrape of metal against metal. Tanta Rose cleaned ashes from the coal stove. No. The sounds were wrong; the room was wrong. The window in the wrong place. Outside there were stars, thousands of stars. I had never seen a sky so full of stars before. Where were the tenements across Chambers Street? Where was the bed with Tanta Rose and Vashti and Libbie and Eve?

A door closed. Opened again. I heard the clatter of wood. The sound of uneven footsteps moved closer. Across the room, the ghostly form of a man took shape. His white beard stood out against a dark vest.

Klaus Gerhard. I was in Klaus Gerhard's house.

I struggled to sit up.

"Good morning, gal," he whispered. "You don't need to rouse yourself yet. I've got to take care of the goats. You go back to sleep awhile longer."

I turned back toward the window, toward the stars. On Chambers Street I would have been getting up to sell news papers.

Klaus Gerhard limped back up the steps and out of the house. The stars faded, and the humped shadow of Wantastiquet Mountain revealed itself on the horizon. I tried using my voice. Nothing came out.

Barefoot, I slowly climbed the three-step staircase, drawn by the smell of cooking. I'd slept in the charity dress from Miss Carpenter. The wrinkles and creases made by my slumber did not improve the dress's appearance.

The dogs heard me coming across the messy sitting room. They reminded me of my sisters, butting against each other, vying for my attention. They bumped their noses up under my hands, leaned against my legs, whimpered with pleasure when I stroked them.

Klaus Gerhard's house had the same disheveled look it wore yesterday. In the kitchen, pans of milk balanced on every surface. The sun slanted across one end of the weedy room. Klaus Gerhard sat at the table, writing in a notebook so much like my own, I glanced down to make certain it wasn't.

"Come by the stove, gal," he called, pulling up an extra chair.

I wobbled across the kitchen toward the woodstove when suddenly my legs gave out. Bracing myself on the back of the nearest chair, I closed my eyes. When I opened them again, Klaus Gerhard hovered over me. "Let me help you, gal."

I put my hand up to show him I could manage. Slowly, I covered the rest of the distance myself.

Once I'd settled into a chair by the woodstove and caught my breath, I took out my pencil and wrote, "You have a notebook, too."

"My journal," he said, lifting the book to show me. "I jot

down the weather, anything about the animals. Not much to keep track of these days. I turned the farm over to the Stockwells last year. They live in a house yonder." He crossed his arms over his beard and sighed. "Folks in town got funny on me. Said, 'We don't do business with Germans.' The Stockwell boys do the farming now." He wrote another line or two in his journal, then closed it.

I wrote in my notebook. "Is that where you do your drawing, too?"

Klaus Gerhart read my question. "I don't draw no more. Haven't for quite some time now."

I looked at him, questioning.

"Took a vow not to."

I leaned forward. "Why?" I wrote.

"When I come back from the Civil War, gal—you heard of the Civil War?"

I nodded.

"Well, when I come back I was fifteen and I felt full of the need to draw. But I found the farm in ruins, the Boss sick near to death. I vowed if I could keep things together, if I could keep the old girl alive, I'd give up everything else. Even my drawing."

I rubbed the side of my nose.

"You must be as hungry as a three-legged cat. How about some corn dodgers, gal?" he asked. "I have a greased fry pan on the woodstove near to smoking." Stirring a mixture of mush, he dropped the batter by spoonfuls into the crackling bacon fat.

While the griddle cakes sizzled, he fixed us each some hot water with a generous measure of cider vinegar splashed in. For the first time I wondered if cider vinegar was trayf and pushed the mug away.

116

Klaus Gerhard slapped his hand on the table, making the mess of seeds and weeds jump. "You been drinking this all along, gal. I aint gonna let you stop now. As long as you're here with me, you'll start every day with apple cider vinegar and you'll end every day the same way."

I inched the mug back in front of me and took a sip. I didn't dare eat his griddle cakes fried in bacon fat, though. In Boston, all the food in Tanta Rose's kitchen was kosher. I didn't have to worry. But as we drove out of Brattleboro, I had seen no sign of a synagogue or a kosher butcher. Here, nothing was safe for me to eat.

While the griddle cakes fried, Klaus Gerhard uncovered a platter of doughnuts from the mess at the table. Doughnuts! Crisp and crusty on the outside, they smelled heavenly, like warm grease and honey. I thought of the doughnut Tanta Rose brought me from Mrs. Rubin. That doughnut was kosher, fried in clean oil. These doughnuts reeked of lard.

I pushed the plate away and sipped my vinegar water, watching Klaus Gerhard at the stove frying griddle cakes. Seeing that long white hair cascading down his back, I longed for Tanta Rose.

He kept checking over his shoulder. As soon as I'd finished my cup of cider vinegar, he immediately filled it again, this time with tea that had been steeping in a glazed brown pot.

I sniffed the tea before I drank. Vashti made a thick unsweetened syrup that smelled the same. Mullein. She made Eve swallow mullein syrup by the spoonful whenever she got sick. The smell of it made me gag. I frowned into my cup.

"Mullein tea. It'll help you heal faster," he said.

Under his sharp eye, I forced myself to take a sip. To my

117

surprise, the tea was good. The honey tasted wonderful with the mullein. And there were other tastes, too, soothing tastes. I breathed in the steam as I put the cup to my lips, and my nose cleared on one side.

Klaus Gerhard shifted the cast-iron skillet away from the heat, pushed the doughnuts toward me again, and made room at the table for the steaming griddle cakes.

I sat motionless at the table, reaching for nothing.

He leaned toward me, his face creased with concern. "Maybe the influenza has ruined your appetite," he said. "But gal, if you don't eat something you'll never get your strength back. Don't any of it look good to them green eyes of yours? I fixed it all for you."

Orville, or maybe it was Wilbur, had been resting his head on my lap. He looked at me with dark wet eyes. Wet and russet colored. They reminded me of Tanta Rose.

I couldn't eat those doughnuts.

Suddenly the dog's head swung up, and both animals rushed across the kitchen to whine at the door.

"Ott's here," Klaus Gerhard said, grabbing a couple of doughnuts on his way out. "Feel free to eat what you will while I'm gone."

He returned a few moments later, surveyed the table hopefully, but I'd eaten nothing. Balancing the newspaper on top of a pile of small tools, he sighed. "Ott sends his regards."

I nodded. I owed a debt of gratitude to Ottiwell Wood. He had started my letter on its way to Harry. But I still didn't like him.

"You ever read the paper, gal?"

The paper. I thought of Chip Pilasky, and Boston, and

North Station. Chip would be on his own now. I missed him, hoped he was doing all right.

"We took the news every day when the Boss was alive," Klaus Gerhard said. He lifted the paper to read, held it between us a few moments, then laid it back down again beside the steaming platter of griddle cakes, puffing a layer of seeds off the table and across the kitchen floor. "Gal, if you ain't eating doughnuts and you ain't eating corn dodgers, what are you eating?"

I stared into my cup of mullein tea.

He snorted, frustrated. He served himself a short stack of griddle cakes, pouring on gobs of brown honey.

Watching him, I felt as if I'd turn inside out with hunger.

Klaus Gerhard speared a forkful of griddle cakes, looked at me, then put his fork down again. He slapped himself on the forehead, rose from his seat and left the table. He opened a door off the kitchen, and his footsteps slowly faded as he limped down a set of wooden stairs. He returned a few minutes later, his arms full of fruit.

Seeing me brighten, he said, "You'll eat this?"

I tore into a peach. Then an apple. I don't know why his fruit tasted so good, but I'd never tasted better. When I finished the apple, my stomach felt good and full.

Grinning, he dumped some roots out of a basket and filled it instead with the remaining fruit. "I'll just leave this on the table, and you come in here and eat again when you're hungry." He reached for his coarse brown coat.

"Are you leaving?" I wrote.

"I'll be out putting the hives to bed for the winter. Brought in the last of the meadow honey last week."

"What should I do?" I wrote.

119

"You? Why nothing, gal. I'll be back around ten or so. You get some rest. First day up's a big one."

Nervous about being left alone, I teetered out of the kitchen, touching the dogs' heads as I passed. Turning, I dragged myself back to Klaus Gerhard and wrote in my note book, "Do the dogs go with you?"

"Sometimes they do, sometimes they don't. Why, gal?"

I wrote, "Could they stay with me?"

Klaus Gerhard nibbled on his mustache ends. His gray eyes swept kindly over my face. "Don't see why not."

Relieved, I started back across the sitting room toward my bedroom.

"Oh, by the way, gal," he called. "You'll find something in the top drawer of your dresser when you have a mind to look."

I picked my way through the messy sitting room, down the three steps, and into my bedroom. My heart hammered from the effort of walking. I didn't know if I had the strength to open the dresser drawer. Leaning against it, I rested.

A dresser all to myself. The dresser on Chambers Street had held Libbie's and Eve's clothes neatly folded beside my own. What had happened to my clothes? They weren't beautiful or fancy. But Tanta Rose had made them, sewing big pockets into the side seams of all the skirts because that was the way I liked them.

Would Vashti leave my clothes in the drawer next to my sisters' things? When I got back, would I find the little undershirts and panties still tucked beside my big ones?

Grasping the knobs of Klaus Gerhard's dresser with shaking hands, I pulled the creaky drawer open. The inside yawned large and nearly empty, except for a pencil that rolled in and out of sight with the motion of the drawer, and a brand-new, beautiful, store-bought sketchbook.

For a moment I could not believe my eyes.

I took the book out and opened it, running my fingers over the clean paper. It was such paper I had never dreamed of: heavy, textured, pure white. Not fish wrap. Real drawing paper, a genuine artist's sketchbook. The book had page after page of blank paper waiting to be drawn on.

I held it to my chest, closed my eyes. I could smell the newness of the book.

Klaus Gerhard giving me that book, it was such a kindness.

But then I thought, he gave up his drawing to save his mother's life, maybe I should do the same. Vow to give up my drawing until I got back to Boston, back to my sisters, and Harry, back with my parents. If Klaus Gerhard could keep the Boss alive so many years by making a vow not to draw, I might keep my sisters alive, my family together by doing the same.

As I swayed in front of the dresser, dizzy with exhaustion, I formed the vow in my mind. Not to make one mark in this beautiful book, not to draw one picture, until I had my family back.

I slid the sketchbook under my pillow, running my fingers over it hungrily. A shiver rattled up my spine. A vow, I thought, might be easier to make than to keep.

chapter eleven

## Tuesday, October 15, 1918

T HIS DAY, in the top drawer of my dresser I found a faded
pair of trousers, a flannel shirt, warm socks. A pair of work
boots sat at the end of my bed.

With the fresh clothes in my hands, I reeled back to the
kitchen, hoping to catch Klaus Gerhard before he left for the
woods. My lungs stinging, I rested at the kitchen door. The dogs
trotted over and rubbed my knees with their wet noses.

Klaus Gerhard came toward me. "You want the dogs again
today?"

I nodded, grateful. But that wasn't what I'd come back for.
Rebalancing the clothes and taking his hand, I dragged him
across the messy sitting room, down the three steps, and to the
left, to the bathroom opposite my bedroom. I knelt beside the
tub, looked back at him hopefully.

"Fancy a bath, gal?"

I nodded.

"I'll show you how it works. Put that boiler in for the Boss
more than ten years ago. She liked her hot baths."

I would have liked the Boss.

After he got the wood boiler fired up and showed me how to open and close the taps and the drain, he left. I brought the dogs into the bathroom with me and closed the door—on Chambers Street, I hated when people burst into the kitchen while I sat naked in the galvanized tub.

After wiping out clumps of dust and dog hair, I opened the taps slowly, filling the large-footed bath with steaming water.

As I removed the charity dress, I smelled my hair and remembered the smell of my sisters; I saw chills on my naked body and remembered the feel of their gooseflesh.

The dogs curled up on the rumpled charity dress as I stretched out in the tub. For the first time since Tanta Rose died, for the first time since I'd left Boston, I wept. I emptied my salt tears into the hot water. Orville came over and put his chin on the edge of the tub and watched for a while. Then circling once and sighing, he lowered himself back beside Wilbur, on top of the sweat-stained dress.

Before the bath could cool, I climbed out. While the water ran down the drain, I dried off and dressed. Kneeling, I wiped out Klaus Gerhard's tub, with plenty of help from Orville and Wilbur. I sniffed the backs of my wrists to see if there was any scent of vinegar. None. Soft and clean, my hair curled more wildly than ever. I thought of how Libbie would scowl at Klaus Gerhard's gift of such boyish clothes. But I loved them. Eve would love them, too, particularly the flannel shirt. She would rub it against her cheek, humming under her breath. And what would Harry think?

An aching loneliness broke over me. Harry. Eve. Libbie. Please, God, let them be all right.

\* \* \*

Miss Carpenter arrived at noon, waking me from a nap as she tripped over the dogs on my bedroom floor. She carried two bags: a small straw suitcase and a black traveling bag. She'd brought me dresses from the Red Cross relief bin and one or two things from her own wardrobe. No pockets in anything.

I preferred the trousers and flannel shirt I had on.

"When will I feel stronger?" I wrote in my notebook.

"You're getting there, Hannah. Don't rush things. You'll end up with a relapse. Are you eating?"

I shrugged.

"How is your voice coming?" she asked.

I tried to speak. Nothing.

When we came up from the bedroom, Klaus Gerhard invited Miss Carpenter to stay and join us for dinner.

Miss Carpenter looked fondly at him and his messy weed-strewn kitchen. "I wouldn't want to impose."

"Ain't no trouble at all, Miss Flo." He cleared a space for her at the table and dished up corned beef carrots, potatoes, all boiled together.

All this food, right in front of me, and I couldn't touch any of it.

"How do you make such delicious meals?" Miss Carpenter asked. "Aren't you rationed like the rest of us?"

"Nearly everything comes right off the farm here. Nothing special to it."

Miss Carpenter turned to me, saw my plate held only a ripe yellow pear and a boiled egg.

"Hannah, isn't there anything else you want?"

I wanted it all.

"Surely you ate more than this before you came here." Miss Carpenter leaned toward me. "Hannah?"

I swallowed a bite of egg, rubbed my nose.

"I never ate much in Boston, either," I wrote.

"Boston," she repeated.

The way she said it, I could tell it was just a word to her. To me it was Chambers Street, Mrs. McCarthy playing the piano, Mrs. Rizzoli hanging out the window. It was Mr. Vaccaro's greasy pole, Mrs. Schwartz's fish, Mr. Shaw's ice. It was eating cat pie at Parson's, the Yankel brothers, Hershel the grocer, and Yossel the insurance man. It was Ovadiah in his prayer shawl, and Nathan and Naomi eating my family's strudel. It was Harry and Chip Pilasky, Eve and Libbie, Tanta Rose and Vashti. It was where I was waiting for Mama and Papa to come home. It was my whole life. To Miss Carpenter, though, Boston was just a speck on a map.

Miss Carpenter wiped gravy from the corners of her mouth with her napkin. Her lower lip was full and red. This was the first time I'd seen her without the gauze mask on. She was pretty in a sturdy sort of way. My fingers itched to draw her, especially without the mask. But I remembered my vow.

"Miss Sullivan suggested you might like to read a novel by our own Dorothy Canfield Fisher." Miss Carpenter stretched her long fingers out to touch the back of my hand. She looked so different without her Red Cross clothes. "But the town closed the library because of influenza. Uncle Klaus, did you know?"

He shook his head.

"I'm sorry, Hannah. I wasn't able to bring you a single book. I hope you won't be too lonely up here."

125

Klaus Gerhard swallowed a piece of corned beef. "Orville and Wilbur keep you company, don't they, gal?"

I nodded.

We pushed back from our plates. Miss Carpenter excused herself, made her way around the piles on the kitchen floor, and outside to her automobile. She came back a moment later carrying a tin full of ginger cookies. Griddle cakes swimming in butter, crisp doughnuts, and now ginger cookies. How much torture could one girl take?

Libbie and Eve would die to see all these sweets.

A shiver ran up my back.

"What is it, Hannah?" Miss Carpenter asked.

Libbie and Eve would die—how could I even think it!

chapter twelve

*Thursday, October 17, 1918*

OPENING THE FARMHOUSE door to the clear, crisp
morning, I blinked at the sunlight. Across my tongue I could still
taste the sweetness of the honeycomb I'd found earlier, wrapped
carefully and set in the top drawer of my dresser. Surely honeycomb was kosher.

A sweet scent of red leaves and wood smoke filled my head.
This was my first time outside since Klaus Gerhard brought me
here.

Orville and Wilbur followed at my side as I came around
the corner of the house. They nuzzled me with their wet noses,
encouraging me.

Stone walls snaked across the fields; disappearing inside a
wood of straight white trees, then emerging out the other side.
A chipmunk streaked over the flat shelf of rocks forming the top
of the wall. From a nearby tree, two blue jays scolded. In the
orchard, Orville and Wilbur, full of energy, crunched windfall
apples, core and all. They rolled on the ground, rubbing their
shaggy backs in the apple mush, paws flapping the air.

Clouds skimmed across the blue sky; shadows slipped lightly

over the fields. The graceful movement of light and shadow made me think of the girl with violet eyes.

Weaving through the sweet-smelling orchard, its trees still holding a bounty of small red apples, I kept my distance from the yellow jackets buzzing around the half-rotten fruit on the ground. Looking back toward the house, I could just make out the rumpled cot on Klaus Gerhard's sleeping porch. Stalks cluttered the porch floor, spilling out the open door, down the steps. It reminded me of a sukkah. Klaus Gerhard sleeping in a sukkah. My body shook in silent laughter.

Turning apples over with the toe of my boots, I searched until I found one that was nearly perfect. After picking off the wet grass, I bit into it. It tasted like no apple I'd ever tasted before. Oh, Libbie.

I pressed on across the orchard to explore the cool flat surface of the stone wall. The rocks fit together, interlocking like the pieces of a puzzle. A greenish-gray moss covered large patches. Looking close, I saw a tiny forest. My palms tingled as I brushed them gently over the low webwork of green.

The different lines of roofs: Uncle Klaus's house, the sheds and barns, together they made a language of angles against the blue sky.

I was alone. For the first time in my life. Truly alone. No one needed me to be anywhere, do anything, take care of anyone.

I was alone in this beautiful place. Alone to think. Alone to sleep or wake.

If I had come upon a place like this with my sisters, with my parents, with my family, I would have thought I'd found heaven.

But in this heaven, I felt nothing but a hollow ache.

I rested against the stone wall, regarding the trees blazing with color, the flaming mountain rising toward a perfect sky, the rich green of the fields, and yearned, above all else, for the crowded, filthy, stinking streets of Boston.

Hearing the snap of branches, I stood quickly. Too quickly. My head spun. As the world settled down again, Klaus Gerhard emerged from the blur.

I waved to him, happy to see him. That happiness startled me. He headed toward the barn, motioning me to join him. I'd heard the chickens and seen the goats from a distance, but I'd never considered coming closer.

"Good to see you out," he said. He took the hat off his head and tossed it to me, motioning me to put it on.

I liked the cap. I liked the way it felt, snugged down over my curls.

"You haven't met my girls yet. This is Mary Pickford here." He pointed to an ugly goat with a white beard. "This here is Gloria Swanson." A mud-stained goat with an expression of mischief in her gold eyes nibbled at his vest tip. "And this lovely lady is Miss Theda Bara." Theda Bara, the goat, had a dark blaze on her forehead. I kept my distance from the animals who shared the small barn with Big Train and the chickens. Naming goats after movie stars. What would Libbie and Eve say to that?

Klaus Gerhard led the goats out of the barn and into the fresh air. Their bony rumps shifted from side to side as they headed away from us, down the hill, toward the brook. He walked back into the barn with a shovel and began cleaning the soiled straw out of the stalls. At such close range, the stench was fouler than a North End outhouse. I didn't even take the time to write, "Excuse me." Even after I'd placed some distance between myself and the barn, the odor still clung to the hairs inside my nose.

Checking my boots, I skated over the grass, hoping to clean them.

I eyed the empty pair of wicker rockers on the planked front porch. Climbing up the stone slab that served as a step, I touched my hand to the back of a rocker. It looked neglected, the paint worn, the seat sagging. Had this chair once belonged to the Boss? I settled into it. As I pushed forward and back in the warm autumn air, the sun cupped its palm to my cheek. My lids grew heavy. A cricket chirped under the porch. Something buzzed around my ear. I didn't fight the exhaustion washing over me. Instead I curled sleepily in the Boss's rocker and let go.

The sound of bells roused me from my morning nap. Up the hill it came like a whiff of wood smoke. The sound grew louder, stronger, as more bells joined in.

"What the devil is that about?" Klaus Gerhard said, coming over and joining me on the porch. "Ain't Sunday, is it, gal?"

I shook my head.

The bells continued to ring as a cloud of dust appeared on the hill and Ottiwell Wood emerged, racing up in his buggy. He drove his horse faster than ever before, and I hoped, though it was so soon it hardly seemed possible, I prayed he had a letter from Harry.

He waved his arm. "Germany surrendered!" he cried. "Germany surrendered!"

Klaus Gerhard humphed.

"Don't you hear those bells?" Ottiwell Wood asked.

"I hear them," Klaus Gerhard said.

"First Baptist said she'd ring all day when news came the war was over," Ott Wood said.

Reaching up, I took him by the hand with all five fingers.

Even if he didn't have a letter for me, his news thrilled me. If the war was over, Mama and Papa could come home.

But as we listened outside in the bright sunshine, one by one, the bells stopped. My hand slipped from Ottiwell's fingers, down to my side.

"You willing to swear on your good name this war's over?" Klaus Gerhard asked.

"Well, I haven't talked with President Wilson yet," Ott said.

"No, I don't suppose you have."

"But it might be over, Klaus. And if it isn't yet, it will be soon enough. Blast it. Can't you work up a little enthusiasm, old man?" he asked.

But Ottiwell's buggy left more quietly than it came, stirring up only the smallest puff of dust as it moved out of the drive way and up Black Mountain Road.

## chapter thirteen

### *Friday, October 18, 1918*

OTT WOOD HANDED Klaus Gerhard the newspaper this morning without saying a word. The headline read: NEWS OF GERMAN SURRENDER FALSE ALARM.

Klaus Gerhard could have rubbed it in. He didn't. He patted Ottiwell on the leg and nodded.

The rumor had fooled people up and down the East Coast. Bells had rung; shopkeepers had closed up to celebrate.

I dragged myself back to the house. Mama and Papa would not be coming home. At least not yet.

Klaus Gerhard served ham for dinner.

Ham.

How many times had my mouth watered at the sweet odor of ham baking in Mrs. McCarthy's apartment? How many times had I longed to cheat and eat this meat, this particular meat. And then Klaus Gerhard places a delicious-smelling slab of it on my plate. On my very plate!

I picked up my fork, my mouth wet with hunger.

But Eve's face floated before my eyes, her voice whispered in shock, "Hannah!"

I sighed, put my fork down, pushed my plate away.

"Won't eat ham either, gal?" He sagged. "Aint there nothing you'll eat? I thought sure you'd take ham."

If he only knew. If I could only tell him I'd take ham every day of the week if I could.

Klaus Gerhard folded his arms across his chest and puzzled over me.

I puzzled back, rubbed the side of my nose. Maybe I could tell him. Some people, like Rocky Keegan, didn't like Jews. But Klaus Gerhard wasn't Rocky Keegan.

I swallowed hard, took out my notebook and scrawled, "I'm a Jew."

He looked at my writing.

I sat very straight, held very still. My heart thudded.

His nose whistled softly in the quiet kitchen as he deciphered my writing. Finally he looked up at me. "A Jew is it," he said. He nibbled on the end of his mustache. "Then Jews are finicky eaters?"

Relief shot through me. He wasn't Rocky Keegan.

"We're not finicky," I wrote. "Jews have rules about food. We can only eat kosher."

"What's kosher?" Klaus Gerhard asked. "Fruit and hard boiled eggs?"

I nodded.

"No pigs?"

"No pigs," I wrote.

"Chicken?"

"Chicken's okay if it comes from a kosher butcher."

"Fish?"

"Fish I can have anytime," I wrote.

"You'll eat fish?"

I nodded.

He jumped up, his whole body hopping with excitement.

"You'll eat fish? Fish!" He smacked his hand against his forehead.

I grinned as he raced from the kitchen. Watching out the window, I saw him head into one of the little barns. Moments later he returned. He was practically clicking his feet in the air. I didn't even notice his limp.

"Smoked trout," he cried, holding the musky-scented fish before me.

I put my nose over the fish, breathing in the wonderful aroma. "Eat!" he urged. He was almost frantic.

I peeled off a piece of the meat, placed it in my mouth, chewed.

"Very good," I wrote.

"Fish!" he fussed at me from across the table. "Anything else? How about vegetables?"

I wrote, "Nothing cooked with lard or bacon grease."

He nodded, reading the words as I wrote them.

"No meat and milk at the same meal."

He ran his fingers absentmindedly through his beard.

"No eggs if there is even a speck of blood."

He waited for me to write more. I put the pencil down.

Klaus Gerhard heaved a large sigh. "No wonder you weren't eating, gal. Well now, let's just see what we can do for you, Miss Skin and Bones."

I smiled, taking another bite of fish. He hadn't said any thing about my being Jewish.

Klaus Gerhard settled back in his chair, ignoring his own

food, just plopped down there watching me eat. Maybe he was strange to look at, and he did have peculiar ways, but I might have been wrong to judge him by those things.

Picking up my pencil I wrote, "Thank you."

I hoped he understood I was thanking him for more than the fish.


After dinner Klaus Gerhard hitched up Big Train. I waited outside the barn, following him back and forth.

"You're worse than the dogs, gal. What are you doing under my feet?"

I took out my notebook. "Can I go to town with you?"

"You ain't strong enough for a trip to town yet," he said.

I nodded, writing, "I am."

He was reluctant to take me with him. But I stubbornly held out. I missed the bustle of a city, even a small one like Brattleboro.

In Brattleboro, Klaus Gerhard hitched Big Train at the post in front of a barbershop. "This is fairly halfway between all the places I'm going. Think you can walk some, gal?"

I nodded. The fact was, I wasn't certain my legs would hold me at all. I waited in the wagon for him to come around and help me down. As he reached my side, a man and a little girl emerged from the barbershop. The man gave off the fragrance of talcum powder and hair tonic. His neck was pink.

Father and daughter were nearly past us when the little girl stopped and turned. She wore a grim scowl on her face. Looking up, she wagged her small finger at Klaus Gerhard. "I know who you are," she said.

"Who am I?" he asked kindly, bending toward her.

"I heard the barber say." The girl backed up a pace. "You're a dirty German." And then she spit on his boots.

I felt as if someone had hit me in the stomach.

Her father looked away, embarrassed.

"Do you know what, Mr. German?" the little girl continued. "If you win the war, I'd rather go live in heaven than stay here with you."

Klaus Gerhard did not move.

The girl's father snatched her hand, mumbled an apology, and led her away.

Klaus Gerhard stood a few moments in the gutter of the street before moving.

Then he came to my side, gathered me in his arms, and gently lifted me down. Once he saw me standing, he limped ahead of me, carrying a heavy basket covered with a cloth, his gait more uneven than usual.

I followed him in and out of stores along Main Street. He paid for everything with honey, or fruit, or goat's milk. All bartered. I couldn't imagine doing something like that in Boston. And yet, Mrs. Schwartz gave me fish paper in exchange for my drawing.

Our last stop was the butcher shop. "Until I can catch you some fresh fish, gal, will you eat what comes from here?"

I wasn't sure. Nowhere on the window did it say anything about kosher meat. Inside, cow carcasses hung from the ceiling. Three white pigs were strung up in a row, the meat hook through their snouts. Raw red slabs of meat filled one large table, where a blond man with a cleaver worked in a blood stained apron. His shoes made a jumbled path in the sawdust at his feet.

Klaus Gerhard and I waited at the counter. A customer came in behind us, was waited on, and left.

Even in my exhaustion I felt anger. "We were first," I wrote. Klaus Gerhard nodded as if this had happened before.

Another customer came in. The butcher talked with her about the false alarm yesterday, continuing to ignore us.

"Those Germans, they just don't know when to give up," he said, tossing his head toward us.

Rage pounded inside my skull. Glaring at the butcher, I dared him with my eyes to continue treating us that way.

Finally, he came toward us and asked what we wanted.

That's what I'd been waiting for. Turning my back on him, I left the shop pulling Klaus Gerhard out after me.

No more was said that afternoon about our treatment in the butcher shop or our abrupt exit from it. In the wagon on the ride home, I dozed off for a little while, my head resting on Klaus Gerhard's shoulder.

That night he tucked me up with a warm brick. "I'm sorry you had to see all that today, gal," he said, making sure the warmth reached my feet. "Don't let it worry you."

But it did worry me.

His humiliation today had been partly my fault. He had tethered Big Train in front of that barbershop so I wouldn't have to walk too far. He'd gone to that butcher shop to buy fresh fish for me.

I had to return to Chambers Street, for his sake as much as my own.

As soon as the house quieted, with the dogs curled on the hooked rug beside my bed, I took my notebook out, and sitting under the window, I wrote a letter by the light of the moon. To Vashti.

137

*Vashti,*

I saw her so clearly. When this letter arrived she would stand, straight backed, under the bedroom window. She would read my letter with the same impatient attention she paid to everything else I did. I swallowed down my anger. This was not to be a letter of anger.

*I know you and Tanta Rose wanted me to go to Albany, but a mistake was made. I boarded the wrong train. While traveling, I fell ill with influenza and was taken off in a town called Brattleboro, in the state of Vermont. While I recover I am staying with a farmer. His name is Klaus Gerhard. You can write me at RFD 1. The letter carrier knows where I am.*

*Please, Vashti, I know you are very busy, but could you tell me how my sisters are? Please let me know they are well. And Mama and Papa, if you have heard from them, please write and tell me what they say. I am all right here. As soon as I am well enough I will find a way home. If you did not use the newspaper money in the jar in the icebox, could you please send it to me? I'm certain there is enough for the cost of my ticket.*

*Sincerely,*
*Hannah*

There was no temptation to sign this letter, "Love, Hannah," the way I had thought of signing Harry's. I was glad I'd written it. That was all. I felt no gladness about returning to the person who would receive it. I felt no certainty that she would even write back.

# chapter fourteen

## *Saturday, October 19, 1918*

OTTIWELL WOOD took the letter I slipped into his hand, the letter for Vashti. He nodded, tucking it into his pocket.

All through the morning, a chilly rain beat against the small windowpanes of Klaus Gerhard's kitchen. I fussed with the fire in the woodstove, peeled and sliced apples, rolled and rerolled pie dough. Maybe I couldn't eat his pies, but I could at least try baking them. Especially with him out in the rain catching fish for me. Spilling flour on the floor, I swept up the best I could in the weed-strewn kitchen. Maybe I was getting used to the smell. And the mess. It didn't bother me the way it had when I first came.

Miss Carpenter drove up at noon to share dinner with us. It was Saturday. Tanta Rose and my sisters would have been Sabbath visiting. Miss Carpenter sat across from me at the table. Klaus Gerhard passed her butter and bread.

"They're keeping schools closed another week," Miss Carpenter announced, dabbing her napkin at a crumb on her lip. "Did you go to school in Boston, Hannah?"

I nodded. "Until the influenza," I wrote.

"Influenza! I planned on stopping here yesterday, but the

motor went bad on the electric railroad and no one could fix it. Every single repairman in town is down with the grippe. Traffic backed up so far I couldn't get through the bridge."

Miss Carpenter stopped talking long enough to sip the tea I'd poured. "You're gaining every day, Hannah," she said. "Living with Uncle Klaus agrees with you."

She was right. I looked at my full plate, fresh fish, hard boiled eggs, slices of fruit, boiled potatoes. I felt Klaus Gerhard's warm clothes on my body, his boots on my feet.

"If you feel up to it, you could put on one of the dresses I brought you, go to town, stop at the Red Cross meeting next Wednesday. It'd be good for you to see some girls your own age. This bread is delicious, Uncle Klaus," Miss Carpenter said, taking a second slice and slabbing thick butter onto it. "The influenza closed two bakeries in Saint Albans this week. You could sell these loaves up there for a fortune."

I listened carefully. Maybe I could bake bread and earn enough money for train fare back to Boston.

Klaus Gerhard smiled softly and shook his head. "Nobody wants my bread."

I remembered him telling me how he had to stop farming because people didn't want anything from a German even if it was just his name that was German; I remembered how the butcher and the little girl had treated him.

"Don't be modest," Miss Carpenter said. "Your bread is wonderful." Klaus Gerhard was not being modest.

"You're not eating ham, Hannah," Miss Carpenter said, looking at my plate.

"She don't eat ham," Klaus Gerhard said. "I got this fish for her special."

140

Miss Carpenter stopped, fork poised over her dish. "You're a lucky girl." She looked at Klaus Gerhard and then she looked at me. "Speaking of lucky girls, one of my patients at the hospital had a story from her brother in France." Miss Carpenter cut her meat into dainty little pieces. "The brother wrote that a French girl had spent three years in a cellar with her mother and grandmother while the Germans occupied their town."

I had lived in a cellar, too.

"After the Germans left, the child found a group of American Quakers, my patient's brother among them, rebuilding her village. She went up to the men and asked how much it would cost to have them build a house for her family."

I thought about Tanta Rose and her aching bones in our dreary tenement apartment. A little French girl knew better how to take care of her family than I did.

"The Quakers built a house for the child, and when they finished, she handed them her entire life savings. Six sous, about six cents American. They thanked her, counted out the money, and gave her two sous back in change."

A little girl, and she'd kept her family together. She'd found a good home for them.

Klaus Gerhard cut the pie I'd baked and served up pieces for himself and Miss Carpenter.

He took a bite. "Pie's interesting without the honey," he said, chewing thoughtfully.

My cheeks burned. How could I have forgotten the honey?

Miss Carpenter nibbled at hers. A piece of tough crust dropped from her fork, landing noisily on the table. "I can't eat another bite," she said, pushing her plate away. She dabbed her lips with a napkin.

My hope of earning the fare back to Boston by baking died a quick death. I rubbed the side of my nose.

Klaus Gerhard didn't notice. He was too busy eating pie. He finished his first piece, and instead of giving the rest to the dogs, to my surprise he reached across the table and cut himself a second.

## chapter fifteen

*Tuesday, October 22, 1918*

WHEN KLAUS GERHARD went out in the morning to bring in the wood, I tried my voice again. I thought today was the day. Today I'd hear from Boston. Today my voice would work. There were things to discuss. Big things like my leaving. Small things, like why he named his goats after movie stars. I ended up asking nothing. I still couldn't talk.

It was a raw morning. I felt sorry for Ottiwell Wood, looking miserable as he pulled up in his open buggy, but still I had hope. Hope that he brought a letter from Harry. Hope that he brought money, or at least news from Vashti.

I ran out to meet the buggy.

Ottiwell wouldn't look me in the eye. That worried me. You couldn't trust a person who wouldn't look straight at you. But maybe it had nothing to do with trust. Maybe he had his mind on other things. He watched Klaus Gerhard coming toward us from the house. "I swear his limp is better. Don't you think, Hannah?"

I turned and watched him approach. His limp had improved.

He caught up to us. "You two sharing secrets?"

"I asked her if you were too stingy to offer an old man a cup of tea on this bitter morning," Ottiwell Wood said.

Klaus Gerhard growled, "Ain't one bit stingy." He motioned Ottiwell out of his buggy and into the kitchen.

"Don't be pouring in any of that nasty vinegar," Ottiwell said, holding his hand over his mug.

"It'd do you good, Ott. Wouldn't it do him good, Hannah?" I nodded.

"Look at the pink in that gal's cheeks," he said, gesturing toward me. "That's the vinegar."

Ottiwell Wood laughed, nearly spilling his tea. His cheeks were covered with hundreds of spidery veins, all bright red. "I've got enough pink in my cheeks without your vinegar, old man."

Klaus Gerhard nodded.

"Found a poem in the paper," Ottiwell said.

He pulled a rough-edged, folded piece of newsprint out of an inside pocket in his great coat.

WHEN I COME HOME

*When I come home and leave behind*
*Dark things I would not call to mind,*
*I'll taste good ale and home-made bread,*
*And see white sheets and pillows spread;*
*And there is one who'll softly creep*
*To kiss me ere I fall asleep*
*And tuck me neath the counterpane,*
*And I shall be a boy again*
*When I come home!*

144

*When I come home, from dark to light*
*And tread the roadways long and white,*
*And tramp the lanes I tramped of yore,*
*And see the village greens once more,*
*The tranquil farms, the meadows free,*
*The friendly trees that nod to me,*
*And hear the lark beneath the sun,*
*'Twill be good pay for what I've done!*
*When I come home!*

*Leslie Couison*
*(Killed in action—October 7, 1916)*

Ottiwell, whose voice had held up the entire time he read, put the paper down on the kitchen table and rubbed the fist missing two fingers into the corner of his eye. "Walt could've written that poem," he said, his voice cracking. "The poor boy." He pulled a handkerchief from his pocket and blew his nose.

Klaus Gerhard sat quietly. "What word you have from Walt?"

Ottiwell looked weary. "Ah, my Walt. He's a good boy."

"They're all good boys," Klaus Gerhard said.

I thought about Rocky Keegan's plan to enlist. Would Klaus Gerhard think Rocky was a good boy?

"Walt says the Germans are starving their prisoners over there," Ottiwell said. "Our own boys down to skin and bones. They have to be carried off the trains on litters. Living skeletons, they are."

Those Germans, I thought. I hated those Germans. I

imagined my father, nearly dead of hunger, being carried off a train on a litter. I wanted to bundle all the food we had here into a tablecloth and send it to the starving American soldiers.

"They're all hungry, Ott," Klaus Gerhard said softly. "French. American. German. Russian. And not just soldiers, either. The common folk, millions of them. They're starving over there. War's a hard thing on the belly, no matter what flag you're flying."

That was the first I'd heard of Germans as common folk. I had only thought of them as the enemy until now.

Ottiwell stood, put his coat back on, drained the last sip of tea from his cup. "I don't know what kind of weed you just fed me, old man, but it's got my fingers warm again and my throat calmed."

Klaus Gerhard stood, too. "That almost sounded like a thank you. You ain't sick, are you, Ott?"

"No sir."

"How much longer till Lowell takes his mail route back?"

Ottiwell shrugged. "Week or two maybe. From the way his missus talks, he just barely knows his own name. Been in a stupor all these weeks." Sighing, he headed for the door.

All this time I never gave up hope, thinking Ott'd pull out my letter from Harry any minute. I was certain he'd forgotten it because of that poem. That poem must have sent every thing else out of his mind.

If only I could talk.

Before he disappeared out the door, I ran toward Ottiwell Wood, opened my notebook. "Is there anything for me?" I held the note between us.

He read my hasty scribble, shook his head. An enormous sadness surrounded him.

Klaus Gerhard came over. "You sure you ain't gettin' sick, Ott?" he asked.

"I'm worried about Walt, is all."

Klaus Gerhard reached out, wrapped his arms around the bigger man, and the two embraced.

Something happened inside my throat as I watched them. I rubbed my nose and looked away.

Late that afternoon, though it was still blustery, the clouds cleared and the sun came out. Some of the trees had lost their leaves, but the woods beside the house, the orchard behind it, and the mountain in front still blazed with color.

Klaus Gerhard sat in one of the wicker porch rockers in the waning light, digesting his supper.

I came out, dressed in his hat, clothes. My boot laces flapped. I handed his shabby coat to him.

"I've got the second milking to do in a piece," he said quietly. "Thought I'd just take a minute or two to help the sun set. Come sit down and give me a hand with it, gal."

I smiled and sat, wrapping my arms around my shins, making a tight knot of myself in the rocking chair. As if human beings could help the sun set. And more foolish, the sun was setting behind us. We couldn't even see it. Looking across the valley to Wantastiquet Mountain, we faced east. Faced Boston.

"War is stinking, gal," Klaus Gerhard said.

I looked over at him.

"The Civil War," he said. "I was fool enough to stick my young nose into that."

Tunneling my hands between my legs, I tried to stop shivering.

147

"Ever hear of Mr. Abraham Lincoln?" Klaus Gerhard asked. He shifted position.

I nodded.

"I heard President Lincoln speak once," he said.

Klaus Gerhard had heard the real and true Abraham Lincoln?

"Mr. Lincoln addressed my battalion on the eve before battle. I was just a kid. But I'll never forget him. He spoke to us boys, real quiet and decent, about the need to show kindness to people we'd got the habit of looking down on."

Klaus Gerhard rocked a while, staring toward the mountain.

"Mr. Lincoln told us a story that afternoon. About when he was a country lawyer traveling some distance from home on a case. It was a bitter night, and he found only a small fire burning when he arrived at his destination. Hogging the heat of that fire were two other lawyers."

I shifted in my seat. The cold gnawed right through the sagging rocker straight to my bottom. The sun had set now; all that remained was the pink-and-orange afterglow.

"One of the lawyers turned to Mr. Lincoln. 'Pretty cold, eh?' he asked.

"Mr. Lincoln answered, 'I'd say it's about as cold right here as it is hot in Hades.'

"'Have you ever been to Hades, stranger?' the first lawyer asked.

"'Why, yes,' Mr. Lincoln replied. 'I have.'

"'What does Hades look like?' the lawyer wanted to know.

"'Why, it looks very much like this,' Mr. Lincoln answered. 'All the lawyers nearest the fire.'"

I laughed. And a sound came out.

Right into the rose-colored dusk, a sound came out.

Klaus Gerhard looked up. He smiled at me, patted my knee. "Well, gal, you either needed a good Abe Lincoln story or the vinegar's finally working."

I unfolded from the rocker and stood, looking straight into his eyes. He looked me straight back, grinning so wide his face nearly disappeared into the creases.

Trying my voice, I got a hoarse, scratchy sound. You couldn't call it talking, but at least it was a sound.

"Speaking of Abe Lincoln and fires, go get yourself in by ours before you get sick again."

Our fire. Klaus Gerhard's and mine.

He slipped his arms into his coat, walked across the yard, moved through lantern light inside the barn, to tend the chickens and Big Train, to milk Gloria Swanson, Mary Pickford, and Theda Bara.

I scurried into the house and warmed my front, then my back, at the stove. My voice sounded like the rattle of rocks in the back of Klaus Gerhard's wagon. But it was something. For the first time in weeks, it was something!

chapter sixteen

*Wednesday, October 23, 1918*

"THE WEATHER'S FAIR. You feel strong enough to come foraging with me, gal?" Klaus Gerhard asked.

I almost choked on the last sip of my vinegar water. Vashti never asked anyone to come with her on her plant-gathering adventures around Boston.

I wanted to go with him. But the thought of being so far from houses, shops, people—I'd never been in the woods before.

"I've got a funeral to see to this afternoon," he said. "But there's a little time for gathering this morning. Do you good to get some fresh air."

"Maybe." It hurt to talk, as if Mr. Izzy, the butcher, had flayed the inside of my throat.

The pluck of hooves sounded as Ottiwell Wood came down the drive.

I raced outside. Please let him have a letter for me, I prayed. I looked into the veined face. Again, Ottiwell did not meet my eyes. He had nothing for me. I swallowed my disappointment and hugged myself against the chill morning.

"You going to see Wallace off this afternoon?" Ottiwell

asked as Klaus Gerhard came alongside the buggy. Ott handed down a newspaper.

"Course I'll be there," Klaus Gerhard said. "Wallace was a friend." He ran his hand over the flank of Ottiwell's horse.

"Doesn't look like too many are going to the funeral," Ottiwell said. "Because of—" He glanced in my direction. "Well, there's the worry over the flu and—and the manner of Wallace's demise."

I waited for an explanation, but neither Klaus Gerhard nor Ottiwell Wood offered one.

"What does that mean?" I croaked. "'The manner of Wallace's demise?'"

Ottiwell Wood swept his cap off his head and banged it against his knee. "She's talking!" he shouted. He turned to Klaus Gerhard. "You old skunk, why didn't you tell me she was talking."

"Figured she'd let you know when she was ready."

"How long have you had your voice back, Hannah?" Ottiwell asked.

"Since last night," I croaked. I wondered if it would always hurt so much to make sound come out.

"Well, good girl." He smirked at Klaus Gerhard. "You've had it nice, Klaus, haven't you? First time you were ever in a position to do all the talking. What are you gonna do now she talks back?"

"Reckon I'll listen."

"Reckon you will," Ottiwell Wood said.

Klaus Gerhard looked over at me, his eyes shining. Then he turned again to Ottiwell. "I'll be leaving for the funeral after dinner. You want to ride with me?"

"I've only got an hour," said Ottiwell Wood. "I'll have to meet you there."

I followed the retreating buggy with my eyes. Tomorrow I was certain to hear from Boston.

Klaus Gerhard headed toward the barn.

"You never answered my question," I croaked to his back.

He turned toward me.

"The manner of Wallace's demise? What does that mean?"

"The way he died," Klaus Gerhard said. He looked down at his feet. "He killed himself."

Ever since the influenza had come I'd been surrounded by death. Mrs. McCarthy's baby. Mr. Weitz. Tanta Rose. What I needed more than anything was a good dose of life.

"Could I go to the Red Cross meeting while you're at the funeral?"

"You want to waste the afternoon with them old gossips?"

"Miss Carpenter said there'd be girls my age."

"You going gathering with me first?"

I put on my—his cap.

Klaus Gerhard handed me a basket. He took another for himself, and a small shovel.

"Can Orville and Wibur come, too?"

"Not those two," he said. "They keep watering the plants before I can harvest them."

Following directly behind him, my feet caught occasionally on the heels of Klaus Gerhard's boots. He never got cross with me, though.

"Good morning, cattails," he said, standing at the edge of a pond, his boots sinking into the muck.

For a moment my interest flared, thinking about drawing

152

cattails. But then I remembered my vow, and plunged my hands deep into my pockets.

"Cattail root makes good flour. And I need some new stuffing for my mattress," he said.

"You stuff your mattress with cattails?"

"Easier to get than feathers, gal, and you have to admit it feels pretty good."

"I've been sleeping on cattails?"

"Sure thing," he said, filling his basket.

I watched him at the water's edge, the dew sparkling in the sunlight, his cheeks pink with cold. If I could only draw Klaus Gerhard and his weeds in my sketchbook, being out in the wild wouldn't be so bad.

Moving away from the water, we tromped through a tangle of brush. A branch snagged my cap and pulled it off. More branches caught in my clothes. In a panic, I struggled to free myself from the undergrowth.

Klaus Gerhard instantly appeared at my side, detaching me from the little trees that had trapped me. "Dang moose maple. Nothing but a big overgrown weed." He lifted my cap from a branch marked with pale stripes and plunked it back down on my head, leading me into a clearing where he stopped again.

"Sheep sorrel," he said, pointing to the ground.

I barely glanced at the clump of small tongue-shaped leaves.

"It's good to eat," he said, offering me a leaf. "Try it."

Reluctantly I bit off a piece of leaf and chewed. It tasted sort of lemony and fresh.

"It *is* good," I rasped.

He grinned at me, then continued walking.

The taste of the leaf pleased me so much, I bent down and plucked another.

Klaus Gerhard stopped me before I could pop the new leaf into my mouth.

"Hold on now, gal. Don't think you can eat any old thing out here," he said. "Jews got their rules about what they can and can't eat. Nature's got her rules, too. Some of these plants will kill you. You gotta know what you're doing."

I dropped the leaf I'd picked, horrified.

"Well, you could have ate that one, gal," he said. "You only had a little piece of Saint-John's-wort. That one's good for you. I just wanted you to know they all ain't."

My heart stayed in my throat a long time while I watched him gather plants. Carefully he dug up roots so as not to break or bruise them.

"How did you learn all this?" I rasped. "How do you know what to pick and what to leave alone?"

He smiled. "I've been gathering plants on Black Mountain my whole life, gal. The land gives you what you need."

I stumbled along behind him through tangled grasses, stepping twice more on the heel of his boots. My foot snagged on a root; I tripped and fell. My hand brushed a prickly-looking plant. Suddenly fire seared the tender skin of my palm.

I tried shaking off the pain. It smarted like a hundred bee stings.

"Nettle," Klaus Gerhard said gently. "Let me see that hand, gal." Within moments, painful blisters had formed. "Got you bad, didn't it? You wait here."

He set off across the pasture, leaving me totally alone for an instant when he dropped from sight. But in a moment, he reappeared, holding an enormous leaf nearly as long as my arm. A good-size chunk was missing from it, and Klaus Gerhard was chewing.

"Burdock," he said, taking the chewed leaf, dripping with saliva, from his mouth. He pressed the leaf against my palm.

My stomach heaved at the touch of it. Klaus Gerhard tied the leaf to me with a clean kerchief. I tried not to think about having something he'd chewed tied to my body. But to my amazement, the pain eased almost instantly. "It's better," I croaked. "Can I take the kerchief off now?"

"Not yet. Why don't you rest a bit while I finish my gathering? I'll be over there. See them shrubs with the red fruit? That's smooth sumac. This may be my last chance to bring it in this fall."

I nodded.

"Look, gal. You've got checkerberry at your feet." He parted the leaves of a pretty low-growing plant, revealing several small red berries. "Some folks call it wintergreen." He crushed the leaf, and a fresh cool scent met my nose.

Vashti made a medicine with this smell.

"You can pick some berries if you feel up to it."

I sat down to rest on the chilly remnants of a stone wall, too cold and tired to pick anything, not even a fight.

After a few minutes, Klaus Gerhard came back to check on me. "Let's get you home, gal. Looks like you've been out long enough. I'll leave the baskets and come back to finish soon as you're settled by the fire." He led me across the pasture.

I was a distraction to him. An intrusion. Like I was to Vashti.

Stumbling over tufts and tangles of grass, I couldn't keep up

155

with him; I couldn't catch my breath. Unable to go another step, right in the middle of the pasture I stopped. If he left me, he left me. I couldn't go on.

Klaus Gerhard took only one step more. He turned, saw me swaying in the path, and came back.

With such kindness in his gray eyes, the vinegary old man stood before me.

A wave of gratitude washed over me. He had not abandoned me. He had not left me alone in this place. Vashti would have left me to rot. But not him. I took a step closer, leaned into him.

He stood still as I nestled my curly head against his chest, against his tickly beard. Then his hand came up and settled on the top of my—his cap.

He smelled of wintergreen and vinegar. It was a good smell.

When we first met, Klaus Gerhard had asked me to call him Uncle Klaus. Back then, I thought *Uncle* was only a name for family. But in a way, he'd become a sort of family to me. Until I could get back to my own.

I breathed in his tart odor. "Uncle Klaus," I whispered to his comforting sleeve.

It didn't even hurt to say it.


The woman in charge of the Red Cross operation, an ancient, coil-haired woman wearing a pince-nez and a locket on a ribbon around her throat, greeted me at the door.

"Hannah Gold?" the old woman asked, briskly looking me over in my charity clothes. All the women in the room wore face masks. The old woman handed me one, too.

I rubbed the side of my nose before putting on my mask. "Yes, ma'am."

"Welcome, dear, I'm Mrs. Page." She led the way into the large room. "Ladies, this is Hannah Gold. She is new in town and newly recovered from influenza. Florence Carpenter and Hattie Sullivan took special care of her at the emergency hospital."

Mrs. Page sat me down at the table with three girls making face masks. "You're doing important work, girls," she said. "Those masks are saving lives all over the country."

One of the girls nodded toward the women at the sewing machines. "The gowns they're making will end up in France, on boys wounded in battle." The three girls looked enviously at the women behind the sewing machines.

Would any of the gowns go to Russia, I wondered—where my father was?

In spite of the awkward bandage over my palm, I quickly learned to take three thicknesses of butter cloth and hem the edges. The girl beside me demonstrated how to make four pleats so each mask opened to cover the mouth, the nose, the chin.

"I met up with Edna Bond this morning," a woman at a sewing machine said. "She's Wallace and Cynthie's neighbor."

I looked toward her. Something familiar about her.

"How's Cynthie doing, Lydia?" Mrs. Page asked.

"Lydia?" I whispered. "Is that Lydia Grant?"

The girl next to me nodded.

I turned in my seat so she couldn't see me.

"She's holding up well," Miss Grant said, "considering."

"Did Edna say what happened?" Mrs. Page asked.

"She thought it was the little girl," Miss Grant answered. "Friday afternoon, before he went behind the shed with the rifle, Wallace's little girl developed pneumonia. The doctor wasn't hopeful. Wallace doted on that child. Poor man, he had pneumonia himself, the doctor said."

Mrs. Page frowned. "No matter what the sorrow, the taking of one's life is a terrible sin."

The girl next to me piped up, "Look at Hannah, Mrs. Page. She's just learned how, and she's faster than any of us."

"Hannah," Mrs. Page said, coming briskly to examine my pile of face masks. "Where did you learn to stitch like that?"

I blushed with pleasure at the praise. "My aunt taught me, ma'am," I rasped.

Tanta Rose and her mountains of hemming. How could I help but learn to be fast with a needle?

At the end of the meeting, Mrs. Page handed me a bag. "If you can stitch so well, you must be marvelous with a pair of knitting needles, Hannah. Bring your finished sweaters next week, everyone," she called to the women as they wrapped themselves in their coats and pinned on their hats. "We don't want our boys freezing through the winter."

That night, after supper, I could barely keep my eyes open as I pulled out the balls of blue yarn given to me at the Red Cross meeting. Klaus Gerhard, Uncle Klaus looked over at me.

"Gave you wool for knitting a sweater, did they?"

I nodded.

"Hope you're a fast knitter, gal. They like these things done from one meeting to the next."

I stuck my chin out, trying to look patriotic. "It's for the soldiers," I said. "To keep them warm in the winter."

"What size needles they give you?"

"Needles?"

Uncle Klaus put his cup down and studied me. "You done much knittin', gal?"

I took a deep breath. It hurt in my chest and my lungs. "I've never knit anything before in my life."

A sly smile crept across his face. "You're thinking to finish a sweater in one week's time, and you don't know how to knit?"

My chin trembled. "Mrs. Page handed me the bag of wool. I didn't know how to give it back. It's for the soldiers."

Uncle Klaus put down the knife he was using to slice roots and patted my arm. "Never mind, gal. I'll show you. But not tonight. You're too tired. And not with that hand of yours. Wool'll bring back your blisters."

He got up and filled a basin with hot water from the reservoir in the stove, tossing in a handful of leaves from a pile in the cupboard.

"Those aren't nettles, are they?" I asked.

"Burdock," Uncle Klaus assured me.

He tested the water until it was cool enough not to scald, then tenderly, he bathed my hand, soaking it in the leaf-steeped water.

"They talked about your friend today," I told him. "The one who killed himself. They said he did it because his daughter was sick."

Uncle Klaus nodded, his beard going up and down. "That all they said?"

"They talked about the war, too. And what the 'German monsters' were doing."

He listened, examining the skin on my palm.

"Uncle Klaus, do you suppose in Germany women talk about what the 'American monsters' are doing?"

Uncle Klaus dried my hand, wrapped it in a clean bandage. "Seems likely, gal."

I looked into his kind gray eyes. "I'm sorry I got in your way today. In the woods."

"You'll like foraging better in the spring. It's warmer. You'll be stronger," he said. "You'll see."

I smoothed out a wrinkle in the fresh bandage. "I won't be here in the spring."

Maybe he didn't hear me. My voice still came and went. He picked the soggy burdock leaves out of the basin.

"I'll be leaving as soon as I get money enough for a ticket," I told him. "I wrote home, asking for it."

He had his back to me, wiping the basin dry. "I didn't know you had a home, gal."

"I don't. Not really, not anymore. But I have two sisters back in Boston. They're waiting for me. And when my parents come back from Russia, we'll have a home again."

"Your parents?"

I rubbed the side of my nose. "Mama got trapped in Russia before the war. Papa signed up to fight so he could get her back."

"Miss Flo told me your mother was gone and your father lost. I thought you were alone." Pain hung at the edge of his voice.

"I'm sorry I didn't tell you sooner, Uncle Klaus."

"How much is the fare from here to Boston?" he asked.

"I don't know."

"How much did you ask them to send?"

"Everything I had. My newspaper savings."

He looked at me, curious.

"I sold newspapers."

Uncle Klaus nodded. "And you expect the money any day. That's why you've been after Ott."

"It may not come at all. Vashti might have spent it. If it doesn't come soon, I'll have to find some other way."

The sorrow in his eyes, the way his back sagged, worried me.

"My sisters," I said. "I left when they were sick. I'll walk back if I have to."

Uncle Klaus waited in silence awhile. Then he spoke. "You ain't strong enough to walk anywhere."

I rubbed my weary eyes.

"You're dead on your feet. Drink your cider vinegar now, gal, and go to bed."

"You'll teach me to knit tomorrow?"

"I'll teach you."

"Uncle Klaus?"

He looked straight at me.

"I—" I started to say something, but I wasn't certain what it was I wanted to say. "I didn't know men could knit."

"There's plenty you don't know, gal."

Giving in to the tug at my heart, I kissed him on the cheek, right where his beard started. I would miss him when I left. "Good night, Uncle Klaus."

"Night, gal."

Slipping between the sheets, my body gradually unwound under the heavy warmth of the blankets. Beneath me was the fluff of cattails, the soft and fragrant fluff of cattails.

chapter seventeen

## Thursday, October 24, 1918

THIS MORNING, THE "SOMETHING" in my dresser was a pair of hand-carved knitting needles. I came stumbling with them through the shadowy light of dawn and found Uncle Klaus in the kitchen straining goat's milk.

"Morning, gal," he said. "You're moving around mighty early."

"Thank you for the needles, Uncle Klaus."

He nodded. "Made them for the Boss years ago." Finishing with the milk, he washed his hands and dried them on his pants.

"Will you show me how to use them?"

He took the end of one of several big balls of blue yarn and wrapped it once around his thumb and forefinger. Then he poked the needle up and down and through the triangle of yarn. Miraculously, a stitch appeared. I watched closely as the needle moved in and around his fingers. "How many stitches does it say to cast on?" he asked.

I dug out the hand-copied instructions from the bag and gave them to him. "May I try?"

Showing me once more, slowly, how to move the needle inside the sling of yarn, Uncle Klaus handed the knitting over to me.

My hand had completely healed from my meeting with the nettle yesterday. No sign of blisters, not even the slightest itch. I wrapped the yarn around my thumb and forefinger the way he had. Moving the needle over and under the wool, though, the yarn simply fell away. I tried moving the needle in a different direction. This time I came up with a knot.

After a dozen failed attempts I slammed the wool and needle down on the table, making roots and dirt bounce to the floor.

Uncle Klaus studied me a moment. "You ain't giving up, are you?" He picked up the knitting from the table and showed me again what to do. "Don't nobody get it the first time," he said.

I took the knitting back.

One tight stitch moved from my fingers onto the needle. Then minutes later another, and then slowly another.

"Keep going, gal," Uncle Klaus said. He sounded kind of choked up. Heading out the door, he came back a few moments later with a load of firewood. Limping across the kitchen, he filled the stove, then stopped to check on my progress.

"You've got it good now," he said.

Sighing, he watched me cast on stitches for the longest time. Then he walked over to the door, his back to me, gazing toward the mountain.

I finished casting on stitches, counted to be sure I had enough, then put the knitting down on the cleanest spot I could find at the table.

"What's the matter, Uncle Klaus?"

"Nothing, I guess. Got all your stitches cast on?"

I nodded. "What do I do next?"

He took both needles this time and showed me how to knit. I picked up the trick of it on my second try.

1 6 3

"You're just a natural born genius, gal," he said.

"Not me. Libbie's the brain in the family."

He nodded, limping away.

I had finished the first row of knitting and carefully laid the needles on the kitchen table when Ottiwell Wood came. He brought the newspaper, but no letters.

After returning to the house, instead of picking up the needles again, I climbed down to the root cellar and gathered a half dozen apples. Back upstairs, I pulled my chair nearer the woodstove and started peeling.

Uncle Klaus limped up behind me. "What you doing, gal?"

"I'm fixing you some cat pie," I said.

"Cat pie?" Uncle Klaus scratched his head. "That one of your kosher things?"

"Not exactly," I said. "Have any raisins?" I turned toward him. The sticky palm of my hand left a crescent-shaped mark on the table.

Uncle Klaus fetched the raisins.

"And walnuts?"

He brought a big jar from off his sleeping porch.

"In Boston, we bought cat pie at the bakery," I said. "My sisters loved it."

My sisters. Eve and Libbie. I stopped. Would I ever fix cat pie for them?

Uncle Klaus put his hands on my shoulders. "How many times you say you've written home, gal?" he asked gently.

"Twice," I answered.

"Write again."

While I put the cat pie in to bake, Uncle Klaus limped out of the kitchen to the front porch. Mug in hand, he settled his skinny bottom on the stone slab that served as a step.

I came out with my knitting and sat in the Boss's rocker. Clouds spread across the blue sky, dark clouds, blowing in low and fast. "At the Red Cross meeting they said the war would be over soon. Will you be sad if the Germans lose?" I asked.

He said nothing.

"When the war's over, that will be good for everyone, won't it, Uncle Klaus? No more fighting. President Wilson promised. This is the war to end all wars."

"I seen what men do to each other, gal. No matter what Mr. Wilson claims, the end of this war holds the seeds for the next. You wait and see."

I went in to get out of the weather and check on the cat pie. Outside, the wind tossed Uncle Klaus's long hair behind him. It looked like angel hair. A chill rattled up my spine. Instead of joining him on the porch again, I pulled the kitchen door shut between us and stayed in.

Sitting in the seat next to the stove I started knitting again. I had finished another whole row when I noticed the newspaper Uncle Klaus had been reading earlier.

A headline read BOLSHEVIKS KILL AMERICAN SOLDIERS IN RUSSIA. My heart banged against my throat. Papa. My papa was an American soldier in Russia.

I raced out the kitchen door. "Uncle Klaus!"

"What is it, gal?" He bolted to his feet, his face pinched with concern.

I shoved the article into his hands. "My father is in Russia!"

He read the headline, sat back down on the stone step. "You think it might be your pa got killed? Could be. That's war, gal."

"That's war!" I cried, furious. "That's my father!"

"Might be your pa's one of the dead, might be he ain't. There are thousands to grieve over, gal. Tens of thousands."

My jaw clamped tight in rage.

"If it ain't your father, it's someone else's. The dead soldiers, they're someone's sons, someone's fathers." Uncle Klaus handed the newspaper back to me. "And what about the Bolsheviks who died in that skirmish, gal? You think those men ain't loved by their kin?"

My hands balled into fists, beating him. "You're wrong! You're wrong!"

He let me pound him, never resisting. "All of us, we're just human, gal."

"Germans are not human," I snapped at him, trying to hurt him with words. "Germans starve their prisoners."

"Germans can't feed their own."

"Then they shouldn't take prisoners," I said.

Uncle Klaus looked out over the mountain. "That's the way war goes."

"Then it's—" I stopped.

"It's what?"

"It's wrong," I cried, turning my back on him. Papa had gone to fight the enemy. But I'd never thought that meant Papa killing another human being. I only thought what a hero my papa was, going off to war. How brave. I did not know what he would have to do over there. I reached for the door, the dogs at my heels.

"You're right, gal," Uncle Klaus said softly, as if he were talking to the mountain. A sorrow burdened his voice, a sorrow so deep I thought it had no bottom. "War is wrong."

I straightened. My fingers gripped the door handle.

The rain started falling, softly at first, then in moments

166

harder, stinging. Uncle Klaus remained sitting on the step.

I came across the porch, pulled on his hand, trying to get him on his feet.

"I'm not ready to go in yet, gal."

"Fine," I said. "Don't." Using my full weight, I shoved Uncle Klaus sideways on the stone slab and sat down beside him.

He took a deep breath. "The day after I heard President Lincoln talk, I got myself tore up pretty bad in a skirmish. Everywhere I looked I saw boys dead and dying. Their side, our side. Under cover of night, I crawled until I found a small cave. I thought I'd hole up there until the pain eased.

"But a Confederate soldier, my age, had beat me to that cave. He could have killed me when he saw me coming. He didn't. He told me he was sick of killing, sick of war. He didn't want no more to do with it. He just wanted to go home and work his daddy's farm.

"That boy, you should have heard him talk about horses. He had a real love. I asked him to fetch out a pencil and paper, and best I could, I drew him a picture of a horse as a gift for his kindness. He folded that picture into his breast pocket and swore he'd keep it as long as he lived.

"Stayed with that boy two days, grew right fond of him. He kept my spirits up. He was the kind that never walked anywhere if he could run. He shared his rations with me, dug a bullet out of my leg, nursed me when the fever set in. I owed that boy my life. On the morning of the third day, my unit, what was left of it, came in sight, marching straight toward us."

Uncle Klaus stopped talking.

Something big festered inside him. Something painful. The rain beat down on our heads.

"My commanding officer spied the boy bending over me in his Confederate uniform. He yelled for the boy to get away or he'd shoot. The boy got up, started toward the officer to explain. He didn't mean no harm, but the officer didn't know that. I should've held on to that boy. I should have kept him by my side. I called him back, yelled for him to stop. He didn't hear the shot for my hollering. That good Southern boy, he died with my drawing of a horse in his pocket."

The sky had gone the color of slate. The rain sliced through my hair, through my clothes, cutting my skin with knives of ice.

"Ever seen someone die in bed, gal?"

I stared at Uncle Klaus through the rain sheeting over my eyes, and in my mind I saw Tanta Rose.

"It's a beautiful thing, dying in bed. A beautiful thing."

I remembered Tanta Rose. I remembered Vashti, her fist in her mouth. It was not beautiful.

Uncle Klaus did not know he was cracking my shell open, that everything was spilling out.

"To die in bed is a beautiful thing," he repeated.

He turned, saw my face.

"Hannah?" Suddenly his voice was tender. He rested his hand on the top of my dripping hair. "Oh, gal." He stood me up. "What did I say?"

He led me out of the rain, into the kitchen, toward the warm comfort of the stove.

Dressed in dry clothes, I went back to the knitting.

Uncle Klaus ate another piece of cat pie. "That's some good food, gal," he said.

A drop of rain slid off the end of a curl and landed in my

lap. Even in dry clothes, I felt like a sodden pillow. "Uncle Klaus, what if my sisters are dead?" I stared at the hard fought inches of sweater lying in my lap.

He brushed crumbs from his beard. "All you've got is this minute, gal. This minute in the kitchen, with cat pie crumbs on the table and a sweater growing on those needles and the stove needing firewood. If your sisters are gone, you can't do a thing to change it. You just got to leave off your fretting and take care of the things you can do something about."

We drove down to Brattleboro after dinner so Uncle Klaus could drop off a basket of fruit to the emergency hospital. I had other plans. I knitted in the wagon on the way there. The rain had stopped, but the sky still hung heavy with clouds.

As we hitched Big Train outside the emergency hospital, a tall woman came along the walk in our direction. She wore a black hat and a long black cape. Tucking my knitting under the wagon seat, I waited, hoping she would pass without noticing us. I'd recognized her immediately. Miss Lydia Grant.

Uncle Klaus recognized her, too. He leaped in front of her, blocking her path, and bowed.

"Afternoon, Miss Lydia."

The woman looked from Uncle Klaus to me, startled.

But she wasn't the only one startled. I stared at her. Her eyes! I'd kept clear enough of her at the Red Cross meeting. I hadn't seen. But her eyes, they weren't two different colors at all. They were both blue, a very pale blue. How could I have been mistaken?

Her expression turned icy as it settled on Uncle Klaus. "Mr. Gerhard."

"How you been, Miss Lydia?"

"These are difficult times, Mr. Gerhard. Though I trust you've been well."

The tone of her voice said she didn't care if Uncle Klaus had been well or not, that she blamed him for being well when so many others had suffered. Maybe her eyes were both the same color, but they made me feel the way I felt when Vashti looked at me. It was the character of a person behind the eyes and not the eyes themselves that needed looking at. I'd have to remember that the next time I drew eyes.

The next time I drew eyes. Would I ever draw eyes again?

"Ain't had a bit of trouble," Uncle Klaus said. "It's the vinegar."

"Yes," Miss Grant said, pursing her lips. "The vinegar." She nodded curtly and proceeded on her way.

Uncle Klaus went back to tying up Big Train. "You know, gal, I saved that woman's life once." He lifted out the basket of fruit covered with a dishcloth.

"You did? Lydia Grant?"

He nodded. "I asked her to marry me—"

"Miss Grant?" I asked. I followed him up the walk to the emergency hospital.

"She turned me down," Uncle Klaus said.

"Well, if she turned you down, how did you save her life?"

"She said she'd sooner die than marry me." He grinned. "So I didn't insist."

All day he had been in a mood. Now, seeing Lydia Grant, the cloud lifted. I didn't understand men. Maybe this was what Harry's mother, Mrs. Weitz, meant when she asked if I had any questions for her while Mama was gone. Woman things. I'd like to ask her a thing or two now.

170

Uncle Klaus headed Big Train back to Black Mountain, agreeing to return to town and pick me up outside the emergency hospital before supper. I walked down Main Street hill, looking for Help Wanted signs on my way to the railroad station.

After being directed by several young boys around to the back, I found the stationmaster, supervising the loading of lumber onto a wagon. He looked, in his tailored uniform, like the actor Wallace Beery.

"Excuse me?" I said.

"Yes?" He glanced over me, then turned his attention back to the workmen.

I intended to ask about the price of a ticket, but seeing the activity at the railroad station, I thought perhaps I'd ask for a job first. "Do you need any help, sir?"

This time he took a closer look at me. "Shouldn't I be the one asking you that question?"

"No," I said. "I mean, I'm looking for work. Do you have any jobs open?"

His eyes moved over my trousers, my boots, my flannel shirt, my cap. "I don't believe I know you."

"I'm Hannah Gold," I said. "From Boston."

The stationmaster thought a while. "You're the little girl the Red Cross took off the train last month."

"Yes sir."

"It's good to see you on your feet again, Miss Gold."

"Thank you, sir, but I was wondering about the job."

"We're only hiring boys," the stationmaster said.

"I can work like a boy, sir."

The stationmaster signed a paper and turned back to me.

"Just because you dress like a boy doesn't mean you can do a boy's work, Miss Gold."

I prickled with anger. "I can do a boy's work."

The stationmaster smiled at me.

I looked away, over at the stacks of coffins. There must have been dozens of them, piled high on pallets by the tracks. A guard stood watch over them.

The stationmaster followed my gaze. "Don't fret, Miss Gold. Those coffins are empty. At least for the moment."

"What are they doing here?"

"The Renaud brothers can't make them fast enough. Folks are stealing them off trains in New York, Philadelphia, Boston. President Wilson ordered guards placed on them. The influenza, it seems, has presented us with more dead bodies than boxes to bury them in."

Thinking about my sisters buried in stolen coffins, I felt the blood drain out of my face.

"Here," the stationmaster said. "Have a seat on this pallet, child. You've gone quite pale."

I shook off his arm. "Sir, can you tell me the fare for a one way ticket to Boston?"

"Why that would be six dollars and fifteen cents, Miss Gold. Are you planning on leaving us soon?"

"As soon as I can pay for my ticket."

The stationmaster nodded. "Sorry I can't be of more help. Austine was looking for a girl to answer their door, but they hired Elsie Price day before yesterday."

"I'll try up there anyway," I said, "if you'll direct me."

"It's a long walk, particularly for a convalescent. Are you certain you want to go all the way up there?"

"Yes, sir," I said.

"Don't you get sick again, Miss Gold," the stationmaster called as I headed up Canal Street.

After the train station and Austine School, I asked for employment at the Estey organ works and Renaud's carpentry shop. No one gave me a second glance.

I was heading back up main street, past the druggist's window, when I noticed a small sign.

# WANTED:
## MOOSE MAPLE BARK.
## PAYING 6 CENTS A POUND.

I stared at the sign. Moose maple. That was the tree that snagged me in the woods yesterday. Could I gather moose maple bark? Enough to buy a ticket home?

Uncle Klaus had planned to meet me before supper, but I was ready to head back early. In spite of the pain in my chest, I decided to try walking home. If I could get from Brattleboro to Black Mountain on foot today, maybe in a couple more days I could get from Brattleboro to Boston. This would be a test. If I passed it I wouldn't have to worry about moose maple or train fare or anything else.

I'd only come a little way up the hill past the covered bridge when Uncle Klaus pulled Big Train up short. It had taken me an hour to come this far and I sat by the side of the road, struggling to breathe. I wanted to cry, but my chest hurt too much. Gently, Uncle Klaus lifted my sorry bones into the wagon. I couldn't

173

draw breath enough to answer his simplest questions. He carried me into the house and settled me in a chair in front of the stove, put a steaming cup of tea in front of me, then went back out, unhooked the rig, and set Big Train to graze.

By the time I'd finished my cup of tea, I felt a little stronger. Making my way out of the house, I found Uncle Klaus in the orchard.

"Tried to get yourself home on your own steam, did ya?" Uncle Klaus asked. Slowly, he led me through the orchard, where he had been gathering windfall apples in a rickety wheelbarrow.

I followed behind him, forcing myself to keep moving. Every inch of my body hurt, especially my chest. "I thought I'd find a job," I rasped. "Nobody wanted me. They called me a convalescent." Leaning against a tree, I fought back my tears.

Uncle Klaus squinted up through the branches of an apple tree. "I know you're hurting right now, gal, but they're right. You are a convalescent. You're gaining, though. When I think on how sick you were the first time I laid eyes on you. I never saw a child in more need than you were."

The weather had cleared off completely from this morning's rain; it was as clear as it had been at dawn.

Uncle Klaus picked up an apple and examined it.

Movement in the woods behind him caught my eye. On the other side of the stone wall, the light glistened off laurel leaves. I saw something move again. It was a girl, with dark hair, and a pale blue gown, running between the birches. Thinking of nothing but catching her, I stumbled across the orchard, and tumbled over the stone wall. But by the time I'd made my way under the trees, she'd vanished.

"Uncle Klaus, did you see her?" I gasped, returning to him.

He watched my slow return, his hands on his hips. "Did I see who?"

"That girl."

"You saw someone in the woods?" he asked.

"Maybe I'm going crazy," I said.

Uncle Klaus laughed softly. "Not you, gal."

"I see things sometimes, Uncle Klaus," I said.

Uncle Klaus threw a rotten apple across the orchard. It exploded into a dozen pieces as it hit the ground.

"We all see things, gal," Uncle Klaus said. "Folks been see-ing things since the beginning of time. Ain't nothing wrong with that. Problem ain't so much with them that sees things. Problem's more with them that don't."

## chapter eighteen

*Friday, October 25, 1918*

SITTING IN THE KITCHEN by the woodstove, I struggled with the Red Cross sweater. I'd finished the first sleeve and spent the last half hour trying to cast on stitches for the sweater's back. All I had to show for my trouble were loops and tangles and snarls. "I can't cast on." I thumped the needle down, glared at the ball of blue wool.

Uncle Klaus picked up the needle from the table.

Wrapping the yarn around his thumb and forefinger, he wove the needle above and below the taut wool, making a loop. The yarn crawled over his fingers. His stitches were tight. I could do better. I took the needle from him, ripped out what he'd done, started again.

I had only needed to see the fingering once more. Casting on my own stitches, loose, easy, regular, I didn't think I'd forget again.

Uncle Klaus stepped back. "Guess you don't need my help after all."

Taking his gathering basket, he left the house.

Immediately I put down the knitting. I noted the direction

he took, then pulling on his ragged jacket, headed out on my own. I stopped first at the toolshed and picked out a saw. Orville and Wilbur nosed eagerly around me as we walked toward the woods, but then I got to thinking about the Public Garden and how all dogs watered trees there. Comforting as I would have found their company, I brought them back and shut them in the house.

I searched inside the woods for nearly an hour before I found my first moose maple. Once I'd discovered that one, though, I began to find others. My worry over being in the woods gave way to excitement. I could do this. I could earn my way back to my sisters by gathering trees.

Sawing down the scrubby maples rubbed my hands raw. And the slender trees weighed more than I expected, as I dragged them, one at a time, out of the woods. But if they weighed a lot, that meant more bark, and more bark meant more money.

I stacked the trees beside the barn, planning on asking Uncle Klaus to help me take them to the druggist. Ottiwell Wood was coming for supper. It seemed as good a time to ask as any.


As the sun sank behind the orchard, Ottiwell drove his buggy up the road.

I should have been exhausted, but my excitement at earning the money for my ticket kept me in high spirits.

"Hello, *o*, double *t*, *i*, double *u*, *e*, double *l*, double *u*, double *o*, *d*," I said. I swung the letters back and forth in my mouth. "I wish I had a name like that."

Ottiwell said, "You've got one better."

He was as clean shaven as Uncle Klaus was bearded, and he smelled of lye soap.

"*H, a,* double *n, a, h.* Like a mirror," Ottiwell said. "I can't do that with my name."

Like a mirror. He was right.

I fried up johnnycake in the kitchen while Uncle Klaus and Ottiwell sat outside on the stone step. Their voices drifted in on the cool brace of an early autumn evening. Uncle Klaus hadn't said anything about my pile of moosewood yet.

"Got a letter from my grandson," Ottiwell said.

Uncle Klaus was quiet.

"Walt's been wounded, Klaus. Near Chateau-Thierry, over there in France."

I heard a paper unfolding.

*Greetings, Papa Ott. Hope you're having a fair autumn and your asthma isn't giving you trouble. I sure miss home. Now don't you say anything to the folks, 'cause I'm not hurt too bad. But I've got a hole in my back and one in my hip an' my left arm's all busted up. I feel fine. That's what gets me. I feel fine. When I came to after I was hit and kind of looked over what was left of me, I just kissed myself good-bye and wondered how it came about that I was still living. Then they bandaged me up and got me inside an ambulance, and when that old bus got to moving I started wishing I wasn't living. Oh boy, did it ever hurt! But I'm all right now.*

Ottiwell stopped reading.

There was silence outside. The sizzle of johnnycake hissed in my ears. I turned toward the door.

That big Ottiwell Wood was hunched over and sobbing, and Uncle Klaus, half that giant's size, had one arm across his back. Uncle Klaus said nothing, just stared straight ahead, straight toward Wantastiquet Mountain.

When they came in, Ottiwell's eyes were as red as the little veins in his cheeks. But by the time he left that evening, his tears had slipped back into that big old head of his.

Uncle Klaus finished milking while I cleaned the kitchen up from supper. I never did mention the moosewood with Ottiwell there. It didn't seem right, my talking about getting back to my sisters while he worried over Walt.

But as soon as I finished putting the kitchen straight, instead of picking up my knitting, I headed out to Uncle Klaus.

He had one arm wrapped around a load of firewood. "Thought you'd be by the stove knitting all day, gal. Instead I see you've been in the woods pruning moose maple saplings."

"I need your help getting them to town," I said.

"I'm happy to help you move 'em, gal, but I'm curious about why."

"The druggist said he'd pay six cents for every pound of moosewood bark I brought him. I figure I've got close to enough right there by the barn for train fare back to Boston."

Uncle Klaus ran his fingers through his beard once, then scratched his cheek. "Gal, did he say he wanted the bark while it was still on the tree?"

I swallowed hard. "What do you mean?"

"Generally, if someone's looking for bark, that's all they want. You've got to peel it off, one sliver at a time."

By now the moon had risen to cast shadows through the branches of moose maple stacked beside the barn.

"You mean I have to shave the bark off every trunk?"

"Every trunk."

"Off every branch?"

"Every branch," he said.

"Off every twig?"

"Well, some of them twigs might be small enough you could squeak by without putting a knife to them."

I couldn't possibly peel the bark off all those trees. All my hopes. All for nothing.

"Come on, gal," Uncle Klaus said. "Don't look so glum. You ever been walking in an orchard in the moonlight?"

He took my hand and swung it as we walked away from the barn, up behind the house, into the apple orchard.

The moon was so bright you could draw by it.

Drawing by moonlight. I crossed my arms hard over my chest to keep my hands from wanting. Heartsick, I turned to Uncle Klaus. "Do you think Ottiwell Wood's grandson is going to die?"

Uncle Klaus shrugged. "Sounds like he got ripped up pretty good. He was making a joke of it so's not to scare Ott. Maybe they'll send him home and finish patching him up here. Ott would like that."

The moon was a round white shiner in the black eye of the night.

"There was a limerick in the paper today," Uncle Klaus said. "I don't suppose you had much time to read it."

I shook my head.

"Let me see if I can recollect.

*A fly and a flea with the flu*
*Were quarantined so what could they do?*
*Said the fly, 'Let us flee.'*

180

Said the flea, 'Let us fly.'
So they flew through a flaw in the flue."

Uncle Klaus kicked aside a rotting apple. He sat down between two gnarled trees, their branches casting moon shadows across his face.

I sat down beside him. "It's Friday night," I said. "The Jewish Sabbath." I shut my eyes, remembering the flame of Shabbes candles, the white light of grace spreading over us, even in our grim basement tenement. "On Friday night after the candles were lit, my aunt, my Tanta Rose, would put her hands on my head and bless me." With my eyes closed I could feel Tanta Rose's hands on my head.

"You ain't mentioned her much before."

"Tanta Rose was my great-aunt. She looked after us, me and my sisters, when Papa went to war. She was so good to us.

Uncle Klaus nodded. "What happened to her, gal?"

"She came home coughing from the factory one day. She died the next morning. From influenza. My sisters, that's when they got sick, too."

Uncle Klaus lifted his hands and placed them on my head. I smelled goat, and earth, and the tang of vinegar.

"I can bless you, gal," he said softly.

My heart raced. "Tanta Rose would say, 'May God make you as Sarah, Rebecca, Rachel, and Leah.'"

Uncle Klaus repeated, "May God make you as Sarah, Rebecca, Rachel . . .'"

"And Leah," I said.

"And Leah."

It wasn't the same as with Tanta Rose. But it was good.

In the apple-sweet orchard I smiled at Uncle Klaus.

An owl hooted somewhere off in the woodlot. Uncle Klaus hooted right back at him.

I felt laughter bubbling up into my chest. It poured out of me like water from a spigot. But the next moment my laughter turned to tears, and I sobbed in Uncle Klaus's goat-tang arms.

## chapter nineteen

### Saturday, October 26, 1918

CLEARING THE BREAKFAST DISHES, I looked out the window at the pile of moose maple trees. During the night I'd wondered how hard could it be to strip the bark off. But seeing the thousands of slender, tangled branches in the morning light, the task overwhelmed me. I came away from the window and brought Uncle Klaus a cup of chicory root tea.

"Making apple cider today," he said. "I know you got your knitting to do, gal, but I sure could use a hand with the press. He beat the dust from the hem of his coat.

The smell of wool suddenly brought Chambers Street flooding back, school mornings, my sisters dressed and waiting for me at the kitchen table, Tanta Rose's coat.

"Hannah? You press some cider with me?"

I turned away, too full of longing for Chambers Street to talk. I washed up breakfast dishes, instead. Uncle Klaus brought over his empty mug, and I reached for it.

It happened so fast. The mug slipped through my fingers. I tried to catch it as it came past my waist, past my hip. But I couldn't. The mug fell, hitting the kitchen floor.

I shut my eyes. Wrapped my arms around myself.

Tanta Rose. I saw Tanta Rose's cup.

Suddenly I felt arms around me. I felt the tickle of beard.

"Hannah, Hannah," Uncle Klaus said. "It's just a mug. It can be mended, gal. Here." Uncle Klaus bent down to pick up the pieces. "Get me a pan of skim milk."

He sat at the table. Carefully he fit the pieces of the mug together. While I held them, he tied them in place with a stout string.

"Now ease the cup into the skim milk, gal," he said. "We'll leave it to simmer on the back of the stove. Remind me to check on it tonight."

I didnt believe his skim milk could mend the mug. How could you make what was broken whole again?

But if it did work. If it did . . .

I joined Uncle Klaus in the orchard. It turned out I liked making cider. With just a crank of the handle, a heavy wooden lid pressed down on the apples, and sweet amber liquid streamed out of a spout into a waiting jug. After I'd lowered the press down to the bottom of the vat, I turned the handle in the opposite direction to raise the press and cleaned out the leavings wrapped in cheesecloth. Uncle Klaus brought more apples over.

"How you doing, gal?" he asked.

"Fine," I said, dodging yellow jackets.

"Those leavings were heavy. I meant to get them for you."

"I managed."

"Why don't you take the wheelbarrow and see if you can find more windfalls."

Gratefully, I accepted his suggestion. I was tired. Sawing

184

and dragging trees all day yesterday, making cider today, and it had only been two weeks since I'd come home from the hospital.

As I searched the ground in the far end of the orchard, I spied Uncle Klaus staring up the road. I squinted my eyes to see what he saw but I couldn't pick out anything.

The wheelbarrow, a quarter full of apples, announced my return with a high, steady squeal. Uncle Klaus hurried over to help.

"What were you looking at before, Uncle Klaus?"

"When?"

"Just now, up the road."

He frowned. "Used to be every soul on Black Mountain came down in the fall to make cider on my press. We had a grand time. Laughing, catching up on news. I thought it would never end. But everything has to end sometime, don't it, gal?"

I nodded. Including us, I thought.

Heading inside, I fixed some dinner. Uncle Klaus was right. Everything did come to an end, from a visit with a friend to a person's life. And then I looked at the teacup in the pan of milk. Had that come to an end, too, or did Uncle Klaus know a way to give things a new beginning?

I tried a recipe from the paper. Honey cupcakes. Honey was the secret to Uncle Klaus's baking. Because of the bees, he always had plenty of honey. If you had honey, it didn't matter so much about sugar rations.

Some of my baking came out on the dry side, but pies and custards and puddings, they went together fine. Uncle Klaus never complained. As I stirred the thick amber honey into the cupcake batter, I thought about Libbie and her sweet tooth. Oh, Libbie, once I get home I'll bake you into a good mood three times a day.

But then who will bake for Uncle Klaus?

chapter twenty

*Sunday, October 27, 1918*

"READY TO TAKE THE MUG OUT?"

I nodded.

We had moved the pan off the stove last night, but Uncle Klaus said the mug had to stay in the milk until the milk cooled. The pan sat on a corner of the kitchen table.

"Go on, gal."

Pulling up my sleeve, I plunged my hand into the pan of cold milk, fishing out the mug. I set it, dripping, on the table, on top of a wad of newspaper.

Uncle Klaus moved around the table, counterclockwise, inspecting the mug from different angles, his hands behind his back.

"She needs setting up another day," he announced. "We'll leave her right here. Tomorrow I'll drink tea from her."

I picked up my knitting. I doubted Uncle Klaus would ever use that cup again. The cracks showed, just as plain as the veins on Ottiwell Wood's face.

Ottiwell made a surprise visit shortly after breakfast. As we came out the kitchen door to greet him, I couldn't help glancing at the pile of moose maple beside the barn. Uncle Klaus threw an arm around my shoulder and guided me toward the buggy.

"What you doing up here on a Sunday?" Uncle Klaus called. "Got a letter from Walt yesterday," Ottiwell called back. He waved an envelope at us as he pulled the buggy to a stop.

*Dear Papa Ott,*

*Everything is sure nice here in the hospital. There's a nurse from Kansas. She says war is nothing compared to tornadoes. If that's the truth, I sure don't ever want to see a tornado.*

*I don't think I explained much in my last letter how I got busted up. With these nurses taking down my words for me, I get so flummoxed sometimes I have trouble remembering which end is up.*

Ottiwell flashed Uncle Klaus a crooked grin.

*I have one of the Quaker men writing for me today, and he's not too pretty. He says to tell you I'm no beauty myself as if you didn't already know.*

*Anyway, we'd been in a dugout for a week, keeping fires going to stay warm, eating two meals a day, and sleeping the rest of the time, when we finally got the orders to march.*

*The people who lived in the town we came to, they'd been waiting for us. For four years they'd been waiting. Wasn't much left of the village when we got there. First we thought wasn't much left of the people, either. We called, but no one answered. Then, an old fella climbed out of a cellar. Two women showed their heads. Then a couple of children. People started pouring out of the rubble. They ran toward us. There were so many of them, they just kept coming. Papa Ott, they were cold. And hungry. We were hungry, too, but nothing like these poor folks.*

Ottiwell pinched the forefinger and thumb of his good hand under his nose.

*The old men stood in the street, staring at us, tears rolling down their cheeks. Women sat on door steps, crying. The children, Papa Ott, they jumped down from the burned-out buildngs and kissed our hands.*

*There was a lot of work to setting that town right so people could get back to some sort of life there. I was helping in a backyard, a family garden. You know how I like digging in a garden. Anyway, I must have hit a booby trap left behind by the Germans. Went off in my face like the Fourth of July. I'm glad it was me caught the worst of it and not the little boy out there helping me.*

Ottiwell Wood put the letter in his lap. "Our army ought to make those German officers they took prisoner clean up these towns: Let them dig up the booby traps their buddies left behind." He looked out over the valley, then turned back to the letter.

*I managed to get some chocolates last Sunday. I also got a can of jam. It tasted mighty good, believe me. But what I wouldn't give for one of Uncle Klaus's apples. You think he could save me an apple or two from down in his root cellar for when I come home?*

Ottiwell folded the letter and slipped it into the pocket of his coat.

"You tell him there'll be apples aplenty waiting for him," Uncle Klaus said. He smoothed his hand through his long hair and looked out toward the mountain. "I can spare an apple or two for that redheaded scoundrel. Used to be he always took what he wanted anyway. Never bothered asking. Guess the war is teaching him something."

Ottiwell flicked the reins of his buggy. "Guess it is."


"According to this story there's a connection between singing ability and the shape of your head," Uncle Klaus said, pointing to an article in the paper. I sat by the stove, knitting, always and forever knitting. Uncle Klaus sliced apples and pears and peaches and laid them on screens. He said they'd dry quickly up in the attic, and we could send them off to Ottiwell's grandson in his Christmas package

He put his hands up and felt all around his head. "What shape am I, gal?"

Leaning forward in his creaky chair, he sang a hymn that people sing in church. Orville and Wilbur trotted over, tails wagging. First one, then the other, joined in with Uncle Klaus, howling.

"Ah. You two have oval heads for sure," Uncle Klaus said, feeding them pieces of piecrust to hush them up. "What about you, gal?"

I shrugged.

"I ain't never heard you sing."

"I sound pretty much like Orville and Wilbur. Eve is the singer in our family. I knew someone once, though. Ovadiah Strauss. He had the perfect head for singing, round as a pumpkin. But if I have to look like Ovadiah to sing, I'd just as soon howl with the dogs."


Driving Big Train down to the emergency hospital after dinner, we dropped off four jugs of fresh apple cider and some custard I'd made.

While Uncle Klaus visited in the hospital kitchen, I headed straight for the ward. Miss Carpenter hadn't been up to visit us in days.

Hattie Sullivan greeted me warmly in the hall outside the big room.

After a hug, I started for the ward door.

"You can't go in there, love," Miss Sullivan cried, blocking the door with her big body.

She startled me. "I won't stay long. I promise. I only need to find Miss Carpenter."

Hattie Sullivan smiled gently. "I never get tired of hearing your voice," she said. "But, Hannah, it's gotten much worse in there since you left. So crowded. And now. Well, Miss Carpenter is a patient herself."

I started to tremble. "Then you have to let me in."

"I'm afraid not, love. You need special permission from Dr. Grace or Dr. Putnam before I let you through that door."

I flew down to the hospital kitchen to tell Uncle Klaus about Miss Carpenter.

"We'll bring some vinegar to her," he said. "She'll be better in no time once we get some vinegar into her."

## chapter twenty-one

## Monday, October 28, 1918

"WHERE'D YOU STICK that mug, gal? We ain't took the string off yet."

"I put it away."

Uncle Klaus frowned at me. "I'm not asking you to believe in miracles. Bring me the mug."

I rubbed the side of my nose, got the mug down from the top shelf where I'd hidden it. Uncle Klaus started unknotting the string.

"You've got those young fingers," he said. "Get in here and untie this."

I worked at the knots until the string sat in a pile on the kitchen table. At least for that moment the cup stayed together.

"Pour me some tea in it, would you, gal?" Uncle Klaus asked. I shook my head.

"Afraid it's going to bust?"

I nodded.

"So what if it does? Come on." He picked the cup up, held it out to me.

I took the cup and placed it in the dishpan, so that when the mug broke and the tea spilled, it wouldn't make a mess. Slowly I poured tea, hot from the stove, into the mug.

The mug stayed together.

Uncle Klaus looked at me from under his white eyebrows.

He made a smacking sound with his lips. "This morning's pie was a little on the salty side, gal. I've got a powerful thirst."

If the mug broke while I carried it to the table, I would surely be scalded. Uncle Klaus wouldn't take a chance scalding me. Carefully, I lifted the mug. As quickly as I dared I brought it across the kitchen to the table.

"Thank you, gal," Uncle Klaus said.

He lifted the mug by the handle and sipped from it.

The mug stayed together.

Tanta Rose's cup. I could fix Tanta Rose's cup.

If only Tanta Rose was alive to use it.

Ottiwell Wood's buggy came slowly up the road. No sooner did the enormous man climb down out of his seat than he doubled over with a wracking cough.

"You're sick," Uncle Klaus accused.

"Just a cold," Ottiwell said.

Yesterday he'd been fine, so excited about his letter from Walt.

Uncle Klaus scowled at him. "You come around this child coughing like that. What if it ain't a cold. What if the influenza's got you. You come infecting the both of us. And every other poor fool on your route."

"Oh, hush up, old man," Ottiwell groused. "I thought you couldn't get sick." His voice sounded deep and hoarse. With my eyes closed I couldn't tell it was him.

192

"Well even if I can't get sick, the gal can," Uncle Klaus said. "Forget the dang mail today, Ott. Drop your bundle back down to the office and let someone else take your route. For criminey's sake. Get home and get to bed."

"I'm not delivering your mail today, you old coot. Lowell Butts is coming along shortly. I only came up to get some vinegar from you before I settled myself in bed. Figured if you're doing so well, and you pulled Hannah through, that nasty cure of yours might not be such a bad thing after all."

"Gal, go wait in your room till Ottiwell's gone," Uncle Klaus ordered.

I scowled.

"Ott, you get out of this weather while I drain off some vinegar for you. Come on, you old fool, into the kitchen."

I listened to their conversation. Ottiwell asked for more smokes. Uncle Klaus told him he had no business asking for anything, muttering under his breath as he fixed up a bag of tonics and teas and vinegar. "Old fool," he kept repeating.

They continued cursing each other the whole time Uncle Klaus limped around the kitchen, gathering things for Ottiwell to take back with him, but their voices held such fondness it frightened me to think what would happen to Uncle Klaus if Ottiwell died.

Within moments they left the house again and crossed the yard back to Ott's rig.

That was a sight, little Uncle Klaus helping that giant of an Ottiwell Wood back into his buggy. The poor man sagged against the seat back. The red veins in his cheeks looked like they'd spread over his face and across his neck.

"I'll be down this afternoon to check on you," Uncle Klaus said as Ottiwell took the reins in his big hands.

I waved from the bedroom window as he pulled away though I don't think he saw me. "I hope the vinegar works," I whispered through the glass.

Lowell Butts pulled up a few minutes later. He left off the paper and a bill from the blacksmith for Uncle Klaus.

"Anything from Boston?" I asked.

The haggard man looked through his leather packet. "Not that I can see, miss."

I had the sweater to finish. The day was short and dark. There didn't seem to be nearly enough light, especially on account of this new business of moving the clocks around.

My hands and fingers ached from so much knitting, and my back and eyes burned. How much worse could skinning the bark off a tree be than this?

I stopped to make Uncle Klaus a carrot loaf for dinner. But he didn't get back in time for dinner. He'd taken Big Train to town to drop off the vinegar for Miss Carpenter and look in on Ottiwell. He didn't get back till late. I fed Orville and Wilbur pieces of carrot loaf and kept the rest in the warming oven. By the time Uncle Klaus got back, took care of the animals, and sat down to eat, it looked more like carrot rock than carrot loaf.

"I've been thinking about that moose maple out there," I said, sitting across from him at the table. I was still knitting, always knitting. "Could you teach me to skin it?"

Uncle Klaus crunched down on his food. "You ain't never used a knife before."

"I'd never done a lot of things before I came here," I said. "But I've learned."

His gray eyes softened. "Yes, you have, gal."

194

"And those trees are cut already. It seems a shame not to use them."

"You could hurt yourself," Uncle Klaus said.

"I could hurt myself walking across the sitting room, Uncle Klaus."

"Bad as the Boss," he said, chewing his way through a mouthful of carrot loaf.

## chapter twenty-two

## *Tuesday, October 29, 1918*

U NCLE KLAUS DROPPED a mountain of branches in the middle of the kitchen floor.

"You want to peel moosewood?" he asked.

"Yes!"

I couldn't believe my ears.

"Then put down that knitting and get yourself comfortable, gal. I'm about to teach you to bark a tree."

Uncle Klaus handed me a pocketknife and showed me how to hold it, how deep to cut. "You work on these young twigs," he said. "Don't have to separate the outer bark from the inner with these tender little things." He sat with me and we worked together, stripping the striped bark off the moose maple twigs.

"What's the druggist use this for?" I asked.

Uncle Klaus shrugged.

"Don't you know?"

He tilted his head to one side, raised a snowy eyebrow.

"You *don't* know!" I grinned. "I thought you knew every thing about plants."

Uncle Klaus nibbled on his mustache. "Oh, he'll be using it

to dry something up, I guess. What does it matter? You trying to earn money or give an old man a hard time?"

"Earn money," I said.

"How much you need?"

"Six dollars and fifteen cents."

At six cents a pound, how many pounds of bark did I have to peel for a ticket to Boston? I tried figuring it up in my head.

I whittled faster. The more branches I stripped, the closer I came to buying a train ticket. My mind tumbled with numbers, and I forgot to pay attention to the knife. It slipped, slicing the side of my finger open. A deep gash.

Uncle Klaus shook his head, pressed a rag against my finger, rummaged around until he found a jar. He dabbed a sticky resin into the cut.

I sniffed. "What's that?"

"Spruce sap and cattail juice," he said. "Stops the bleeding, keeps out infection."

It numbed the pain, too.

Uncle Klaus finished dressing my finger and cleaned up the blood. Rubbing his beard with the back of his hand, he studied me.

"Why don't you finish that sweater and let me strip bark awhile, gal," he said.

I reached for my knife. "I can do this."

"Stubborn," he muttered under his breath. But he didn't take the knife away.

Summer returned that day. The temperature rose into the high seventies, and we moved ourselves out onto the porch. Sweat trickled down the inside of my flannel shirt as I whittled. I didn't mind. I could always take a bath when we finished. So we kept going, peeling moose maple.

Finally, after supper I put the pocketknife down. "I'd better finish up this sweater for the Red Cross meeting tomorrow."

"Coming down home stretch with it, ain't you, gal."

I nodded. "None too soon, either."

Finishing the last few inches of stocking knit, I set about ribbing and binding off the front collar. When I slid the last stitch off the needle and knotted it, I studied the four separate pieces, front, back, and two sleeves.

"What's that face for?" Uncle Klaus asked.

"How do I get them together."

He laughed. "It ain't so hard as it looks, gal. Watch." Uncle Klaus showed me how to weave the pieces together with a blunt wooden sewing needle and a piece of blue yarn, catching a stitch from the front collar, then a stitch from the back.

"It's like hemming!" I said, as the flat seams began to form.

Sewing the front to the back at the shoulders first, I then wove the caps of the sleeves on and finally joined the side seams.

I closed my eyes for a moment, then smoothed the sweater out. "It's done."

My palms sweat onto the blue wool of the sweater as I ran my hands over it.

"You did it, gal."

"We did it, Uncle Klaus. Do you think it's good enough?"

He nodded. "Plenty good enough."

I smoothed it once more. "It is good, isn't it?"

"I'd wear it."

I sighed. Uncle Klaus would wear anything.

"Come on over and give me a hand here, gal."

198

I washed the sweat and wool from my palms and helped Uncle Klaus. He'd stopped working with the maple, too, turning his attention to packing the dried fruit for Ottiwell Wood's grandson. "How's Ottiwell doing?" I asked.

"He's fretting about Walt's Christmas box instead of concentrating on getting better," Uncle Klaus said. "The dang boxes don't have to be off till mid-November. I told Ott he's got time. But he wants the box sent now. I'll drop it at the Red Cross tomorrow when I leave you off for the meeting."

"I could take care of it for you," I said.

"Ott won't be happy less I do it, gal."

I trusted Ottiwell Wood with my letters. The least he could do was trust me with his box.


Uncle Klaus went to bed while I soaked in the tub. The house had settled down for the night, when, in my nightgown, I crept back to the kitchen, where the sweater waited amid the mess of moosewood bark. I pinned a note inside the collar. "For American Soldiers in Russia." I wanted my sweater to go to my father. I wanted him to know I'd made it for him.

Before heading to bed, I tiptoed to the door off the kitchen and peered around the corner into Uncle Klaus's sleeping porch. A steady draft blew through the room, startling my feet with cold. Goose bumps rose up and down my back under my nightgown. Uncle Klaus slept curled tight on the sagging cot.

I crept back to my room, took the quilt off my own bed, and brought it in to cover him.

"Take care of the things you can do something about," Uncle Klaus had once said.

It was good advice.

## chapter twenty-three

*Wednesday, October 30, 1918*

Today, the "something" in my dresser was my quilt, folded neatly, returned to me.

Except for when he was down in Brattleboro with Ottiwell, Uncle Klaus stayed pretty close to home. I couldn't help notice how he studied my fingers as they twitched out the stitches of the sweater or cramped around the pocketknife. He silently watched as I traced the crack lines in his mug. I would find him crossing his arms over his dusty brown vest and chewing on the ends of his mustache, staring at nothing. He was preparing himself for my leaving.

After a morning of stripping bark, I put on a charity dress and placed the finished sweater in the bag that had once held balls of wool.

Uncle Klaus dropped me off at the Red Cross. "I'll take this load of moosewood bark to the druggist first," he said. "Then I'll be back with the box from Ott."

Mrs. Page clapped her hands with delight when she saw the finished sweater. Her clap made a soft padded sound in the busy room. "Where did you learn to sew seams like this, Hannah?"

"Klaus Gerhard," I said.

Mrs. Page turned the sweater from front to back, inside and out, admiring my work. "This is just wonderful."

It really was wonderful. Just a week ago I'd brought home a bag of yarn. Now I'd made a sweater. I rubbed the side of my nose.

All the women, even the ones at the sewing machines, came over to admire my handiwork. I wished Uncle Klaus could hear them fuss.

Placing the sweater into the "completed" bin, I glanced at the others deposited there, comparing mine. Mine wasn't as good. Especially not the first sleeve. But it would hold together, it would keep someone warm, it would not shame anyone to wear it. I had pinned the words *For American Soldiers in Russia* to the sweater last night. This morning I'd removed the note. The sweater could keep anyone warm. Anyone. Even a German.

"Ladies," Mrs. Page said. "Today, some of you will stay here with me to inspect and tag Christmas boxes, while the rest of you go out into the neighborhoods. We musn't neglect the need for cleaning up after the influenza. Families all over town need our assistance."

I heard the familiar sound of Uncle Klaus's limp coming up the steps and onto the wooden porch of the Red Cross. He poked his head inside the door.

The ladies looked him up and down. I realized what it meant to him to come into a place like this, not knowing what treatment he would receive.

"Klaus?" Mrs. Page asked, catching sight of him. "Klaus Gerhard?"

Uncle Klaus looked down at the box in his arms.

Mrs. Page motioned him closer.

"We were just talking about you. Are you sending off a Christmas box?"

"Favor for—I'm—it's not for me—Ottiwell's grandson, Walt. For him. From Ottiwell." Uncle Klaus tangled his words.

"No alcohol in there, eh, Klaus?" Mrs. Page asked. "Nothing flammable? No note? No written material?"

"Yes. No. Well, there's a book," Uncle Klaus said.

Ottiwell had wrapped a small book in a khaki-colored hanky. "You'll have to remove that," Mrs. Page said.

"Ott's just sending the boy something to cheer him," Uncle Klaus said softly. "Walt likes to read."

"No books allowed," Mrs. Page said. She bent closer to him and whispered. "Don't worry, Klaus, the American Library Association is seeing to the boys' reading needs over there in France. Young Walt won't want for a thing."

Uncle Klaus kept his eyes down. He shuffled his feet.

"Keep in mind how long it is until Christmas, Klaus. Will everything in here keep?"

He nodded.

The regulation-size box couldn't have held one more package, even with the book removed.

"I see Ottiwell has wrapped everything in handkerchiefs. Very good." Mrs. Page continued inspecting the package. She had a list in front of her of what was allowed, what wasn't.

Occasionally she looked up and smiled at Uncle Klaus, but he didn't notice. He was too busy watching his feet. I'd never seen him act that way. Shy. Uncle Klaus was shy with Mrs. Page.

"It all looks in order, Klaus," she said. "It's very thoughtful of you to take care of this for Ottiwell. How's he doing?"

202

"He's coming along," Uncle Klaus said. He kept shifting from one foot to the other.

"We'll just seal this up then, Klaus. It has to go a great distance." Mrs. Page spoke slowly, patiently, as if talking to a small child.

When the box was wrapped, the Christmas label attached, and the name Walter Wood printed in dark ink above the address in France, Uncle Klaus fastened the stamps, and Mrs. Page affixed the Red Cross approval label.

"There we go. Tell Ottiwell we'll see this gets to his grandson," Mrs. Page said. She smiled at Uncle Klaus. "And you take good care of yourself, Sonny."

I bit my lip.

Sonny?

I had to pass Uncle Klaus as my group, led by Mrs. Sullivan, headed out the door for cleanup duty. I grinned at him. I couldn't help it. "So, Sonny, how much did we get for the moose maple?" He fixed me with his gray eyes, and stroked the fringes of his mustache. "Not even a dollar," Uncle Klaus said.

My smile disappeared. All that work, all those hours, and we hadn't even made one dollar. Well, I'd just have to peel more. I'd just have to peel ten times more. A hundred times more. Whatever it took to get me back to Boston.

## chapter twenty-four

*Thursday, October 31, 1918*

HALLOWEEN.

Last Halloween I dressed Libbie and Eve like little soldiers. They carried canteens and wore boots. I rubbed ash on their faces to give them beards. We hadn't moved in with Vashti and Tanta Rose yet. Papa was still home.

Papa laughed and laughed when we came into the kitchen in our costumes He pulled himself up straight and saluted Libbie and Eve just like in the real army.

I had dressed up, too. Like a French painter, with an easel and a long paint-stained shirt.

So much had changed since last year.

I looked over the newspaper as we finished breakfast. "Schools here open again on Monday." I thought about schools opening in Boston. Who would get Libbie to class? Who would braid Eve's hair and tie her ribbons? How far behind would I fall in my studies?

"You thinking about going to classes in Brattleboro?" Uncle Klaus asked.

"If I went to school I wouldn't have time to strip moose bark."

"You can't keep stripping moose bark at this rate for too long, gal. You're wearing yourself out. Getting careless. Look at your pile from yesterday. Druggist won't take it unless the inner and the outer bark are separate."

I sighed.

"You need to break the work up a little. Do some other things. You still have your book?" Uncle Klaus asked.

I put down my knife, stepped over the mess in the sitting room. I brought him the book Miss Carpenter gave me when I couldn't speak.

There were pictures scattered around the words. My hands, my fingers remembered drawing them.

Uncle Klaus waved away the little notebook. "That ain't the one I meant. Where's your artist's sketchbook? Didn't you ever do nothing with that?"

I balanced my whittling knife so I could rub the side of my nose. The artist's sketchbook.

"I took a vow, Uncle Klaus. Not to draw until I was back with my family again. I never made a mark in it."

"You took a vow?"

I nodded. "Like you did with the Boss, to keep her alive. I vowed not to draw till I was back in Boston, till I was with my family again."

"Oh, gal. I don't know that my swearing a vow made any difference with the Boss. Maybe she was meant to live to her nineties and my giving up drawing didn't have one thing to do with it."

"But how will you ever know?"

He smiled. "I won't."

"I can't break this vow, Uncle Klaus. I can't take a chance.

Not hearing from any of them, it's so easy to think the worst. I can't break my vow now, it's all the hope I have. You understand?"

He nodded. "Me, I've learned a thing or two about vows. The Boss is gone her way. And you, you'll go yours. It don't make no difference if I take a vow or not."

I ran my knife down the striped bark.

"I'm drawing again, gal." He didn't just smile. He beamed. "Started making sketches in my journal."

"May I see?"

Uncle Klaus dug his book out from under the mess of moosewood and handed it over. The back half of the book exploded with drawings. I turned page after page, admiring them.

The drawings were mostly of me.

Uncle Klaus hummed as he set off for the bathroom. He spent a long time in there. When he finally came out, his hair and beard dripped with water.

"What do you think?" Uncle Klaus asked.

"I think it's odd your taking a bath this time of day."

His hair smelled fresh, like leaves and flowers.

I reached out to touch it, held a long strand of it against my cheek. Like Eve with her silky. I took a deep breath. "It smells nice."

"Strained nettles," he said, trying to get a comb through his tangles.

Looking down at my hand, I remembered the sting from the nettle plant. I regarded his scalp with alarm.

"No sting in strained nettles," he said. He struggled with the comb, yanking it through his long hair.

"Sit," I ordered.

I took the comb from him, sat him down in the kitchen chair in front of the stove and stood behind him. Gently, slowly, I worked out his snarls. When the comb finally slid through Uncle Klaus's long mane, I began to count the strokes.

One, two, three—

"I'm getting it cut today." He surprised me. "Get my hair cut once't a year. Cut it and sell it. Usually hold off till spring, but I'm ready now."

I stared at Uncle Klaus, trying to imagine him without his hair.

He laughed. "If you could see your face, gal. Ain't never met a man cut his hair before?"

"Not so he could sell it," I said.

"Some poor old girl will ride to church beaming this Christmas under a new wig made from my old locks."

I wondered if it could be Miss Lydia Grant.


We didn't stop at the barbershop where the little girl spat on Uncle Klaus. We passed right by it and climbed down some steps to a small shop tacked onto the side of a brick building.

Only one barber chair, carved from wood with a padded footrest, graced the small shop. Shelf after shelf of numbered shaving mugs framed the mirror. The barber sold postal cards, too. A whole wall of different scenes, some of covered bridges, some of farmhouses in the snow, some just plain fun. If I'd had any spending money I'd have bought a funny one and sent it to Libbie and Eve.

The barber, a Negro, had a kind smile. "Afternoon, Mr. Gerhard," he said in a respectful voice.

"Afternoon, Mr. Green," Uncle Klaus answered.

"What can I do for you today?" Mr. Green asked.

"I'm here for my haircut," Uncle Klaus said.

"It's a little early, isn't it, Mr. Gerhard?" Mr. Green gathered towels from the arm of his barber chair. "You telling me we're not having winter this year?"

Uncle Klaus frowned. "Oh, winter's coming, Mr. Green. I calculate it'll be here within the week."

"I'll let Suzannah know," Mr. Green said. "If you say cold's coming, she'll start cooking her soups for the restaurant. But if that's the truth of it, how come you're getting shorn now?"

Uncle Klaus folded his arms across the front of his wool vest. "Getting in my way, I guess."

I had the feeling I'd just seen Uncle Klaus lie for the first time. He didn't look comfortable doing it.

Mr. Green looked down, embarrassed. "None of my business, Mr. Gerhard. None of my business at all."

Why was Uncle Klaus cutting his hair?

"Uncle Klaus—" I started.

He looked over at me, stern, his eyebrows creased low over his gray eyes. My voice caught in my throat.

Uncle Klaus leaned back against the marble slab sink on the opposite wall from the chair. The sink was spotless. The whole tiny barbershop gleamed. Even Vashti would have approved.

"How much you figure you can give me for it, Mr. Green?" Uncle Klaus asked.

Mr. Green combed his dark fingers through the silky white hair. He measured it. Gathered it in his fist. The pure white hair coming out of that black fist was like a gush of clear water from the rich dark earth.

"I figure four dollars, Mr. Gerhard," Mr. Green said. "It's not as long as usual. Four sound fair?"

Four dollars. Why did my hair have to be so short? So wild and short and worthless.

Uncle Klaus shook hands with the barber, and Mr. Green swung the chair around for Uncle Klaus to sit in. The big chair nearly swallowed up his thin old bones in their baggy trousers.

In less than an hour he looked like a different man. No hair. No beard. Just the bushy mustache on his upper lip.

Uncle Klaus had given me his cap a long time ago to wear on my head. Right there in the barbershop, I gave it back to him.

# chapter twenty-five

## *Friday, November 1, 1918*

"Looks like the nice weather may end soon." Uncle Klaus slid his cap off and scratched his bald head with a pencil before slipping the cap back on. "Can't get over how long the color stayed this year."

"Someone's looking out for you, Uncle Klaus," I said. "Keeping it warm till your hair grows back."

Uncle Klaus snorted. "More likely the world's just so het-ted up with this war it can't cool down." He carried his empty mug to the sink. "I'll be up on the mountain this morning. See if I can bring down some spruce sap. I heard the druggist pays good money for spruce sap."

Haircuts? Spruce sap?

Tanta Rose had sold things from the old country to take care of me and my sisters. Was I forcing Uncle Klaus to sell things, too?

Slipping from my pocket the eighty cents I'd earned so far whittling moose bark, I held the coins out to him.

Uncle Klaus looked squarely into my face. "What's this for?"

"Room and board," I said. I couldn't look right at him. "I never meant to be a burden on you."

Uncle Klaus said nothing for a moment.

My hand trembled. If he took my money, that would begin to make things right with him. But what about my sisters? Would I ever get back to my sisters?

"Keep your pennies, gal," he said.

Still I held my hand out to him.

He wrapped my fingers around the coins, closing my fist inside his. "Keep it," he said.


While Uncle Klaus gathered spruce sap on top of Black Mountain, I took a break from whittling and made my first solo trip into Brattleboro to see Miss Carpenter. It would still be a while before I'd peeled enough bark to earn my fare back to Boston, but I wanted to see her, to thank her, to tell her good-bye.

At last, as I trudged past Wells Fountain, the steeple of the church connected to the emergency hospital came into sight. I headed straight to the parish house and up the stairs. Dr. Grace had given me permission to visit Miss Carpenter as long as I wore a mask.

"Hannah," Miss Carpenter said, perking up as she caught sight of me coming around the screen. "I'm so glad you came.

I handed her an apple from Uncle Klaus's root cellar and placed a flask of vinegar water on the table beside her.

Miss Carpenter smiled and held the apple in her two pale hands. "Does Uncle Klaus know you've been raiding his cellar?"

I nodded.

Miss Carpenter began coughing. I stepped back behind the

screen until she'd finished. Afterward, her voice sounded weak. She kept struggling to clear her throat. It seemed like a lifetime ago I was sick like that.

"Remember when you couldn't talk?" she asked.

I nodded.

"And I gave you the notebook?"

"I brought it today." I pulled the notebook from my trouser pocket.

"May I see?"

I gave her the notebook turned to the page with her face, the drawing Uncle Klaus said had the chin right but not the eyes.

"Will you remember me?" she asked, her gaze fixed on the picture.

I gripped the frayed hem of my sweater.

"How could I forget you?" I said.

She put her hand over her heart. She was looking now at my drawing of the girl with violet eyes. "I can't explain it really. I could look at this one forever."

A chill climbed my spine.

Miss Carpenter started to cough again, and again I waited behind the screen. When I came back, she'd fallen into a light sleep.

Gently, I set the notebook on the little table beside her. "You keep this," I whispered.

Through the mask, I kissed Miss Carpenter on her burning forehead. Accidentally, I bumped the flask of vinegar with my elbow as I backed away. It fell with a thud and she woke. "Hannah? You're still here?"

"Yes," I said. "But for only a little longer. Let me get you some water and vinegar before I go."

212

Miss Carpenter groaned. "It's so vile."

"It's not bad once you get used to it."

""I'll never get used to it, Hannah," Miss Carpenter said, weakly taking a sip. She shuddered. "Never."

After supper, Uncle Klaus finally let me come with him to visit Ottiwell Wood.

We put on gauze masks before we entered his bedroom. It was possible I'd made those masks myself at the Red Cross.

"It's about time you came," Ottiwell whispered.

"Good to see you, too, Ott. You been drinking your vinegar?" asked Uncle Klaus.

"Pugh." Ottiwell's voice sounded like it came from far away. "I drink it. But I don't like it."

"No one said you had to."

Ottiwell gasped, then coughed. Uncle Klaus held him as Ott spit out some blood.

"Can't see as it's done me any good," he whispered, breathless.

Uncle Klaus was silent. He'd nursed Ottiwell Wood every day since he'd shown up on our doorstep coughing, asking for vinegar. He'd seen him rally and he'd seen him fail.

Uncle Klaus eyed the empty woodbox. "Don't you stop drinking that vinegar. You hear me, Ott?"

"There's nothing wrong with my ears," Ottiwell whispered.

A week ago, he was a great, hulking giant. Full of noisy good health, good humor. In the bed now lay a bony husk of a man. "Got a letter from Walt," Ottiwell whispered.

I was almost as happy that Ottiwell had heard from his grandson as I would have been if I'd heard from Chambers Street.

"I don't have the breath to read it. You do it, Hannah."

I took the letter from the hand with the missing fingers.

*Dear Papa Ott,*

*I'm mending faster than the doctors thought. I tell them it's because of the nurses. They've got fine-looking nurses here.*

*Could be some time before I return. Even when we stop fighting, getting all the boys back home will take a while. Just unraveling all the barbed wire the Germans put up could take years.*

I wondered if there was barbed wire in Russia, too.

*I'm patched up enough, I'll be returning to the front in another week. I'm nervous about going back. I don't remember much good about living in those trenches. The damp rotted my feet. And the gas. There's nothing good to say about mustard gas.*

All those fruit pits, did they really protect the soldiers from mustard poison?

*There's one nice thing I remember. The candles. All those candles inside the trenches, lighting the French night. Now that's a pretty sight. A downright comforting sight.*

Folding the letter back up, I placed it on the table beside Ottiwell.

Uncle Klaus tramped down to the cellar and came up again with an armload of firewood. "Lowell Butts says to tell you they miss you down at the post office."

I followed Uncle Klaus's lead and brought up several armloads of wood myself

Checking Ottiwell's kitchen, we found food on the shelves, food Uncle Klaus brought on his last visit.

"Ott, you ain't eating." Uncle Klaus glared at his patient. "Here's some custard Hannah made for you just this afternoon. It's still warm."

"You made me custard, Hannah?" Ottiwell whispered.

I nodded.

"Not burnt is it?"

"No, it ain't burnt," Uncle Klaus said.

"I thought maybe it was something you didn't want," Ottiwell whispered to Uncle Klaus.

"You old fool," Uncle Klaus said. "The girl baked this custard just for you. If you ain't nice I'll take it home."

Ottiwell's hand moved shakily to the dish held before him by Uncle Klaus. He lifted the towel off the custard, grinned. "It's perfect, Hannah."

"I'll put some in a dish for you," I said.

"Not now. Not too hungry."

I nodded.

"War's over soon, Hannah," Ottiwell whispered. "Before long we'll have those old Germans walking the plank."

Uncle Klaus crossed his arms over his chest and turned to look out the window. The baldness of his head still startled me.

Ottiwell looked up at me, his eyes glazed with fever. "Hannah, you haven't heard from home." It was a statement, not a question.

I shook my head.

Ottiwell Wood sighed. "Who knows if Walt'll ever get back."

Uncle Klaus continued staring out the window.

"It costs dear. War. It sure costs," Ottiwell said. "Hannah?"

I came closer to Ottiwell's bed.

"You haven't heard from Boston."

Why did he keep saying that?

"I suppose I have to die of something. If it isn't grippe, it'd be something else."

"You know what they say about the pessimist," Uncle Klaus said, talking to the window. "Stands under the tree of life and grumbles when the fruit drops on his head."

Ottiwell grabbed my hand. "Hannah. I never sent those letters of yours."

I stared at him.

"It's a terrible thing I did. Terrible wrong."

My mouth went dry.

"I'm probably going to hell on account of it."

Ottiwell's words blurred in my head. My heart hammered. "You didn't send my letters!"

Ottiwell wept quietly. "I did it for Klaus. I did it for you, Klaus." He turned his head away from me. "He doesn't even limp anymore."

Uncle Klaus stood rigid at the window.

"Hannah, you were better off here," Ottiwell cried.

"Old fool," Uncle Klaus said under his breath. He turned to me. All this time I'd been waiting to hear from my family, and they hadn't known where I was. If Ottiwell Wood wasn't sick to death I swear I would have killed him right then and there.

"Go home, Hannah," Uncle Klaus said.

"No." Ottiwell reached for my arm. "I have something for you."

"I don't want anything from you."

"In the drawer. Klaus, open the dresser drawer."

Uncle Klaus did as he was told.

"Bring me the blue stocking. The one with the knot in it."

Uncle Klaus brought over a stocking, knotted at the top.

"Take it, Hannah," Ottiwell Wood whispered. "It's for the train. It's all I've got. I know it's not enough to make up for what I did. But—"

My body trembled with fury. I gripped the stocking in my fist for only a moment, then threw it down on the floor.

Ottiwell Wood wept, without sound. Too weak even to make a sound.

Uncle Klaus came up beside me. "Go home, gal. Go on. Take Big Train. She knows the way. I'd best stay here tonight. You think you can drive the wagon?"

I felt such rage I could hardly look at the dying man. All these weeks he had stood between me and my sisters. Every day I had run to him hoping for news. Every day the silence had made my sisters' fate seem more uncertain. Every day I had cursed Vashti, feared for Harry. And all along it had been Ottiwell Wood.

Sitting in Uncle Klaus's wagon, I couldn't stop trembling. I'd never driven Big Train before. I'd never driven any horse and wagon. Flicking the reins across the horse's broad back the way Uncle Klaus did, I clicked my tongue. Big Train stretched her huge neck forward, and we started to move. Before long we were trotting through the dark along the common, toward the Putney road, the road out of town. Big Train knew the way.

But as we turned the corner of Park Place, an automobile

appeared out of nowhere. I gripped Big Train's reins, pulled hard. The horse reared, balanced for a moment, listed to one side, and then fell. The wagon teetered and flipped; the shaft snapped. I found myself sprawled on the cold hard earth of the town green. The automobile spun around twice and came to a halt on the grass only a few yards away.

The driver waved his fist. "You fool! Where's your lantern!" Angrily, he checked every inch of his automobile for damage.

My heart wouldn't stop pounding.

"How's a body supposed to see you out here in the black of night. Blasted child driving a wagon. You horse-and-buggy people! If this dang flu doesn't kill you, driving at night without a light on your rig surely will."

The man, satisfied his automobile showed no sign of damage, got back in, and drove away, still ranting.

My hands remained locked into fists, as if I still held the reins. I walked over to Big Train, already back on her feet. "You all right, girl?" I asked, running my hand over her side, down her legs. My heart thudded in my chest. "You all right?"

The wagon lay smashed on the green, a total loss, but the reins still dangled from the horse's bridle. I took hold of the leather grip with one hand and rested my other on the horse's big neck. "Let's go home," I whispered.

And slowly Big Train led the way.

## chapter twenty-six

*Monday, November 4, 1918*

I STARED OUT THE KITCHEN WINDOW as snow fell. The sky was flat and gray. I could smell the cold in Wilbur's and Orville's fur. Big white flakes drifted slowly down, then smaller flakes, coming faster, harder. I pulled on my coat, my hat, and ran out into it.

I'd tended the chickens and Big Train, milked and fed the goats, strained the milk, brought in the firewood, loaded the stove. I'd put things as straight as they could be in Uncle Klaus's kitchen, in Uncle Klaus's house.

I'd even scrubbed his clothes on the washboard and hung them to dry over the kitchen chairs.

With the chores out of the way, I danced through the orchard in the swirling flakes. I wanted to shout, to sing. Snow caught in my eyelashes. Stung my cheeks. I opened my mouth and stuck out my tongue. And all the while I spun around in the falling snow. This was the third day I'd been alone here. At first I'd planned to set off for Boston right away. I was strong enough. But I couldn't leave the animals without someone to care for them. I couldn't leave Uncle Klaus without explaining about the wagon; I couldn't go without saying good-bye.

I had not seen angels here, soaring up the Connecticut River the way I had seen them over Chambers Street. But I had felt

219

them. I had felt the presence of the girl with violet eyes. In the silence of Uncle Klaus's house she was very close.

I lay down in the dusting of snow and spread my arms and legs to make a powdery angel of my own—a bell-shaped skirt, a curve of wings.

The stubbly ground showed through.

All around me angels, even in the brown earth.

My shoulders were wet, my hair glistened with snow. My boots dripped, making small puddles in front of the woodstove. I caught sight of my reflection in the glazed brown surface of Uncle Klaus's teapot. It distorted my face, made my big nose bigger, but it also gave a wonderful shine to my eyes.

Pouring tea into Uncle Klaus's mended cup, I cocked my head. For a moment I felt as if someone had come into the room.

I had been thinking about Ottiwell Wood. The white fury had cooled. Now, in my heart I felt only relief. I hadn't heard from Vashti, from Harry, from my sisters in all this time because my letters had never reached them. Not because they didn't care, not because they were dead.

And I had had this time with Uncle Klaus. This precious time with Uncle Klaus.

Remembering Walt's letter, I turned over in my mind what he said about the one nice thing in the trenches of France. The candles. I shut my eyes, imagining France lit up by hundreds of candles, thousands of candles, millions of candles—strings of light shining up from the trenches as if the earth itself had cracked along a thousand splintery veins, and through those veins flowed endless streams of light.

Uncle Klaus returned on foot after supper. From a distance, I barely recognized him without his hair and his beard. But no one else had that limp.

Waiting at the door, I let the eager dogs out to greet him. They raced to his side and brought him on home.

"You hungry?" I asked, putting a mug of hot apple cider vinegar and water down in front of each of us.

He shook his head. "Ate at Ott's before I left."

"How is he?"

Uncle Klaus wrapped his delicate hands around the mug. "A might better."

I took a deep breath. "I wrecked the wagon, Uncle Klaus."

"I thought that might be my rig on the common. You and Big Train all right?"

"We're all right. So's the man in the automobile."

"Yell at you for driving without a lantern, did he?"

I nodded.

"That was my fault, gal. I should have never sent you off like that from Ott's. I wasn't thinking."

"Is Ottiwell going to die, Uncle Klaus?"

"Not if I can help it, gal."

My chest felt tight.

"You still angry with him?"

I shrugged.

"Ain't none of us angels. We each got a little of the angel in us. And a little of the other, too."

"Uncle Klaus, did you know all along? About the letters?"

He looked at me. Beneath his eyes, small pouches swelled with exhaustion. "No, I didn't, gal. But I can't say I'm entirely sorry he did it. Oh, I'm sorry for the sorrow it caused you, and for the trouble it caused your people, but I wouldn't trade nothing for these last few weeks."

I rubbed the side of my nose, trying to hide the tremble in

my chin. I wouldn't have traded, either. "I'm leaving tomorrow, Uncle Klaus. On foot. I'll follow the railroad track to Boston."

"I half feared you might be gone already."

"I wouldn't have left the animals uncared for."

He nodded. "I thank you for that, gal."

"I belong in the city, Uncle Klaus. My family, they need me," I said.

"It's good being needed," Uncle Klaus answered. "No doubt about that."

"It's more than that, though. What am I really, without my family?"

Uncle Klaus chewed on the fringes of his mustache. "Seems to me you're quite a lot, gal. Quite a lot indeed."

"I'll write to you."

"That'd be good."

"Not for a while though. I'll have my hands full, taking care of my sisters until my parents get back."

"And if your parents don't get back?"

"I'll find a way."

"You and those sisters of yours, you'll always have a home here."

I nodded.

Klaus Gerhard's long johns and overalls and shirts hung stiff and dry on the backs of the kitchen chairs. "Once I told you there was a lot you didn't know. You remember, gal?"

"I remember."

"Seems like there's not a one of us ain't got something to learn. I'll get you back to Boston, gal. I'll take you there myself."

"How can you do that with the wagon broken? Besides, who'd take care of the goats and the dogs? Who'd keep a fire in the stove? Who'd look after Ott?"

"Those are my problems, ain't they? You've got problems of

your own waiting. I'm not sending you back to Boston without knowing what will happen to you once you get there."

I didn't know what to say.

"Get some rest, gal. It's a long way to the coast on a horse's back."

"Good night, Uncle Klaus." It grieved me to think I would never say those words to him again.

"Good night, gal." It grieved me even more to know I would never hear him say those words to me.

I couldn't let Uncle Klaus take me to Boston. He was needed too much here. In the thick and silent dark, I slipped, fully dressed, from bed.

"Hannah!"

The voice startled me. "Eve?"

"Hannah! "

The voice echoed in my ear.

I moved silently to the window. It sounded as if the voice came from somewhere outside.

No! My sister couldn't be calling. In my excitement to get home to them, I had imagined it.

I stared out into the night. Wantastiquet Mountain sprawled under a spray of stars.

"Hannah! Hannah!"

I heard the voice again.

Trembling, I stole from the bedroom and made my way up the three steps, across the sitting room past the sofa and chairs covered in old blankets.

The dogs stood in the kitchen, wagging their tails in circles.

I reached down to them, my heart pounding. No one was there.

Walking across the kitchen, toward the porch where Uncle

Klaus slept, something caught my eye up in the orchard. In the distance, I saw a blue light.

I walked past the sleeping Uncle Klaus, out the porch door, down the steep steps, and across the orchard.

I knew who she was instantly. Not Eve. Not Libbie. Brightly, before me, stood the girl who saved me from stepping in front of a streetcar, the girl who took care of me on the train from Boston, the girl with violet eyes.

A blue light surrounded her shoulders and her head.

I ran toward her.

She stood, so simple, in her bare feet, in her pale gown. Starlight reflected off her, dancing in her hair. The dark, dark hair reflected the blueness of starlight.

She must have been cold, her feet numb. I took her hand and pulled her toward the house. I wanted to give her something warm to drink, something warm to wear.

As we lit on the first step, I looked up.

Uncle Klaus stared down at us from the doorway of the sleeping porch. He was fully dressed. His arms crossed over his chest. His new beard made a soft fuzz over his chin and cheeks.

I led the girl up the steps two at a time toward Uncle Klaus. Uncle Klaus, eyes wide, stepped back to let us in.

Upon reaching him, the girl stopped and turned her full attention his way. Her eyes. Her eyes shone like sun dancing in the water of the Charles.

Uncle Klaus's cheeks were wet. His beard was wet.

The girl touched his face.

I ran back to my room, grabbed my bags.

From under my pillow I pulled out the sketchbook. It still held the warmth from the bed. Not one mark had I made in it. Not one.

224

I opened the top drawer of the dresser.

Tomorrow, there would be something in the drawer for Uncle Klaus. Tenderly, I placed the sketchbook in the drawer, then the pencil on top of it.

I grabbed my boots and the suitcases and raced back to the sleeping porch.

Uncle Klaus sat on his cot.

I put the suitcases down, set the boots before the girl.

Silently, she slipped her bare feet inside them. She looked odd in them, as if she'd never worn anything on her feet before. She walked the way you do with a stone in your shoe. But I felt better seeing something on her feet.

Uncle Klaus fingered the straw suitcase. "Looks like you're leaving."

I nodded.

He led the way into the kitchen.

Orville and Wilbur followed behind the girl.

From the sugar tin, Uncle Klaus removed four dollar bills. He handed the money to me.

"I can't take this," I said. "This money was for your hair."

"I cut that hair for you, gal."

The girl rubbed her hand over Uncle Klaus's scalp. He groaned like Orville and Wilbur when they get scratched behind their ears. He stood there a few moments, a sweet smile on his face. Reaching into his pocket, Uncle Klaus brought out another fistful of money. "And this is from Ott. He's almighty sorry for what he did to you, gal."

The girl turned her violet eyes on me.

It was hard to breathe. The light in the room left no space for air.

Ottiwell had only been acting out of kindness. "Tell Ott I understand. Tell him it's all right."

Uncle Klaus nodded. "That'll mean the world to him, gal. I'll fetch him up here tomorrow to keep an eye on him full-time. I'll tell him then."

My knees felt rubbery. Slowly, I came forward and leaned my head into Uncle Klaus's chest, nestling my curls into his vest. His right hand came up and stroked back my hair. I shut my eyes. I could smell goat and woods. I could smell a lifetime of vinegar in his bones.

"You know, gal, denying the thing that gives you joy, your God-given gift, that's a wasteful thing. Don't bargain your life away with vows."

I could hear his heart beating. His wool vest rubbed against my nose. "Uncle Klaus—"

He nodded. His head moved up and down above mine.

"Will you be all right?" I asked.

"I will. For better or worse, gal, we each got something waiting on ahead."

I took a step back. His eyes shone with a light that was part sorrow and part something else.

"I don't want to leave you," I whispered.

He folded me into his arms. Held me tight. I smelled Big Train on his clothes; I smelled nettles in his new hair.

"Get on with you, gal," he said. "You'll be fine. No matter what's waiting, you'll be fine. And so will I."

"Come with me," I said.

"I don't belong in that city of yours any more than you belong here."

And then, he reached for his cap sitting on the kitchen table, and backing me away, he set the cap on top of my head.

The girl with the violet eyes waited on the slab of rock Uncle Klaus called a front step, playing softly on her harmonica, until I came to her, barefoot, dressed like a boy in trousers and cap, ready to go home.

* * *

I heard the approaching train whistle as I stood in line at the ticket counter, trying to read the schedule.

"One to Boston, please," I said, putting Uncle Klaus's money, Ottiwell Wood's money, my moose maple money under the grill.

A small crowd of people gathered on the station platform.

Within moments, the ground shook beneath my feet as the locomotive pulled in, hissing, squealing, steaming to a stop.

The girl with violet eyes led me to my train.

The night shimmered with angel light; my chest exploded with it.

The girl looked down at the two suitcases, the small straw case and the black traveling bag. She looked at the boots on her feet. My feet had turned white with cold. So white they felt warm. "You keep the boots and the clothes," I said. Or maybe I just thought it.

The girl with violet eyes kissed me on my closed lids. When I opened them again I saw things with such clarity.

The conductor put his metal stool down in front of me. He checked my ticket, helped me aboard.

I looked around for her, but the girl with violet eyes had gone.

"Board!" The conductor yelled up and down the platform.

From the front of the train, the whistle blew once, twice. Uncle Klaus could hear it up on his hill.

I boarded the train. People waved sleepily out their windows.

I walked down the aisle between the rows of seats, settled near the back of the car into the padded cushions. Across from me, a man in a striped suit nodded.

I let out my breath.

I was going home.

Wantastiquet Mountain rises in the dark. Her evergreen boughs comb the twinkling underbelly of the night. A brooding moon sulks unseen in the star-filled sky.

The sweet perfume of wood smoke and brown leaves climbs upward.

A harmony of stars thrills the darkness, when suddenly the chorus is silenced.

The stars go out.

And once again the sky opens, revealing the light of heaven.

Up into the brilliant light, through the vast rupture, figures stream, ascending on silver ladders.

A legion of angels.

In a steady upward flow, angels ascend.

And in that flow of angels, there is one.

She carries a harmonica in her blue sleeve. She holds a straw suitcase and a black traveling bag in her hands. She wears a pair of work boots on her feet.

As she disappears through the radiant opening, a bag and suitcase fall away.

The two objects drop down, at the entrance to heaven seals itself shut.

Down, as the stars are rekindled.

Down, to land gently on the rugged shoulders of Wantastiquet.

part three

chapter twenty-seven

*Tuesday, November 5, 1918*

I STEPPED THROUGH THE BIG DOORS of North Station into the early sunlight. Boston rushed up to meet me. Nothing had changed. The crowded streets teemed with honking automobiles, clanging trolleys, horses and wagons jangling over cobblestones. People streamed up and down the street on their way to businesses, factories, schools. A gust of wind blew a cinder into my eye. I wrapped my arms around myself for the pure joy of being home.

Lifting my face toward the narrow strip of sky, I wondered how I could have survived without the height of these buildings, without the crowds.

I looked for Chip Pilasky, but a boy I didn't know hawked the morning paper in my old spot. Where was Pilasky?

Two months ago I'd sold newspapers here. Two months ago I'd never heard of influenza or Brattleboro, Vermont, or Klaus Gerhard.

"Pa-per! Pa-per! Mornin' pa-per." The boy wore his fair hair parted in the center. Deep shadows under his eyes crept halfway down his cheeks. I remembered forcing myself out of my cot before dawn, determined to beat Pilasky to the pickup. That all seemed like a lifetime ago. The blond boy had only a couple of papers left under his arm.

He approached me. "Paper, mister?"

Did I look like a mister in trousers and flannel shirt and a cap?

The boy looked at me strangely. "In case ya didn't notice, mister, ya forgot yer shoes."

I looked down at my feet. On the train I had tucked them up on the seat to keep them warm, but out here I had no place to put them. The muscles in my feet cramped with cold, the skin was turning a reddish purple. My feet felt miserable. The girl with violet eyes had never seemed miserable.

"Where's Chip Pilasky?" I asked.

The boy gave me an odd look. "Who?"

"Chip Pilasky. The boy who used to sell here."

The newsboy shrugged. "He got the flu or something. It's my corner now."

Maybe Pilasky was selliing somewhere else. Just because he had the flu didn't mean he was dead. I had the flu. I wasn't dead. Not everyone died from the flu.

"You should get some shoes, mister," the boy said, turning to sell a paper to a man heading into the station.

I wouldn't think about my feet, only about my sisters. In a few minutes I'd see them again, see Harry again. I crossed the street carefully, keeping pace with the jangling West End crowds.

Taking in the rows of familiar tenements, the shop fronts, Joe and Nemo's, the fruit peddlers, it was like I never left. The West End had its own smell. Not like Brattleboro. It was a smell of city and salt air. I loved the smell. It was the smell of home.

A gust of wind lifted and pushed me a couple of inches, raising my cap. My curls escaped, and I turned my head upside down and tucked them back under the hat again.

What would my sisters say when they saw me? I imagined their eyes wide with surprise.

What would Vashti say?

The sun inched over Chambers Street. I tried not to wince at every pebble, every rock between the station and home. The wind blew cold.

Wrapping my arms around myself, I thought longingly of Uncle Klaus's heavy jacket. Everyone here had coats to bundle in. What was I thinking, boarding the train in nothing but a flannel shirt and trousers, and yet, I hadn't really noticed the cold then.

I walked past Mr. Izzy's butcher shop, past Mrs. Schwartz's fish shop, past Parson's Bakery. Outside Murry's Pawnshop, I recognized Yossel Yankel, the insurance man, but he rushed away. The shadow of his hat concealed his face. He didn't notice me.

At last, I came to our tenement. Dark windows, five flights, flat roof where Harry took me once to kiss me. Mrs. Rizzoli's window was shut against the cold. No more hanging over her sill and gossiping, until spring. Mrs. McCarthy's windows had new curtains. Leaves danced in the corner of the entranceway at the top of the stoop. The steps needed sweeping. Our building looked drearier than I remembered. The low front window, the window looking down into the bedroom of our basement apartment, was dark.

Maybe they were all in the kitchen.

I glanced up at Harry's apartment. How many mornings had he stood there waving to me? Seeing me safely home from

235

North Station. But he was not there now. No one was there. The curtains were drawn.

Quickly, I backtracked to the corner of Chambers and Brighton. I raced to our alley, tore past the ash cans and garbage at the back of our building.

My heart skipped to see the kerosene lamp flickering on our kitchen table.

That lamp, it had shone on Eve singing her nonsense songs, on Libbie reading among the dirty dishes, pushing her glasses up onto her freckled nose, on Tanta Rose bent over, hemming trousers, on Vashti standing at the stove, preparing her decoctions.

I promised myself I'd try harder with Vashti.

Taking the three steps down to the door, I forgot altogether about breathing.

Through the window to our kitchen, I expected to see them, Libbie, Eve, sitting at the table.

But I saw only Vashti, sitting in the spotless kitchen, her straight back turned to me.

I lifted my hand to knock. For a moment I cradled in my heart the hope that Tanta Rose would come bustling from the sitting room across the kitchen to welcome me. That she would come, wiping her hands on her apron.

But Tanta Rose was not there. Could never be there again. Vashti stood, put out the lamp.

She must be going now to get my sisters, to wake them for school. If they didn't hurry they would be late.

I shivered on the back steps, trying to breathe, waiting for Libbie and Eve to race through the swinging door.

Picking up one foot, I pressed it against the opposite leg, warming it. Then the other foot.

Surely my sisters would be out any minute.

Any minute.

I had shifted my feet three times, four times, and still my sisters did not come.

Stumping back up the alley and around and down Chambers Street, I stopped at the front of our building again, just as Vashti came into the bedroom. She placed something on the dresser, then left.

Libbie and Eve, those slugabeds. Could they still be sleeping? How had they ever managed without me?

I was telling myself this thing, that they were well, that they were safe, lumped up in the big bed, that they were just sleeping late, but inside, panic rose higher in my chest.

Vashti came out through the front door of the tenement, down the steps, striding past without seeing me, her arms looped with baskets.

I waited, watching her move swiftly away.

She had left them alone? What was she thinking? They were too young to be left alone.

Tearing up the outside steps, across the hall and down the stairs to our basement apartment, I burst into the sitting room.

Desperate, I searched for my sisters, any sign of my sisters, a flash of hair, a snippet of braid. I saw nothing, nothing.

I ran to the bedroom.

A half-straightened blanket humped up the big bed. I tore the blanket away. The bed was empty. The room was empty.

My eyes swept over the dresser. No sign of Eve's hairbrush or Libbie's tin of barrettes. Opening drawers, I could not find their nightgowns, their underwear. No blouses, no sweaters, no stockings. I did not see Libbie's eyeglasses.

My hands trembled. A wave of cold washed over me. Horrible cold. Colder by a thousand times than my naked feet. A pain shot through my right eye. The eye began to twitch.

Not only were Tanta Rose's things gone, not only were my things gone, but Libbie's and Eve's things were gone, too.

My sisters.

I ran into the street.

Harry. I wanted Harry.

I couldn't catch my breath, running two, three buildings down to Mrs. Weitz's dressmaking shop. I stepped on something sharp. I didn't care.

Tearing up the steps of the shop, I pushed open the door. Mrs. Weitz was talking to a customer. Her grizzled head flew up to stare at me standing in the doorway. Her eyes moved over me. From the cap on my curly head to my blue bare feet. An expression spread across her face, pulling her mouth crooked, making her tremble. An expression of horror.

"*Go!*" she shrieked. "Go from here!" And she spit on the floor of her shop.

The horror on her face, the terror in her voice, pushed me out, back outside into the cold, back down the steps, away, away from Mrs. Weitz, away from Chambers Street.

I ran, though my feet screamed for me to stop, I ran and my chest burned with fire.

Why did Mrs. Weitz look that way, why did she chase me away, why did I frighten her?

Had I changed that much? Would I have frightened Harry, too?

My heart wouldn't unclench. To lose my sisters, to lose my home, and now to lose Harry, too.

I didn't know where to go, what to do. I ran to our old apartment, the one on Wall Street, the one we lived in before Mama went away, before Papa went away. A young woman with a baby on her hip and one more clinging to her skirt answered the door of our old flat. She looked frightened to see me. I could not catch my breath to speak. While I stood gasping, she shut the door, locked it against me.

I ran blindly through the West End of Boston, over the cobbles and bricks. With every step my feet grew more foreign; it was the same with the pain in my heart, as if this body, this sorrow belonged to someone else. I ran in the long shadow of the tenements. Then turned and ran to the Charles. I was on the other side of my pain. I was simply running. Running over a bridge, more running, then another bridge. Running, until I collapsed at the cemetery in Everett, the Jewish cemetery where dozens, dozens of fresh graves disturbed the ground.

Panting, I dropped down in the frozen grass. The cold pushed up from underneath to harden inside of me. I shivered, surrounded by fresh graves. I didn't know which were my sisters', which Tanta Rose's. Was Harry here, too, with his father? I couldn't remember the prayer for the dead.

If only I could dig open the earth and join them.

My hands stung as I plunged them into the frozen dirt. They cracked, then bled.

Someone was sobbing. Over the sound of my desperate digging I heard someone sobbing. At first I thought the sound was coming from me. My ears stung with cold. I did not trust what I heard. But the sobs could not have come from me. They were too deep. They were the sobs of a man.

I looked up.

Ovadiah.

He stood a few yards from me, tears rolling from his bulging eyes.

"Nathan," he said, staring at me.

Nathan was his brother's name.

Ovadiah sunk to his knees, crawled on his knees over the rough frozen earth to me. He gathered me to his chest, pulled me to him. He embraced me. I felt the rub of his coarse whiskers against my cheek. I smelled his unclean breath.

"Nathan," Ovadiah repeated.

"I'm not Nathan," I said, pulling away. "I'm Hannah. Hannah Gold. Ovadiah, tell me please what has happened to my sisters? Please tell me. Where are my sisters?"

He wasn't listening to me.

He moaned. "Oh, Nathan, I knew you wouldn't leave me."

He hugged me again, sobbing into the chills on my neck.

My cap hid my curls. I wore the trousers from Uncle Klaus. I did not look like a girl. Unless you looked closely. Ovadiah was not looking closely.

There was some resemblance between myself and Nathan. People had said so. Our curls dark and wild. Our eyes large and green. Perhaps this was Nathan's grave.

I pulled away from him, stood up.

Ovadiah stood, too. Slung over his shoulder was a paper bag tied shut with a string. He looked old. Much older than his nineteen years. His flat black cap was too small for his huge head; it smelled dirty. All of him smelled sour, neglected. He was still big and broad, but he had lost something. He was like an empty shell.

"Come, Nathan," Ovadiah said gently. "You must be hungry. You've gone a long time without eating."

240

Ovadiah was crazy.

Something had happened to drive him crazy.

He took a roll from the bag tied with a string, placed it into my hand. The roll was harder than the ground I stood on.

"I'm not Nathan," I said. I turned to leave him, but he caught my arm. He held onto me with a desperate grip.

I had always loathed Ovadiah.

But now, looking into his face, I could not find the contempt I once felt for him. And when I looked to my heart I found only pity.

"Ovadiah," I said gently. "This influenza has taken your sister and brother from you, hasn't it?"

Ovadiah stood there, beaming down at me. Such a look on his face. Just once, I wish Vashti had looked at me with such a look.

"Tell me, Ovadiah. My sisters, Harry Weitz, they're dead, too, aren't they?"

Ovadiah's face clouded over. "So many dead." He shook his huge head back and forth so that his black beard brushed across his coat. Ovadiah wrapped his sadness around his shoulders like a prayer shawl.

But then he looked up, his eyes shining again. "No. Not dead. I have you. Come. We will find your sister, too."

He did not take me straight back to Boston, to the West End, to Chambers Street. He led me, instead, through Chelsea, East Boston, the North End, through the business district, across the Common to downtown, along the Charles. Often I stumbled and fell, unable to feel my feet. He removed his coat and wrapped it around me. He had another beneath the first.

Under cover of night, we stole into the West End, to the old neighborhood. The darkened street rose to meet my frozen feet, but I couldn't feel it. Ovadiah moved cautiously toward his building. He whisked me up the stairs, all the way to the roof.

"Where are we going, Ovadiah?" I asked.

Up on the roof, against the wall of the stairwell, leaned the remnants of a sukkah, with brittle cornstalks and dried flowers entwined in the framework.

Ovadiah welcomed me inside the sukkah, as if he had brought me to a great palace.

Inside he'd moved a bare mattress, a tattered blanket. The roof opened right to heaven. A light rain fell.

Ovadiah lifted the blanket from the mattress. "Rest, Nathan," he said, steering me to bed. "You are tired."

I stared at him in disbelief.

He had been living in the sukkah?

"When did Nathan and Naomi die? When did my sisters die, Ovadiah?" I asked.

He sat on the mattress, looking lost. He turned to me. Stared at me.

His eyes settled on my feet. He let out a low long moan. Standing, he began to pace. Finally he came to the front of the sukkah.

"You want your shoes, Nathan. Rest. I'll find your shoes."

He came back into the sukkah, took me by my shoulders, and laid me down. Tenderly he covered me with the tattered blanket, tenderly he covered my bruised, torn feet.

"Don't go anywhere," Ovadiah said. "I'll find your shoes. I'll find your sister. We'll be together again."

We'll be together again. I shut my eyes.

After all, we had wanted the same thing, only to keep our families together.

I didn't dare move until the heavy sound of his footsteps faded.

Wrapping the blanket across my shoulders, I hobbled out of the sukkah into the icy November drizzle.

At this time of night Uncle Klaus would be sitting by the woodstove, chopping cattail root or burdock root or some other root he'd dug up. He'd be warm, safe. Orville and Wilbur would be sleeping at his feet under the table. The three goats would nuzzle one another in the barn.

With the blanket still wrapped around me, I climbed down the steps, set my naked feet back on Chambers Street. The street stayed busy, even at night. People along the sidewalk, hanging out at street corners.

If only I could get past Mrs. Weitz to Harry, talk with Harry. But what if Harry was dead, too? I was stung by the memory of Mrs. Weitz's face when she saw me. She lost Mr. Weitz to influenza. Did she lose Harry, too? Did seeing me remind her of losing Harry, her precious Harry, her miracle Harry?

I stole back to her building, peered in through the window. Darkness shut me off from the inside of the shop. Normally Mrs. Weitz came down at night to work. I'd see her bent over her sewing machine. A tape measure hung around her neck, a pincushion by her wrist. She wasn't keeping evening hours now.

Once more I returned to my apartment through the front door, smelling the stale cooking odors from the different flats. I felt like a ghost, drifting down the steps to the basement, into the darkened sitting room. I didn't care if Vashti was there. I didn't think she would see me even if she was. I was invisible.

Moving slowly through the rooms, it felt like walking on the bottom of the sea. All traces of my family had vanished, even in the dark I could sense the difference, smell it, feel it. It was as if we had never been.

Tanta Rose's teacup. I found it, still in pieces, still wrapped in a towel, but no longer hidden on the high kitchen shelf. I found it on the table, beside the empty bed. Vashti had moved the broken teacup beside the bed. But Libbie's glasses were gone. Eve's silky was gone.

All I had left of my family was a shattered teacup.

I took it.

I took the pieces. And with a heaviness I carried in my arms like a sleeping child, I left.


Dirt ringed the underside of my fingernails. It stung. Everything else felt numb.

Limping down Chambers Street, wrapped in Ovadiah's tattered blanket, I stared into faces, looking for Harry, for Eve, for Libbie. I searched for the girl with violet eyes. She wasn't there.

I missed the quiet company of Uncle Klaus, the comfort of his table, his hot water and vinegar. I missed my cattail-fluff bed, the view over the fields, the humped mountain called Wantastiquet.

I was too tired, too used up, too cold to care what came next.

Exhausted, I headed up the many steps to the pitiful shelter of Ovadiah's sukkah.

I found Ovadiah sitting on the bare mattress.

His hands covered his face and his body shook silently. For a moment I remembered Ottiwell Wood on the step with Uncle Klaus after Walt's first letter from the hospital in France.

"Ovadiah?"

He did not hear me.

I touched his filthy sleeve. Gently shook his shoulder. "Ovadiah?"

His hands came away from his eyes.

He blinked, staring at me, then he rose. His expression shifted like the sun coming out from behind a cloud. He enveloped me in a great hug. I thought I would suffocate in the huge arms, in the stinking coat.

"I told you not to go," he scolded, bending down and picking up a pair of boy's boots.

I could not answer. In gratitude I reached my hand out, took hold of the boots. But I couldn't feel my feet to put the boots on. Carefully, gently, one at a time, Ovadiah put the boots on my feet for me.

# chapter twenty-eight

## *Thursday, November 7, 1918*

I PEERED OVER THE EDGE of the roof. Mr. Izzy's wife, Bubbe Sadie, sagging breasts, soiled apron, sat in her coat on a folding chair, giving orders, taking up the whole sidewalk.

I wanted to rush down to her, to hug her simply for being there. I wanted to ask her about my sisters. I needed to hear the truth. I could not believe they were gone until I heard it.

But I knew the news should not come from Bubbe Sadie. It had to come from Vashti. I would hear the truth from Vashti. The one thing she had always given me was the truth. She had never held me or shown the smallest kindness to me. She had built a wall of silence around herself, a wall I could not tear down. But she had always told me the truth.

I was torn in half about my sisters, needing to know, not wanting to know.

As I watched Mr. Izzy come in and out of his store, I wondered why no one had missed Ovadiah. Why no one looked for him. Perhaps with all the confusion from the influenza he had been overlooked. But perhaps it was something else. Perhaps they didn't look for him because they didn't want to find him. If they found him he would be sent to France. With his sister and brother gone he had no choice but to go to war.

A truck wound its way up the slippery street.

On the sidewalk, two girls hunched together, one red-headed, the other brown curls. For a moment I saw Eve and Libbie. But then, laughing, they tipped back their heads and I saw their features. They were not my sisters.

The two girls looped their arms and continued on their way.

When I was in Brattleboro with Uncle Klaus, I remembered only shadows of my sisters. Here, in the West End, on the street where we lived, on the streets where we walked, my sisters' faces came so clear to me. I would have liked to draw those faces, before I lost my sisters forever. But there was my vow, my vow not to draw again. What of my bargain with God? My bargain for my family? For Libbie and Eve?

Libbie and Eve were gone.

I had no paper to draw on anyway. I could go to Mrs. Schwartz. I could ask for fish paper. But what would Mrs. Schwartz say about a girl who abandoned her sisters? Would she look at me the way Mrs. Weitz had looked at me?

Ovadiah grabbed me by the coat and pulled me back from the ledge. As soon as he looked away, I inched toward it again, as close as I dared. I hungered for the sights, the smells, the sounds of Chambers Street.

As I looked on, farther down the block, Carla Foti, dressed in sheet, halo, and wings, rehearsed for the Christmas celebration. She floated across Chambers Street on a strong cable stretched from one window to another. Halfway across, hanging over the street, she released homing pigeons out of a basket before being pulled to safety inside the window across the way. Her sister had played the Christmas angel for the neighborhood last year. There were so many Foti girls, they could have supplied the neighborhood with angels for a lifetime.

I backed away from the edge of the roof to ask Ovadiah a question. "Why doesn't Mrs. McCarthy play her piano?"

Ovadiah shrugged.

How many nights had I hemmed trousers to the sweet sound of Mrs. McCarthy's playing? There were no hems to sew now. How could I have left without burying Tanta Rose? How could I have left without burying my sisters?

Ovadiah studied a sheet of paper. He made notes. His body trembled with music but he did not let the sound out.

I had felt such contempt for Ovadiah before I left Boston. Because he would not fight in the war.

Who did I think I was to judge him?

My heart ached with each distant glimpse of a neighbor, Mrs. Schwartz, Mrs. Rubin, Mr. Yankel. I longed to call down to them from the roof. To be hugged by them, welcomed by them. Found by them.

But if they had judged me the way I once judged Ovadiah . . .

Finally, in the dark, Ovadiah took me by the hand and led me from the sukkah, down the stairs, and cautiously onto Chambers Street. We slipped through the West End without stopping, until we reached the steps of the Joy Street synagogue, then sat and rested. Ovadiah opened his bag, the bag that had held the stale roll. I hoped for some food, but from the bag he pulled a piece of sheet music. A pencil dangled from his ear by a string. He made some notes on the sheet and placed it in the bag again.

I sat next to Ovadiah.

A dandelion grew beside the synagogue steps, in November, in the dirt, along the wall. I picked the entire plant except the root, offering Ovadiah the leaves. He shrugged me off.

Slowly I chewed the gritty greens. The dandelion made my mouth bitter.

"You know what we need, Ovadiah?" I looked him squarely in the face, though he never looked directly at me. We got up and started walking again.

"We need vinegar. Apple cider vinegar. That's just what we need."

I thought he didn't hear, but after a few moments he left me outside and went into Vaccaro's. He came out minutes later with a small bottle of amber-colored vinegar.

Back at the sukkah, I served him the drink Uncle Klaus had served to me. I could not warm the water. I did not have honey to cut the bite. I served the vinegar to him, unsweetened and cold. How different my offering was from the apple strudel Vashti had fed Ovadiah at our kitchen table that Sabbath morning. The strudel had been still warm from the bakery. Vashti had fed it to Ovadiah and to Naomi and Nathan.

Ovadiah refused to drink the vinegar.

"Ovadiah, it's good for you."

He lifted it to his lips. Put it back down again. "What are you pulling, Nathan? This stinks."

Neither of us had bathed in days. We stank. The vinegar smelled sharp and clean.

I yearned for the tang of it in my mouth. When Ovadiah

249

walked away from the cup I drank it down myself. It was not good in cold water. Not good at all.

"Sing to me, Ovadiah," I asked, tucked up on the mattress under the tattered blanket, wearing Ovadiah's overcoat and Nathan's boots. One of the things I had missed most while I lived with Uncle Klaus was the sound, the sound of Mrs. McCarthy's piano, the sound of families yelling, children playing, even the sound of Ovadiah's singing.

Ovadiah's head was perfectly round. The best shape for singing. But I had not heard him sing since I came back.

"I vowed that I would not," Ovadiah said. "I gave my word." He thumped his fist over his heart and lifted his bulging eyes. "To God, I made a vow. No singing until the children return to me."

Vows!

In the synagogue everyone could hear Ovadiah. His voice had soared in the high room, filled it with sound. Even the cantor did not sing with the passion of Ovadiah. He would look so comforted by his prayer shawl wrapped across his broad back, his head covered with the velvet yarmulke that once had been his father's. Where was that yarmulke, where that prayer shawl now?

We had all made vows. Uncle Klaus, Ovadiah, and I. We had all made bargains with God. What good had it done?

"You shouldn't have made such a vow, Ovadiah," I said. "The world is better, people feel better when you sing. You should sing."

And Uncle Klaus should draw.

And me? What about me?

chapter twenty-nine

*Monday, November 11, 1918*

I AWOKE TO THE SOUND of bells ringing, whistles shrieking.

I knew instantly what it meant. I knew in every part of my body what it meant.

"The war, Ovadiah," I cried. "The war is over!"

I shook him. He slept on his feet, leaning against the side of the sukkah. His heavy eyes looked dazed.

"The war's over," I repeated. "Listen."

Ovadiah shook his head slowly.

"It's the real thing, this time. I know it, Ovadiah," I said. "No false alarm."

I hurried over to the edge of the roof, looked down over Chambers Street. People flew out of doors, hugging, kissing, shouting.

I ran back to Ovadiah, took his hands, tried to dance with him.

"You don't need to hide anymore, Ovadiah," I said. "The war is over. They can't make you fight. Come down with me. Come down, Ovadiah."

251

He didn't understand.

I pulled on his hand. "Come, Ovadiah. You need to come down from here. It's safe for you to come down now."

Dark circles ringed his eyes, he was dangerously thin, dangerously tired.

"Come, Ovadiah. People won't be angry now. Not if there is no more war."

I raced down the stairs, and with a cry of desperation, Ovadiah followed after me.

"Nathan!" The sound of his voice clawed at my heart. "Come back, Nathan. Don't go out there."

"It's all right, Ovadiah," I called over my shoulder.

I hit the street and found myself surrounded by people. They hugged, kissed, cried. The bells kept ringing, the whistles blowing.

The excitement swept me along. Shouting, I threw Uncle Klaus's cap into the air. It landed in front of me. A boy tromped past at that moment, leaving the mark of his boot on it.

Uncle Klaus.

The bells would be ringing in Brattleboro. Uncle Klaus would be standing at the kitchen door. "The end of this war holds the seeds for the next."

Breaking away, I gathered the hat from the sidewalk, climbed the steps to my tenement, stood on the top of the old stoop, running my fingers through my hair.

I wept, though I couldn't hear myself for all the noise. I didn't know why, but amid all the happiness I wept.

"Hannah?"

I looked up.

"Hannah!"

Harry's voice. I heard Harry's voice.

"Hannah! Hannah!"

I strained to see over the crowds, caught sight of his dark hair, waved wildly. He was alive. Harry was alive!

He was three buildings away. A crowd of people stood between us.

I pushed through the crowd, straining to reach Harry.

Ovadiah called me back. "Nathan, Nathan." He bellowed like a cow, looking for a lost calf.

"Hannah!" Harry called again.

Ovadiah clutched the collar of my coat. He was dragging me away, away from Harry, away from my tenement, away from Chambers Street. His desperate strength locked onto me, onto Nathan.

Rocky Keegan brushed past, shouting, waving a flag in each fist. "Hey, Banana Nose!"

The crowd swept him away.

"Hurry, Nathan!" Ovadiah cried, dragging me away from Harry. Cutting down Spring Street, he pushed against the crowd. People laughed, danced, yelled. I could hardly see around me for the crowds of delirious people.

And then I did see. I saw a straight back. A short crop of salt-and-pepper hair. For a moment I had mistaken those two girls for my sisters. But there was no mistake this time. Ahead of me, just ahead of me, was Vashti.

I looked up at the tall straight back. I could remain silent, let her disappear into the crowd. Avoid a confrontation with her. She would never know I had trailed only a step behind her. But I turned to Ovadiah. Vashti could help him. She treated him kindly when others wouldn't talk to him. She knew the ways of healing. Different from Uncle Klaus, but still she knew.

253

"Vashti."

She spun around like she had been slapped.

I looked into the two different-colored eyes. "Vashti." I stood before her, wearing the same trousers I had worn the night I left Uncle Klaus.

Vashti looked down on me in silence.

I felt rage boiling up. It pulsed behind my eyes. Now I would tell her how I felt. What she'd done to me. I would make her tell me of my sisters.

Ovadiah had been separated from me by the crowd. "Nathan," he cried. He sank to his knees in the filthy gutter.

I pushed the questions about my sisters behind the banging of my heart. I swallowed my fury. "Vashti, Ovadiah is sick. He needs help. He doesn't eat; he doesn't sleep; he thinks I'm his brother Nathan. Tell him it's safe to come out now. The war is over."

With crowds pushing and yelling on all sides, Vashti made her way to the curb, knelt beside Ovadiah.

He looked lost, on hands and knees at the edge of the throbbing street.

"Ovadiah?" Vashti said gently.

Ovadiah tried focusing his eyes on her. He reached out a trembling hand, placed it on Vashti's shoulder. "I found Nathan."

"No," Vashti said. "Look closely, Ovadiah. This is not Nathan. This is Hannah. See?"

Ovadiah started shaking his head, shaking his head. He shook it until I thought he'd shake it off. His shoulders trembled.

I took his hand. It was filthy.

"Ovadiah, it's true. I am Hannah. Hannah Gold."

Ovadiah struggled to stand. He touched my wild curls. He stroked my smooth cheek. His dark eyes stared into mine. For a moment I saw the curtain lift. I saw a flicker of understanding. I saw also a crushing sorrow.

Ovadiah sat down on the curb with all the chaos of celebration going on around him. He sat on the curb, took out his sheet of music and his pencil, and started making marks. He hummed to himself.

"Ovadiah?"

He was humming Kol Nidre. He was breaking his vow with God. God had not given him his brother and sister back.

I turned from Ovadiah to Vashti. "Help him."

Vashti was silent.

"Vashti, can you help him?"

I felt the vibration from Ovadiah, humming Kol Nidre on the cold curb.

Then Vashti bent toward him. "Come, Ovadiah," she said. She helped him to stand.

"Come with me," Vashti said to Ovadiah, ignoring me, as if I wasn't there. She was leading him back to Chambers Street, back to the basement apartment where her brown bottled tinctures still lined the sitting-room wall.

Nothing had changed.

The silence had simply grown greater.

I was following behind them when Mrs. Schwartz called, "Hannah? Is that you?"

She ran out of her shop and wrapped her fish-scented arms around me, kissing me on both cheeks.

"Look at you in pants," Mrs. Schwartz said. "I've been saving paper, saving paper. Joe says to me throw out the paper, she's gone. But I said no. She's coming back. And look at you. Hannah, look at you."

Her eyes were shining, and she hugged me again.

I planned on staying in her arms for as long as she would hold me, when I heard his voice, close. "Hannah?"

I turned.

His dark hair still fell softly across his forehead. He'd grown taller, just in the time I'd been gone.

"Harry."

He stood unwavering in front of me. His eyes swallowed me.

I smoothed my hair, felt embarrassed by my clothes.

"Where have you been?"

I didn't know where to start.

"Hannah." His hand reached out. I stretched my own hand toward his. Our fingers touched halfway.

Around us the whole world exploded in celebration.

Mr. O'Brian rushed past. "This is the greatest day in the history of the world," he announced, taking Harry by the shoulders.

"Yes sir," Harry agreed.

Children ran between the legs of their parents, were lifted and kissed by neighbors, passed along from one cheering adult to another. People waved flags, beeped horns, marched up and down the streets, yelling.

Someone started a bonfire at the corner of Chambers and Ashland. Hundreds of people crowded around the bright warmth, singing. "And we won't come home till it's over, over there."

As Harry led me along Chambers Street I saw CLOSED signs

hanging in shop windows. A truck carrying a load of women from the textile factory honked as it passed. The men from the machine shop banged mallets against huge pieces of sheet metal.

Harry never let go of my hand. He pulled me up the steps toward Mrs. Weitz, who stood weeping in her doorway.

I was afraid at first that she would spit at me again.

But there was no horror on her face now. Only tears. Only kindness. "Hannah," Mrs. Weitz cried. "Forgive me. When I saw you barefoot, standing in the doorway of my shop, I thought you were a ghost."

She swallowed me into her arms. The worn tape measure around her neck pressed against my cheek.

"Come, Hannah," Mrs. Weitz said. "Come, my darling, out of this craziness." She climbed the steps to her apartment. "Come," Mrs. Weitz insisted, and Harry climbed behind us.

The rooms now were filled with November light, the curtains opened. The cot where Mr. Weitz had died was gone. The apartment was a home again, full of cheer and life.

A door opened.

I saw the red hair.

The braids, neat, the glasses slipping down the freckled nose.

Libbie.

She looked straight at me, adjusted her glasses.

"Hannah? Hannah!"

I broke open with joy. Running to her, I swept her into my arms. Swept her up and swung her around. "Libbie, Libbie, Libbie!" Kisses, angel kisses all over her face.

And then I heard a small voice. A beautiful small voice. "Hannah?"

Standing in the doorway. Eve! My sweet soft Eve.

I sank to the floor. My sisters slid down with me.

"Where have you been, Hannah? Where have you been?"

I didn't trust myself to speak.

We moved to the sofa, unwilling to let go of one another. I shut my eyes and smelled my sweet sisters. Their bones dug into mine as they scrambled over me. They both talked at once, telling me everything, and I could not hear their words. Outside bells were ringing, people cheering.

My arms were not big enough to hold them. We were a tangle of legs and hands. I couldn't figure out where I left off and they began.

Mrs. Weitz stood beside Harry, wiping her eyes and her nose on her handkerchief. That handkerchief. I remembered how it moved through Mrs. Weitz's hands as Mr. Weitz lay dying.

After a while, Mrs. Weitz brought us into the kitchen. "Eat," she said, bringing out a kugel.

Uncle Klaus never tasted kugel. I should have cooked him kugel.

Outside the noise continued. But in the apartment, I felt surrounded by a cushion of calm.

"How?" I asked, looking up into Mrs. Weitz's face. "How did my sisters come here?"

Mrs. Weitz touched Eve's head tenderly. "Vashti asked if I could look after them after Rose died. She still had so many patients to care for. She asked if they could stay with me. I was honored. For Vashti to ask such a thing of me! When I inquired about you, Hannah, she said you were gone. I didn't know what to think. I thought you were gone. You know, dead."

Harry looked at me. "I knew you weren't dead, Hannah."

I swallowed. "Vashti sent me away. I've been all this time in Vermont."

"Alone?"

"With an old farmer, his dogs, his goats, his horse."

"You stayed all this time in Vermont with an old man?" Mrs. Weitz asked.

"He was very kind."

Harry reached into his pocket, brought out something silver, shiny. He opened my hand and dropped a necklace into it.

"My Jewish star."

"I found it beside the Charles River the day you disappeared," Harry said. "I thought you left it for me. A sign."

You owe me, Harry had once said. You owe me your star.

I remembered the girl with violet eyes. I hadn't left Harry a sign. She had.

"Mrs. Weitz. You're so good to look after my sisters—"

Mrs. Weitz smiled. "It is all I ever wanted."

"But they fight—"

"These angels?"

"And they eat—"

Mrs. Weitz nodded. "How they eat."

I looked at Libbie. She was fatter than I remembered.

Getting up from the sofa, I walked across to the window, looked down on the frenzy of celebration in the street, wrapped my arms around myself.

"What is it, Hannah?" Harry asked, coming up behind me.

"It's all too much. All these weeks I've worried about Libbie and Eve. How I could get back to Libbie and Eve. And now I am back and I don't know what to do. It's all too much."

"Nonsense," Mrs. Weitz said. "You are together with your

sisters. Your mama and papa will come and find you safe and well. Nothing is too much."

I looked at Mrs. Weitz. She was right.


The noise of celebration continued throughout the day. I stared down on the merrymaking from the Weitzes' window, Harry's window.

Eve clung to my leg.

"There is something I need to get," I said. "Uncle Klaus, the man I stayed with in Vermont, he showed me a trick with milk and broken teacups."

Harry and Eve and Libbie insisted on coming with me. Eve made up a little song about the armistice as we pushed through the crowds, across the street, and up to the roof, to the abandoned sukkah. Libbie wanted me to spell *armistice* for her.

On the roof the sukkah leaned against the side of the building. "You slept here?" Harry asked.

I nodded.

I folded Ovadiah's tattered blanket. From behind the mattress I slid the tea towel with the pieces of Tanta Rose's cup inside. I also gathered up the bottle of amber-colored vinegar. There was little else I wanted, little more to take from this broken nest.


Libbie and Eve and Mrs. Weitz went out to join in the celebration after supper.

Harry stayed in the Weitzes' apartment with me.

In the kitchen, Tanta Rose's teacup soaked in a pan of skim milk on the back of the coal stove.

Below, whistles shrieked; church bells rang; bands played.

Flags waved everywhere. The lights out ban had been lifted for the night. Strings of Japanese lanterns decorated the dark. Sticks of Red Fire flashed, lighting up the neighborhood. Below, Libbie crashed tin pans together. Eve tooted a horn and spun a grager. Neighbors threw confetti, shot off guns, firecrackers. Cans and pails rattled over the pavement. The night thundered with celebration.

"What I could use right now is a little peace and quiet," I said. It surprised me.

Harry put his arm around me, gazed out at the celebration.

"The sound of Mrs. McCarthy's piano would be nice. Harry, why doesn't Mrs. McCarthy play her piano anymore? I listened for it when I was on the roof with Ovadiah. I couldn't hear it."

Harry led me back to the kitchen window looking out over the alley. On top of a pile of trash lay a carcass of wood, the battered, broken body of a piano.

"Mrs. McCarthy died of influenza," Harry said. "The new tenants didn't want the piano. They said the piano was made in Germany. They didn't want a German-made piano in their apartment. They destroyed it."

I sat at the Weitzes' kitchen table, across from Harry. Was Uncle Klaus looking out over Wantastiquet? Maybe he was walking in the moonlight through the orchard with Orville and Wilbur, keeping a safe distance from the celebration down in Brattleboro. Maybe he was swapping insults with Ottiwell Wood, as Ott convalesced in the cattail bed.

I pulled the old fish-wrap book of my drawings toward me from the center of the kitchen table. Eve and Libbie had insisted on bringing my drawings with them when they moved to Mrs. Weitz's apartment.

Eve had tucked inside the last page of my sketchbook the drawing I'd given her of Tanta Rose, carrying her bundle of hemmed trousers down Chambers Street.

I sighed, touching Tanta Rose's back with my finger.

"I have seen angels, Harry," I admitted for the first time. "I wouldn't have made it back to you without the help of angels."

## chapter thirty

*Wednesday, November 13, 1918*

THE CUP WAS READY. I untied the string, and Eve and Libbie and Harry and Mrs. Weitz held their breath, but the cup stayed together. I smiled, remembering how I'd doubted Uncle Klaus. Libbie looked at me with new respect, and Eve, her eyes rounded with wonder.

"What will you do with it?" Mrs. Weitz asked.

"The cup should go to Vashti." No matter how I felt about Vashti, she loved my Tanta Rose. The cup belonged to her.

Eve and Libbie and Harry went ahead of me to school, but I stopped at the old tenement.

Instead of letting myself in, I knocked at the door. This was no longer my home.

Vashti answered.

She was as tall, as straight as ever.

"Hannah," she said, looking down at me.

"May I come in?"

Vashti stepped aside.

Her shelves of tinctures and roots were nearly empty.

"How is Ovadiah?" I asked.

Vashti motioned me into the kitchen. It felt odd now, this kitchen. Familiar and strange all at once.

"Ovadiah is lost," she said, sighing sharply and sitting. She didn't offer me a seat.

I looked at her until her eyes met mine. Opening my schoolbag, I carefully removed the tea towel wrapped around Tanta Rose's cup. Vashti lifted one eyebrow, questioning.

"Open it," I said.

She frowned at me, but she unwrapped the towel, found the teacup whole again.

She studied it a long time as it sat in the center of the table, though she did not touch it.

"I can see the cracks," she said finally.

I should have been angry. I should have taken the cup back, taken it away from her. I should have smashed it against the kitchen wall to hurt her the way she had hurt me. But I saw something in her face. I remembered the night in the kitchen, the night Mr. Weitz died. I remembered her fist in her mouth after Tanta Rose died. Vashti's pain groped in the dark, putting out its hands, recoiling from everything it touched, trying to find its way to the light. Trying to survive anyway it could.

She stared blankly at the cup, not seeing me or the kitchen. She did not look inside the cup at the piece of folded paper, the drawing of Tanta Rose carrying her hemmed trousers along Chambers Street. That, too, belonged to Vashti, whether she wanted it or not.

I got up to leave.

Seeing her sitting at the table, so straight, so unbending, I felt my heart open. She couldn't hurt me. I had my sisters. I had

264

Uncle Klaus. I had Mrs. Weitz and Harry. I had my parents. What did Vashti have?

I went over and stood behind her. Gently, I placed my hands on her stiff shoulders, lay my head on her prickly hair. The coarse ends stabbed my cheek.

She was unyielding. But she did not shake me off. Under my hands I felt her shoulders tremble.

I came around and knelt in front of her. Her long, thin hand moved to my face. She traced the high bone of my cheek, the arched line of my brow. She tucked a rope of my hair behind my ear. Then she looked away.

I stood. Walked across the familiar floor.

"Wait," Vashti said.

She led me to the front room where Ovadiah sat on the edge of the big bed. He was staring without blinking. He sang softly, his voice rising and falling in a song I did not know. It sounded ancient and holy, and yet, Ovadiah sang it the way a child would sing a nursery rhyme.

I had trouble looking away from him. Finally Vashti led me back to the sitting room and closed the bedroom door.

"You had no love for Ovadiah and yet you took care of him, Hannah," she said. "Why?"

I thought about those days on the roof with Ovadiah. I thought about my time with Uncle Klaus. Listening to the muffled chanting behind the closed door, I sighed. "We took care of each other."

Vashti nodded.

"Can you help him?" I asked.

She looked directly into my eyes. Truth, I could always count on Vashti for the truth. "No," she said.

*  *  *

At dusk, Mrs. Weitz came up from her dressmaking shop.

"It smells like heaven up here," she said. "Whatever you're cooking, Hannah, I think my last three customers were hoping for invitations."

The kitchen glowed with the warmth radiating off the coal stove. Mrs. Weitz stood with her back to the heat.

Snow fell silently outside. Mrs. Weitz kissed Libbie and Eve, she hugged me, ruffled Harry's hair, then sat down at the table.

In the other apartments in the Weitzes' building, neighbors were doing the same thing. All through the West End people were sitting down to share a meal. In Germany and Russia, too, families sat together and ate.

Libbie rested her chin on her hands, watching me serve.

Harry sang the *motzi* and we began eating.

"What a cook you turned into, Hannah Gold," Mrs. Weitz said. "Your mama and papa won't know what to do with themselves."

Harry chewed. He ate my food as appreciatively as Uncle Klaus. I smiled at him. He wiped his mouth on his napkin.

Eve climbed into Mrs. Weitz's lap after dinner, and Mrs. Weitz leaned her head on Eve's hair and hummed. Eve made up words to Mrs. Weitz's tune.

After dinner Harry went outside with the boys to give us some privacy.

I heated water for baths.

"I love having someone to bathe again," Mrs. Weitz said, undressing my sisters. "I haven't bathed Harry since he was a little *pisher*."

266

How much more she would love bathing Eve and Libbie with a bathtub like Uncle Klaus's.

Tenderly, Mrs. Weitz washed my sisters as I looked on.

I held out the towels, and they climbed out of the tub. Libbie and Eve ran bare and giggling into my arms, then back to the bedroom to dress in their nightclothes.

While Mrs. Weitz tucked my sisters into her big bed, I washed myself, my knees drawn up to my chin in the galvanized tub.

Outside, Rocky and Harry and Sugar and Pauley Cohen harmonized on the stoop, singing songs from before the war. The shadows from automobile lights moved across the darkened sitting room.

When I was clean and dressed in my nightgown, I headed back to the bedroom.

Eve and Libbie had already fallen asleep, snuggled against the lightly snoring Mrs. Weitz.

After all these weeks of worry, they were all right. My heart beat with relief. They were all right.

A sound echoed through the apartment, floating toward me from the front room. A flutter, a whisper.

Turning from the bedroom where my sisters slept in the warm embrace of Mrs. Weitz, I came back down the hall and looked out the front window.

Standing beneath me on Chambers Street was the girl with violet eyes.

Her head tilted softly to one side as she gazed up at me. Her blue dress fell lightly around her.

My heart tapped wildly as I slipped out the apartment door to meet her. I followed her across the street and climbed up, up onto the roof above Mr. Murry's pawnshop.

The snow had stopped. The girl with violet eyes took my hand. As we ran above Chambers Street, her velvet hair brushed my cheek. I smelled a perfume sweeter than Uncle Klaus's honey.

She led me across roofs, one after another, until we reached Ovadiah's sukkah.

Entering the sukkah, she filled it with a radiant light. The dried stalks of the shelter rustled eagerly in her presence.

I stood before her, embraced by angel light.

"Hannah?" Harry stood outside the sukkah.

I knew it was Harry. It was Harry's voice, Harry's mouth, Harry's eyes, but looking into his face I saw so much more than Harry. I saw Eve and Libbie, Mama and Papa, Uncle Klaus and Mrs. Weitz, Ovadiah and Vashti. I saw my entire world. With all its joy, all its pain. All of it waited for me outside the sukkah. But within the sukkah I was embraced by angel light.

It all balanced before me in a moment.

And in the next moment there was Harry again, just Harry, and the girl with violet eyes was gone.

Stepping from the sukkah, I looked up into Harry's eyes.

He wrapped his coat around me and held me.

As I watched, angel light faded from the sukkah. Slowly, the broken shelter took back the night.

But left behind, on the floor, was a pair of boots.

I picked the boots up, held them to my chest.

Inside one boot, the glow of something white.

I reached in. My fingers closed on a piece of paper.

The paper, heavy textured, was from a sketchbook. On it was a drawing: of Uncle Klaus and myself and the girl with violet eyes. She was looking out of the picture at me. Uncle Klaus had drawn her eyes just right.

And in his familiar handwriting, the writing I had seen each morning as he wrote in his journal, I read:

*She keeps both beneath her wings;*
*One wing o'er thee, and one o'er me,*
*So we are near.*

I folded the drawing and slid it inside my pocket.

"Leave the boots here," I said, and Harry placed them beside the mattress, inside the sukkah.

I looked up through the open canopy into the Boston sky, ordinary sky, ordinary night. My hand curled around Uncle Klaus's drawing.

My other hand I offered to Harry.

Slowly, making our way back across the rooftops of Chambers Street, Harry and I went home.

Over the night streets of Boston, angels fly. Angels soar in their shimmering robes. Their eyes shine. Their wings stretch tip to tip across the narrow streets: Lowell and Leverett and Allen. Angels glide slowly on the cool currents of wind, while beneath them the city murmurs in sleep: the rich beneath thick quilts on Louisburgh Square, the poor in their drafty North End flats. The Common is brushed by golden light as angels drift over. Beached swan boats gaze skyward in hushed wonder, their feathered backs reflecting angel light. A thousand children sleep sweetly, the movement of angel wings loosening the grip of their sorrow. A grocer dreams of speckled cod; a scholar dreams, lamenting God; and a young girl dreams of reunions sweeter than fresh cider——while angels sweep over alleys, over rooftops, over spires. In the still November night, angels sing like snow drifting past the darkened windows of Chambers Street.

AUTHOR'S NOTE

When Austria's Crown Prince Ferdinand died of an assassin's bullet in June 1914, his country used his death as an excuse to declare war on Serbia. Neighboring nations quickly took sides, depending on old grudges and anticipated financial gains.

From 1914 to 1917, Americans hotly debated whether the United States should enter what came to be known as World War I. Many Americans wanted the United States to stay out of it.

Nevertheless, in 1917, after the sinking of three U.S. merchantmen vessels and the British interception of the Zimmermann telegram, a telegram that revealed Germany's intention to attack the United States along its Mexican border, President Woodrow Wilson joined the battle.

War is expensive. It is paid for not only with money but with enormous cost to human life. By the time the armistice—a mutual agreement to cease fighting—was signed on November 11, 1918, nearly eight and a half million people had died.

Now, eight and a half million people is a lot. But even more people were destined to die as the war ended. Twenty-two million more, to be exact. These people didn't die on the battlefield or in tent hospitals; they didn't die in air attacks or from starvation; they didn't die from bullet wounds or mustard gas. Twenty-two million people died because they caught the flu.

It started at an army camp in Kansas in the spring of 1918. Not many people paid attention to it at first. Diseases like diphtheria posed more danger than flu. U.S. troops, carrying what seemed a harmless bug, were sent overseas. Until late summer of 1918, the flu remained strictly a military problem, but then, on September 3, 1918, a civilian case showed up in Boston. By the time the month ended, ten thousand citizens had lost their lives to it.

It's no wonder the flu spread quickly. Children slept crowded, several to a bed. Raw sewage often ended up in alleys. Restaurants scraped food left on one customer's plate into the soup pot to serve again. Efforts to finance the war meant parades, meetings, door-to-door pleas. Thousands of people rubbed elbows, coughed, sneezed, breathed on each other daily.

New laws were enacted to battle the rapidly spreading illness. There were fines for spitting in public, fines for sneezing or coughing without a handkerchief. People wore gauze masks at work and on the street.

Movie houses closed; schools closed; libraries, dance halls, churches, and saloons closed; even phone booths were padlocked. But the flu went where it pleased, killed who it would.

Doctors worked frantically to find a cure. People tried a variety of home remedies, from red pepper sandwiches to wearing strings of onions.

Coffin makers couldn't keep up. Grave diggers couldn't keep up.

The pandemic—worldwide epidemic—reached the point where almost everyone either had the flu or was taking care of someone else who had it. Some young children prepared food, cleaned, tended their sick parents and older siblings. Other little ones wandered unsupervised through the streets.

Doctors and nurses worked beyond their physical limits, traveling to the homes of the ill, tending to their medical needs, and then tending to the needs of their farms and their homes, feeding and milking livestock, bringing in firewood, banking stoves. These overburdened physicians slept upright in their buggies, their horses following the road from house to house, patient to patient.

Emergency hospitals sprang up in hotels, private clubs, churches. The vehicles of the wealthy became ambulances for the poor. The Boy Scouts went door-to-door checking for those too sick to call for help.

If the epidemic had continued at the rate of spread and mortality of that fall, the human race would have been extinguished. But just as quickly as it came, the influenza left.

Though some of my material came from books such as Richard Collier's *The Plague of the Spanish Lady*, much of the information came directly from people who survived the influenza pandemic of 1918. Now in their eighties and nineties, their recall of the particular details of their experience is astounding. I also spent months poring over books about and newspapers from the period: at the National Jewish Historical Society on the campus of Brandeis University, the Brattleboro Historical Society, and in my own home, thanks, in particular, to the editors of the *West Ender.*

In Vermont folk medicine, apple cider vinegar was used to cure just about everything. I use it myself and find it does a great job ridding me of stomach pain, helping digestion, and stopping or easing colds and headaches. Using plants medicinally is a skill and craft nearly lost in the years since medical science has taken such great strides, but plants are still used today in some conventional medications, and a growing number of people are taking another look at the medicinal benefits of "common weeds."

As for angels, it is said that during World War I, a battalion of celestial soldiers once led the Allies to victory on a battlefield in France. When I was a child, I saw the sky open and angels descend on ladders. I saw it only once, on a special night of the Jewish calendar, but it was an experience I will never forget.

Finally, it is true that a straw suitcase and a black bag mysteriously appeared on the top of Wantastiquet Mountain in early November 1918. Though thoroughly investigated by police, to my knowledge, no one ever figured out where the suitcases came from.

**Kol Nidre**—CULL NID-reh. A prayer chanted as the sun sets on the eve of Yom Kippur. The deeply moving prayer allows for the repenting of vows made rashly between the worshiper and God.

**Rosh Hashanah**—RAWSH ha-SHAW-neh. This holiday, celebrating the Jewish New Year, begins the Ten Days of Penitence, during which the individual, heart and soul, is examined by God.

**Shabbes**—SHAH-biss. The Jewish Sabbath, running from sunset on Friday to sunset on Saturday each week. It is a time of miracles, visions of heaven, and the glimpse of angels.

**Sukkah**—SOOH-kah. A temporary structure where meals are eaten during the feast of Sukkoth. The sukkah symbolizes the time when Jews, during their wanderings, erected temporary shelters in the wilderness. The roof, covered with cut vegetable stalks, is left open to the sky.

**Trayf**—TRAYF. Food that is not kosher.

**Yarmulke**—YAH-m'l-kah. A small round cap worn during religious services and ceremonies.

**Yom Kippur**—yum KIP-per. All food and drink are forbidden during this last day in the Ten Days of Penitence. The most solemn and sacred day of the Jewish calendar, it is said on this day God seals the fate of every person for the coming year.